CANDLELIGHT
RECIPES *for* MAGIC

ALSO BY MARIAN SINGER

Dancing the Fire

Magic for Wild Women

Everything Wicca & Witchcraft

CANDLELIGHT RECIPES *for* MAGIC

KITCHEN WITCHERY & ENTERTAINING

Marian Singer

CITADEL PRESS
Kensington Publishing Corp.
www.kensingtonbooks.com

For hearth and home gourmets everywhere to whom cooking is a passion that offers its own kind of magic. Salute!

CITADEL PRESS BOOKS are published by

Kensington Publishing Corp.
850 Third Avenue
New York, NY 10022

All Kensington titles, imprints, and distributed lines are available at special quantity discounts for bulk purchases for sales promotions, premiums, fund-raising, educational, or institutional use. Special book excerpts or customized printings can also be created to fit specific needs. For details, write or phone the office of the Kensington special sales manager: Kensington Publishing Corp., 850 Third Avenue, New York, NY 10022, attn: Special Sales Department; phone 1-800-221-2647.

CITADEL PRESS and the Citadel logo are Reg. U.S. Pat. & TM Off.

First printing: August 2005

10 9 8 7 6 5 4 3 2 1

Printed in the United States of America

Library of Congress Control Number: 2005922706

ISBN 0-8065-2668-8

CONTENTS

PART II

Gather Round the Fires: The Recipes

ACKNOWLEDGMENTS

The author would like to thank Bob for his patient attention to detail in making this book something truly special. Also to my family for diligently sitting through hundreds of meals just so I could proof recipes. (So much for that diet, guys!) Finally, special gratitude goes out to new friends in the community—Renee, Chuck, Caroline, Sadie, George & Sterling—each of you inspires something wonderful in me. Consider this an open invitation to come on over for dinner! Love to you all.

INTRODUCTION

There is no event greater in life than the appearance of new persons about our hearth.

—RALPH WALDO EMERSON

My mother always had good recipes on hand, even for those moments when ten people showed up unexpectedly at our door. She would whip out meals with an uncanny elegance, then serve them out with candles and a smile on her face that made everyone feel welcome. She taught me that those special little touches and sense of joy can become a tradition—something that can be part of every meal and every menu you create. It can also inspire magic! After all, happiness is a kind of spell unto itself. All that warm, positive energy saturates whatever you happen to be working on with very little extra effort. So it is that this book was written with my mother's tradition as its heart, and a little magical know-how as a guiding force.

Candlelight Recipes for Magic blends the beauty, simplicity, and symbolism of two metaphysical methods—candle magic (making, lighting, and burning candles for magical goals) and kitchen witchery (a hearth and home approach to spirituality that finds potent symbols and components in everyday things)—into a harmonious consortium. Burning candles generate a special warmth and sense of hospitality, which cannot be imitated by modern light. Hearthside magic generates that same warmth because it starts with each person's unique spiritual vision. Together these two traditions make a powerful ally for making and manifesting magic from components that abide in the sacred space of your home.

To understand this better, consider for a moment the symbolic value given to candles in particular. Numerous global traditions from Judaism to Wicca use candlelight as an emblem of both the human and the divine spirit. Because they gave off light in the darkness, candles were associated with the power of the sun and solar gods and goddesses in Greece and Rome (among others). Moreover, in Buddhist tradition the lighting of a candle is a willful act with purpose—one chooses to put fire to the wick and transform reality and the spark of one's soul—a spark that this book hopes to nurture.

Now add to this foundation kitchen magic. Around the world the hearth-and-home approach to spirituality were the most well known and time honored. Born from people's everyday lives and experiences, kitchen witchery begins at the heart of the house (the stove) and ends with your creativity. Combining candles with kitchen magic, ultimately, results in simple, no-nonsense, time-effective approaches for weaving magic into daily moments, specifically cooking!

I remember early in my own spiritual practices learning how to work with candles as a focus or a component to spells. At the same time I was also desperately trying to learn to cook for my then new fiancé (who is now my husband of twenty years). Romantic candlelight dinners were regular, and they got me to thinking about taking my enjoyment of candle magic and mingling it with my culinary adventure. Before I knew it there were always candles burning in my kitchen, lighting the way toward manifesting spiritual goals while I cooked.

This book celebrates that discovery process by sharing it and adding magical methods to the blend for powerful, life-affirming results. To begin, part I of this book provides a hands-on primer for the candle-lighting kitchen witch. We'll review common pantry folklore and superstition and how you can apply both to your own candlelight recipes. We'll also talk about the philosophies of kitchen magic, which include making your own energized candles, creating just the right ambiance to support your goals, and blessing or prayers to top everything off. Since we have to make meals anyway, we might as well whip up some magic too! To me, this is the ultimate in clever multitasking and pragmatics! See, both candle magic and kitchen witchery were designed by everyday people who usually didn't have time for complex spells or rituals—folks like you and me who wanted spirituality to be part of their daily life without fuss and muss. Consequently, the ultimate goal here is having the entire meal, from preparation to cleanup, become a worshipful act that manifests what we most need and want.

Next comes the fun part—the recipes. What metaphysical cookbook is complete without a tantalizing assortment of food and beverages that serve the mind, body, and soul? Unlike an everyday cookbook, however, this one is a little different—it's assembled by the need or goal you have in mind. Thus, when you want to integrate prosperity-oriented foods, drinks, and candles into your menus, for example, you would turn to chapter 8, Providence Platters, and find recipes for money, employment, and abundance.

About the only words of caution I have is that kitchen-candle magic can quickly become addictive. You'll naturally find yourself perusing supermarket and pantry shelves for gadgets and ingredients that can fill your sacred pantry so that it's more conducive to spiritual tinkering. I've recently redone my entire kitchen with candlelight recipes in mind. Having said that, please know you don't really have to turn your life upside down to use and enjoy this book. Ultimately your intuitive nature will guide you through the rituals of cooking in ways that make sense regarding your environment, means, and time constraints.

Rather than delay any longer, let's get right to the basics. Turn the page and let's get cookin'!

PART I

Lighting the Candle

MEALTIME MAGIC

Thousands of candles can be lighted from a single candle, and the life of the candle will not be shortened. Happiness never decreases by being shared.

—BUDDHA

1

Pantry Philosophy

THE IDEALS AND METHODS OF KITCHEN WITCHES

All good moral philosophy is but the handmaid to religion.

—FRANCIS BACON

Before we begin examining how to effectively blend candle magic with kitchen witchery, it helps to define what constitutes the quintessential kitchen witch—ethically, philosophically, and practically for readers new to this concept. The three keys to functional kitchen magic are inventiveness, simplicity, and meaningfulness. Our methods aren't carved in stone—rather, they're born of a combination of folklore, superstition, and common magical methods, to which foundation we add a heaping helping of personal flair and vision. This personalization is what makes kitchen magic meaningful, and also what drives manifestation. As in any form of magic, if a spell, ritual, or other technique doesn't make sense to you, it's not going to work!

For kitchen witches, life itself is the magic—meaning we try to blend our spirituality into every moment of every day. We look to our common routines and actions, including cooking and candle lighting, to provide us with opportunities to raise and direct energy in very intimate ways that respond to the moment and our needs or goals. For example, when you're perking up coffee how about adding a "pick me up" style incantation to blend the mundane goal with the spiritual one? Here's an example:

Coffee strong, coffee fine
Perk with energy
RISE AND SHINE!

You might also light a bright red candle (red traditionally represents vitality and power) at the end of the incantation for vibrant energy.

Now the first reaction some people have to this type of illustration is that it sounds too simple to work, or it seems kind of playful. Well, simplicity is a powerful thing. It releases us to focus wholly on our goals. Better still there is nothing stodgy or gloomy about kitchen witchery—it is truly a joyful celebration of sacredness in our homes and hearts. Laughter is good "soul" food!

With that in mind, kitchen witchery always reflects your space, your ideals, and your ethics. In this philosophy your living space is truly your sacred castle, fit for a god/dess! Which one? The hearth god/dess, of course—the spark within and without that burns with hospitality, graciousness, quick-wittedness, and proactive flexibility. You are about to become the guru and god/dess of your space, and it doesn't require any fancy equipment, expensive accoutrements, or turning your life inside out.

There is literally nothing in the world or in your home that cannot be used in magic should you wish to—in other words, unless you want something special or different, you have all the goodies you need to be spiritually successful right now in and around your living space (especially food and candles!). In particular, your kitchen stove becomes a magical hearth, a pot your cauldron, a candle your focal, and a wooden spoon a wand with which you'll wield and direct magical energy so it lands in every bite you eat!

Additionally, since this book focuses on cooking—the phrase "you are what you eat" takes on new meaning. Now you have the opportunity to bring focused energy into everything from cereal or snacks to a five-course meal. Eating then neatly internalizes those transformative vibrations, releasing them to every cell of your being. If all this sounds good to you, or sounds like what you already do every day—welcome aboard! You're a kitchen witch in the making already!

2

Threshold of Belief

CANDLE AND KITCHEN LORE AND SUPERSTITION

Cooking is at once child's play and adult joy. And cooking done with care is an act of love.

—CRAIG CLAIBORNE

I mentioned earlier that kitchen witchery uses folkways as one foundation for spells, rituals, and other magical methods. By definition, folklore is the beliefs, stories, and traditions of ordinary people—people like you and me. Folklore integrates into our cultures and lives often without anyone realizing it. For example, no one thinks twice about blowing out candles on a birthday cake and making a wish. Likewise, hardly anyone notices that most folks pass food sunwise around the table during meals, or when someone tosses salt over their shoulder after spilling it. All of these simple actions are repeated partially out of habit and tradition, but they are also all things that have a purpose (wish fulfillment, inspiring blessings, and protection, respectively).

Kitchen witches believe that folkways have a power all their own—power that isn't minimized in the face of modern conveniences. On a mundane level, most folkways became traditions thanks in part to old-fashioned observation. If an action or prediction worked once, then people used it again. Those actions or predictions that worked repeatedly were handed down from generation to generation.

On a metaphysical level, folkways have a lot of power. For one thing we have a natural psychological connection to these actions. We already trust in them, so they're "user friendly." Additionally, consider the energy generated by one person's will and belief in a specific tradition, such as the necessity of bringing a small gift when we visit someone's home. At one time people did this to appease the hearth god or goddess of that home so those that lived there would continue to enjoy those blessings. Now, consider hundreds of people all believing that so doing will have the same results. That's a lot of raw energy resonating through the halls of tradition and lore, and pooling in the collective unconsious—energy that a clever witch or pagan can tap and direct if they so choose. And in kitchen witchery, that's exactly what we do!

So let's take a moment to explore where many such household traditions originate, and how we can use or adapt them in our candlelight recipes

CANDLE FOLKLORE

As an item readily available around the house it's not surprising to find a lot of folklore and superstition surrounding candles (it could literally fill volumes!). I'm only sharing a few examples here to get you started and to help you understand how the recipes and magical instructions in part II came about.

GENERATING LUCK

To improve your good fortune, light candles with your right hand and let candles burn themselves out naturally. If you can't do this safely, consider blowing out your candles with a silent prayer or wish for luck. Thus, if you're preparing some of the luck recipes in part II, using your right hand to light them is one way to support that goal.

Another luck rule is not blackening the bottom of your candles when you put them in a holder. This turns good fortune away. To avoid this problem, light the top of the candle and let wax drip into the base and secure the candle that way before beginning your recipes. In addition, if your luck has been really bad, you can turn the candle upside down to literally turn around the energy. Just remember to focus on your goal!

On special occasions it's said the gift of a bayberry candle brings with it a wish for serendipity. I happen to really love the smell of bayberry and enjoy having one small candle per guest when I have company. That way we surround ourselves with fortunate energy and everyone can take a little of it home with them.

PROTECTION

Blessed candles placed in your windows or around your magical working space provide protection. It's the same idea people use in creating the sacred space, whether that be a Wiccan altar or a magical circle. Now you can use this concept in your cooking area, which is soon to become a sacred space thanks to your focus and intention.

DIVINATION

People worldwide observed candles as part of divination efforts. There are various ways that candles participated in fortune-telling. They include the ancient art of pyromancy (divination by observing fire), lychnomany (observations of the whole candle together—fire, wax, and wick) and carromancy (divination by wax patterns when dropped on a surface like water).

There are at least two ways to use this information in your candlelight recipes. First, light a candle when you begin cooking. Watch the candle's behavior. If the flame glows bright and clear throughout, it means your energy is likewise focused and clear! Alternatively, you could use candles after making recipes intended to heighten psychic awareness. For example, take one of the candles that you've burned while preparing and serving the food and drip it onto a smooth surface while thinking of your question. Now look at the resulting patterns. You can interpret this much in the same way one interprets tealeaf patterns or ink blots!

WORSHIP

On a personal level, I cannot help but think of both my spirit and the divine each time I light a candle. That simple, single

BLESSING A PANTRY CANDLE

Many neopagans like to have a special candle that honors the spirit of their home and everyone who lives therein. In this case, we're going to bless a candle specifically to use in your kitchen. I suggest using a white candle enclosed in a glass container. White is the color of pure intention and protection, and it's also an all-purpose color when you don't have other candles handy.

To bless something means to call upon the divine to set apart this tool for a specific purpose. In this case, your purpose is to energize all your pantry enchantments with the best possible intentions and overall good energies. The blessing can take place at any time of day, but dawn is nice for its upbeat vibrations. Hold the candle in both hands, close your eyes, and visualize gold-white light filling it from above. Talk to your vision of the divine in words that are comfortable to you, expressing your desire. For example, "Great Spirit, fill this candle with your clarity. Each time it's lit, may it shine with love, hope, joy, and positive energy for the good of all. So be it."

Put the candle near your stove and light it whenever you're working on magical foods.

flame that shines gently from the darkness and chases the shadows puts me in a different, more spiritual, frame of mind. In my sacred pantry, I light a candle to honor the god/dess and also to honor the spark of the divine in my soul. So, if you have a deity that you follow, having a candle to welcome them into your kitchen witchery is one option to consider.

I'd like to ask you to take a moment and think about what the light of a candle represents to you. Were there any traditions in which candles were (or are) important to your family? Do those customs still hold value to you? If so, integrate them in your kitchen witchery. For example, if you always lit a candle during mealtime prayers with your family there's no reason to stop that custom now. Just give it more meaning. What god or goddess would you like this to represent? This is a perfect opportunity to continue nurturing your relationship with deity and with your family traditions.

KITCHEN FOLKLORE

From a mother's advice to get up on the right side of bed and eat an apple daily for health to the saying "keep the home fires burning" there's a richness of superstition surrounding our daily routines, including cooking. While we might not have a fireplace to keep burning so emotions stay warm in our homes, we do have pilot lights (or long-burning candles), for example. Or, while we may not always bake and brew by the waxing to full moon (so things rise and age properly), we could put together the basic ingredients for a recipe during that time frame, store them, and use these energized components when it's more convenient. And the custom of never throwing away bread because it's "throwing away your prosperity"? Well, how about saturating stale bread with your wishes, then giving the pieces to the birds (who in turn carry your wishes on the winds!)?

I'm sure many people reading this book remember the elders in your family doing "quirky" things, or sharing quaint sayings.

Now's the time to try to remember those, write them down, and see which ones you can use. My grandmother, for example, always baked early in the day. At first I thought it was just pragmatic—it was cooler then. But when asked about it she told me that she liked getting up with the sun. It made her happy and hopeful. I've always remembered that and use dawn as a time to prepare meal components aimed at generating hope and joy. She also whistled while she cooked. I now know that whistling is one way that ancient witches raised the winds and other types of power, and I enjoy joining in that custom.

Although I could easily fill a book with kitchen lore, it's much more functional to adapt those things with which you're already familiar—those that bring a gentle smile to your face and positive memories. In my case, dawn came to represent a fresh start for my soul, a time of renewal when I can listen to the divine, a time to honor my ancestors (especially Grandma) in my workings, and a time to prep the magic for the day to perfection. Whistling became more than a simple musical diversion; now it was part of my candlelight recipes. I'm sure as you look over your list of traditions, and test the practices, you'll come up with similar positive results that you can apply for a variety of spiritual goals.

3

Hands On, Heart's Afire

MAKING YOUR OWN CANDLES

An original is a creation motivated by desire. Any reproduction of an original is motivated by necessity . . . It is marvelous that we are the only species that creates gratuitous forms. To create is divine, to reproduce is human.

—MAN RAY

Besides using folkways, kitchen witches often like to make their own tools. There's always been a certain pride attached to something you've made with your own hands. Additionally, with candles you can fashion them from the ground up with the energies you need, salvage any extra wax, and recycle it, thereby building power with each new candle incarnation. See, the vibrations you put into the candle remain in the wax even when the spell or ritual is done. If you collect and save the wax (label it by the goal or theme of the magic), then you always have a ready supply of pre-empowered media with which to work when preparing another recipe.

What I'd like to do is give you fairly fast, effective methods for candle making that adjust to your time constraints. Before we can make a candle, however, we need to consider the component parts to the process. You'll need to assemble these beforehand, and bless or charge them according to your goal.

Component Parts to Candle Making

1. *Base Component—Wax:* I personally love beeswax because it burns slowly, cleanly, and evenly. However, it's more expensive than paraffin, so buy according to your budget. Note: The paraffin available at the supermarket is often intended for canning and not really suitable for candles. Instead, buy completely opaque paraffin at a hobby supply store for best results. Or it's perfectly okay to mix beeswax and paraffin.
2. *Wick:* In purchasing accompanying wick, these will be labeled according to the size of the candle in which it should be used. If you're working in beeswax, try square braid wicks. You'll find these are good multipurpose items whether you're shaping the wax into a fancy design or just making a block. Oh, and you don't have to make the candle with the wick inside of it! If you use a hot piece of metal to puncture a hole in the middle, you can thread your candle like a needle, moving the wick through that hole. Afterward add a little extra wax to hold it in place. I like this method when there are children and cats around, both of whom love to tinker with craft items at the worst possible moments (like when the candle is still hot).
3. *Additives:* Potential additives for your candles include stones, shells, and aromatics. All of these can give you extra symbolic value (like adding powdered or whole seashells to a water-oriented candle). Remember, however, that a lot of additives can hinder how evenly the candle burns (causing sparking, smoke, or other problems). For aromatics—no more than a half teaspoon of oil to a pound of wax is good. I have used powdered aromatics, but the results have been unreliable at best. Sometimes they seem to make it harder to unmold the candle or cause difficulty in the wax setting up right. Also, powders can cause flare-ups, thereby representing a potential fire hazard. Please keep this in mind during your experimentation. Overall don't exceed

more than about one ounce of additive to two pounds of wax.

4. *Colors:* For color most hobby shops have coloring specifically designed for candles and they give you instructions on how much to use. This changes from brand to brand, and wax to wax, so I recommend knowing how much wax (and what type) you're planning to use in advance of buying coloring agents.

   Coloring comes in liquid, powdered, cake, and chip form. Cakes seem to give the best results, but it's hard to get consistent colors. Liquid dyes seem easier but often smell nasty. No matter the type of wax, too much liquid dye leaves that odor, so use it carefully.

5. *Tools:* Potential tools for candlecraft include a spoon, ladle, and molds, if you want them. Because many ingredients for candle making aren't edible, having some tools set aside just for your candlecraft avoids mixing these items with your culinary adventures.

MAKING THE CANDLE(S)

I recommend rolled and poured candles as being the quickest to create.

ROLLED CANDLES

Rolled candles require buying rolling sheets of wax at the craft store (choose the color according to your goal). Sheets of wax come in different sizes, so you can either get the size you want or cut a larger sheet into the length desired (with twice that in width). Lay the sheet in sunlight or use a blow dryer to warm it to the point where it's pliable. Rub the inside of the wax with whatever aromatic you've chosen, put down a length of wick (leaving some out at the top), and then just roll it on up! It should naturally hold its shape, but if you find it releasing, add a dollop of hot wax to the bottom or edge of the candle.

POURED CANDLES

Poured candles require a mold. You can use wood or glass, and even the traditional milk box, but please make certain that if you plan to take the candle *out* of the mold at the end, that you oil the inside first with any type of cooking oil (I've even used spray oils with successful results). As mentioned earlier, you need not suspend a wick in the middle of your mold if you don't mind the alternative piercing process (piercing the wax with a pin or thin metal rod and threading the wick through)—however, this is very difficult if you're not taking the candle out of the mold before burning it.

Self-contained candles are more easily threaded during the pouring process by suspending a wick in the middle of the mold. I accomplish this by placing a piece of aluminum foil on the bottom of the wick and tying the top to a pencil. Lay the pencil across the top of the mold to allow the wick to hang in the center. Size wise, avoid an enclosed candle (one with a non-wax side) larger than six inches, as these tend to burn out unless you're using dripless wax.

The process for the poured candle is pretty straightforward. Set up your mold and wick, melt the wax, add aromatics, cool a little and pour it in very slowly and evenly! Leave the candle at room temperature because cooling it too quickly causes cracking. Furthermore, try not to bump or move the candle after you've poured the wax. It needs to harden, and movement can create air bubbles. I usually give it a full day to settle before blessing and trying to use it. Should you wish to remove the candle from the mold, soak it in a bit of hot water (don't let the water over the rim onto the wax). That should loosen the wax around the edge so you can slide it right out.

Don't forget that you can add all manner of magical elements including color and aromatics, or specific metaphysical processes like blessing, charging, and prayers. Examples of these additions are included in the next chapter.

4

A Magical Ambiance

CANDLELIGHT RECIPES FROM SETUP TO CLEANUP

For alchemy means: to carry to its end something that has not yet been completed.

—Paracelsus

Now that we have the elements of kitchen magic in one hand, and candles in the other, let's consider how to put these together for the best results in our recipes. I say "our" recipes because I fully expect readers will want to use their own favorite foods as part of their pantry magic too. Accomplishing this isn't too difficult.

First, let's look at your work space. Just as you don't think of churches as being dirty or cluttered, your sacred kitchen should be clean and ready for the task at hand. Beyond the health considerations, this is a way to begin putting yourself in the right frame of mind for working magic. It's also a way to saturate the pantry with positive energy that will support your goal. So tidy up and lay out all your tools and ingredients as part of your ritual. If you wish, you could also bless your components and implements at this juncture. One little ditty that I like to use goes like this:

Kitchen god/dess, hear my wish
Bless these items
Bring magic to this dish!

Usually I repeat the blessing three times (once each for body, mind, and spirit), then get to work.

A second consideration, and a very important one, is your own attitude. Don't go into your kitchen angry unless you want a lot of angry people after dinner. Similarly, avoid candlelight recipe creation when you're ill, stressed out, weary, or just plain "off" somehow. No matter how adept a kitchen witch you may be, those negative energies can boil over into your food, creating quite a metaphysical mess. The last time I cooked when I was angry we were all fighting by the end of the meal. Of all the suggestions I'm providing, this one I consider "essential." You shouldn't compromise when it comes to spiritual energy.

The third consideration is the recipe itself. Not every recipe you have, and not every recipe in this book, is going to be perfect for your goals or personal tastes. Don't let that stop you! I have often said that baking is like chemistry whereas cooking is like alchemy—because cooking allows more flexibility and tinkering (and in fact playing with the recipe often improves the result). If you want to adapt and adjust a personal or candlelight recipe, do so; just bear in mind that any changes you make also change the energies with which you're working.

There are two ways to tackle candlelight recipes. One is to create the recipe around your goal, the other is to look at a recipe as it stands and find the magical potential. The recipes in part II were fashioned around specific goals. But what if you want to make spaghetti tonight using Mom's tried-and-true instructions? What magical potential does it have? Well, the main ingredient of tomato sauce has associations with love (tomatoes having once been called "love apples"). The red color also ties into love and passion. Therefore, if you wish to improve the loving energies in your home and relationships, focus on that key component and your goal while you cook. Light a red candle in keeping with your theme. With very little fuss, you've just given your food a boost of warm energy that will bless everyone at your table. And, of course you can add other symbolic touches that support your goal too.

AROMATICS

Consider bringing magical aromatics into the mix. This can be accomplished by adding herbs to the recipes, putting out potpourri or incense in the kitchen, dabbing your candles with essential oil, or even adding some fresh flowers to your countertop. Just because an aroma isn't *in the food, per se, it's still part of the overall working energies of your space.*

Now, since this is "pantry" magic—let's focus on aromatics that are already filling your spice shelves. Almond extract generates insight, allspice powder brings good fortune, apple supports well-being, and bay helps with prophetic vision—just to name a few! Want more ideas? How about cinnamon for passion, ginger for an overall energy boost, lemon for purification, mint for the conscious mind, orange for dedication, sage for wisdom, and thyme for bravery! Don't forget that if any of your chosen herbs can't be used in the food (because it would affect the flavor) you can boil them or mix them with wood powder for incense, dab them on candles, or even use them as a personal anointing oil to release their energies into the room and the food just the same!

Abbreviated Aromatic Correspondence List

- *Allspice:* improved fortunes
- *Apple:* health, wisdom, focus, decision making
- *Basil:* love, relationships, peace, accord
- *Berries:* prosperity, abundance
- *Cloves:* romantic energy, safety, power enhancer
- *Coriander:* the rational mind (improving)
- *Garlic:* protection, banishing

- *Lemon:* clarity, happiness, devotion, longevity
- *Nutmeg:* psychic awareness
- *Orange:* devotion, dependability, good health
- *Pepper:* cleansing
- *Rose:* love, divinatory awareness, dedication, health, friendship
- *Rosemary:* memory improvement, the conscious mind, well-being
- *Vanilla:* insight, energy, love

COLOR

Another component for your consideration is that of color. We know that color speaks to our conscious mind visually, and to our subconscious as well (just by our reactions to light, darkness, and various predominant color tones in a room). Color symbolism gives you a little extra flexibility in your pantry magic. Though you may not always have the exact ingredients desired for your spell-recipe, you may have items in the right hue for symbolic purposes!

In using color for personal candlelight magic, I suggest considering how color affects you and what personal associations it holds. For example, if your mother was a very nurturing soul who loved pastel hues, then you're likely to associate pastel colored foods, beverages, and candles with that type of energy. Using color symbolism in candlelight recipes for your family or another group, however, is a little different affair.

With groups I suggest falling back on more traditional symbolism for color. Most people associate red with energy, love, and the sun. Therefore, if you're making candlelight recipes for a Summer Solstice celebration—red's a great color to integrate throughout the meal: red candles, red pepper, red cabbage, red grapefruit, tomato juice, and so forth. Bright orange of course, would be another good choice that blends nicely with the red such as might be found in orange-colored sweet peppers or orange juice.

Abbreviated Color Correspondence List

- *Black:* Reversing energy. Rest. Earth-oriented energy (for grounding and foundations). Endings and closure. When you need these strong, cornerstone energies look to edibles like black beans or Russian black bread.
- *Brown:* Foundations. Another earth-oriented color. Safety. Confidence. Diligence. Ideas for foods that have this color include beef stew and rye bread (or any toasted bread).
- *Gold and yellow:* Solar and fire magic. Conscious mind. Communication. Talent. Learning and mental focus. Good fortune. Prosperity and success. The God aspect. Note, however, that pale yellow is more strongly associated with Air energies. Food ideas that highlight yellow energy include yellow bell peppers and anything with a butter base or sauce.
- *Green:* Financial matters. Steady growth. Destiny. Renewal and health. Earth-oriented magic, especially herbalism. Think lettuce, celery, green pepper, baby greens, etc.
- *Dark blue:* Insight and psychism. Water-oriented energy. The dreamscape. Dedication and meditation. (Note that while finding dark blue food is difficult, you can use beverages with food coloring or your candles as the keynote for the energies.) Eat blueberries when you're working magic intended to bring spiritually oriented dreams.
- *Orange:* A blend of red and yellow, this brings steady energy to fulfill hopes and dreams through tenacity. Acceptance of change. Gentle motivation. Try sweet potatoes and oranges for focusing on these goals (if you want to blend the two together, they taste divine!).
- *Pink:* A calmer version of red that inspires friendly energy and kinship. Emotional matters. Metered improvements in emotional, physical, or mental health. I recommend pink grapefruit for this because it also comes in a lovely circle, the symbol of completion.

- *Purple:* Regality, leadership, charisma. Spiritual authority and insight. Communing with spirits. Discernment. Try grapes for this, naming each one after your goal as you consume them, or purple onions for a truly zesty personality (just don't forget the breath mints).
- *Red:* Vigor, zeal, passion, courage, the ability to succeed in the face of great odds, willfulness, fire. Red peppers, pomegranate seeds or juice, and tomatoes are good examples of food with the right colors for these goals.
- *Silver:* The goddess and lunar energy. Safety. Metaphysical awareness and insight. Creativity and imagination. In this case, how about your silverware? BTW (by the way), I also have some gold-toned knives, forks, and spoons when I wish to have more solar energy.
- *Pale blue:* Happiness and hopefulness. A fresh start. Harmony and understanding. Here you might want to consider blue-toned beverages. There are numerous sports drinks now with colors that will suit your goals.
- *Violet:* Discovery (sometimes adventure). Honed talents. Improvements. Balancing karma and personal energies. Future-telling. Perhaps decorate your table with violet-petaled finger bowls!
- *White:* Purity and safety. Cleansing. The moon's energy. Honesty and honor. Clarity. Spirit. The first thing to come to my mind is milk—a perfect representation of the goddess.

Don't forget that you can mix and match colors to get the right harmony of energy you want. For example, use yellow and violet (communication and peace) when you need to balance out your energy within a group. Now, it may not always be possible to find foods in the right color (there's not a lot of blue and purple food!). However, the culinary industry helps us there. There's nothing wrong with adding food coloring (so long as it doesn't look bad when it's cooked). Nor is there anything wrong with using decorative accents around the preparation and serving space in the colors that reflect your goal. Stay flexible and go with the creative flow!

CRYSTALS

Speaking of decorative touches, what about crystals, metals, minerals, and other similar items? It's relatively easy to set a tiny crystal into the base of a homemade candle to augment the vibrations it produces. You can also set crystals around a candle or set them up as part of the dining centerpiece (effectively creating an informal altar). Now, being a frugal witch, I typically choose stones that I either have at home or that aren't too expensive. Most of the stones in the following list can even be purchased at a science shop in the mall, so you shouldn't have too much trouble finding them.

Since you won't be using stones and metals in your recipes, I suggest instead that you add them to your sacred kitchen space. Use them in the base of your candles. Put them by the stove, countertop, or in your pocket while you prepare the meal. Use them as a decoration on the dining room table, or perhaps have one stone per person to hand out as an after-meal gift so that guests carry the energy home with them.

Stone Correspondence List

- *Agate:* Messages (clarity of), improved finances, hopes and dreams, peace, courage, understanding dreams.
- *Amber:* Overcoming fear, the sun's energy, strength, success, and improved health.
- *Amethyst:* Inner beauty, dedication, awareness, peace with self, honing the mind.
- *Beryl:* Ironing out red tape, especially legal. Motivation, learning. Excellent for hospitality in the kitchen space.

- *Bloodstone:* Opportunity, foresight, honesty and candor.
- *Brass:* Solar-oriented energy, improved prosperity and overall vitality.
- *Copper:* Communing with spirits, improved conscious awareness, a healing stone.
- *Coral:* Longevity, encouraging positive dreams, children's safety, overall water-oriented energy.
- *Iron:* Grounding, intensity, banishing (especially devic entities).
- *Jade:* Good fortune, love and devotion, a blend of earth and water energies, meditative ability.
- *Lodestone:* Passion, the power of attraction (magnets).
- *Moonstone:* Intuitive nature, a gardener's friend, the moon.
- *Onyx:* Balance, protection, wish magic.
- *Quartz (clear):* Akin to white candles, this is an all-purpose stone that can be blessed with any type of energy. Also good for clarity.
- *Quartz (rose):* Friendship, gentle love, and self-love. Healing emotions.
- *Quartz (rudilate):* The lines of the rudilate help disperse energy where it needs to go.
- *Seashells:* Transformation, accepting change. Water-oriented energy, divinatory insight, and ongoing cycles.
- *Silver:* Also lunar and water oriented, this is a goddess stone even as is the color.
- *Tin:* Luck, especially on the road.
- *Turquoise:* Another travel stone that provides protection, dispels fear, and brings achievement.

I sometimes use conglomerates and whatever other rocks I find in the yard, too, based on their shape or color. An oval equates to goddess energy, a square is earth oriented, a triangle is fire/god energy, and a circle is the moon (to me, anyway). This is one case where beauty is in the eye of the beholder along with the symbolic value. Moreover, remember when you don't have the "right" stone for the energy you want to create—you can, again, use the stone's color instead.

DECORATIONS

Continuing with our decorating theme, the magical ambiance of your kitchen and dining room can be rounded out even further by small touches added into the preparation and/or serving space. I realize that not everyone has a plentiful kitchen or dining space, so let's look at space-saving items (like the stones) that will provide more supportive energy with which to work.

By far, my favorite touch is fresh flowers. Here you've got the aromatic symbolism, color correspondence, and the metaphysical association of the plant itself from which to choose! This type of multilevel flexibility is a crafty witch's dream come true! Just a bud vase will do!

What about things that would normally be in your space anyway? I'm thinking place mats, dishes, cups, and hot pads. I often peruse second-hand stores and find some of the most wonderfully witchy designs you can imagine just right for cooking and serving special magic! To illustrate: If your family is anything like mine, keeping blue place mats and other highlights helps when "keeping the peace" becomes an issue.

About the only caveat here is to think about placement in your overall plan. For example, place mats go under a dish so they create a foundational energy, while cups go beside the food creating a secondary accompanying energy. In addition, cups with symbolic colors or patterns might be more suited to those meals where you've prepared a magical beverage as an accompaniment. I'm trying to take you from the mundane use/construct of an item to seeing its correlation metaphysically. Once you begin making those connections, it will become quite natural and your entire candlelight recipes will run smoothly from start to finish!

Speaking of start to finish, don't overlook service as a component in your candlelight magic. The way an item is placed on a plate, and the smile that accompanies, makes a difference in the overall ambiance. I think presentation counts for a lot because it impacts us visually, while the aroma and taste excite two other senses. For example, if I've made a chicken dish for health, I might serve it garnished with three spears of broccoli across the top to represent body, mind, and spirit. The final piece to this dish is a bit of fresh orange zest, which supports the goal of health. Looks beautiful, tastes good, and wasn't overly hard to assemble!

As you read part II of this book you'll see most recipes include some serving suggestions to get your creative juices flowing. Use those as a guideline, not an edict. The finishing touches should be fun for you—not drudgery. Top off your dish in whatever way feels right at the moment, and then hum a little tune, put out the plates, and internalize the wonders you've created!

TIMING

In reading old tomes of magic it's not unusual to find very specific instructions that include what time of day to gather or mix components. This was because that time frame supported the magic astrologically. Nowadays, we know that certain meals come at certain times of the day, and it's not going to be feasible to always cook during the best astrological influences. Don't sweat it! What you can do instead is choose symbolic timing in which to prepare a small, easily stored part of the meal (like dry ingredients or sauces). That way, if you feel auspicious timing is important to your plans, you have at least one component that's been prepared in that time frame. Here's a list of traditional correspondences for your consideration:

Cooking or Prep Work Time Frame	*Energies Created*
DARK MOON:	turning energy, quiet, thoughtfulness, rest
NEW MOON:	a fresh start, steadily growing energy
WAXING MOON:	progress, change, drawing specific energy to yourself
FULL MOON:	maturity, awareness, understanding the mysteries, profuseness, wisdom
WANING MOON:	decreasing energies, slowing things down, releasing
BLUE MOON:	wonders, wishes
ARIES MOON:	overcoming; house cleaning personally or literally, self-improvement
TAURUS MOON:	hard work paying off, abundance
GEMINI MOON:	release the old, embrace the new, and bring balance
CANCER MOON:	strong lunar energy for inventiveness
LEO MOON:	focus on inner strength and how you use your words
VIRGO MOON:	monetary gain, success
LIBRA MOON:	symmetry, discernment, truth revealed
SCORPIO MOON:	sexual energy, passion, fiery awareness
SAGITTARIUS MOON:	reaching goals in wise ways, budgets, self-mastery
CAPRICORN MOON:	inner workings support outward manifestation
AQUARIUS MOON:	motivation, adventure, pursuing a dream
PISCES MOON:	water-oriented energy, fruitfulness, movement
DAWN:	similar to a new moon with more solar energy; renewal and hope
NOON:	complete mental awareness; fire, management ability

Cooking or Prep Work Time Frame	*Energies Created*
DUSK:	releasing and closure, endings
MIDNIGHT:	the in-between time, good for nearly any type of magic.

Having said all that, we should remember that magic works forward and backward in time because it's considered existing outside of normal frameworks. That's why we use the phrase "out of space, out of time" in conjunction with magical circles and sacred spaces. Honestly, if a spell that you're adapting for pantry magic calls for something to be prepared at 4 A.M.—it's certainly that time *somewhere* in the world, even right now! So, it's all good! In other words, don't get so hung up on the details that you forget about *why* you're making this candlelight recipe and subsequently lose your focus.

PRAYERS, CHANTS, AND BLESSINGS

It takes me forever to say my prayers these days, but I don't care, because this time around, I want to make sure God doesn't have to do any guesswork.

—TERRY MCMILLAN

Mealtime prayers, chants, and blessings are a bit like the icing on the magical cake you've created. While the tradition of praying before dinner seems to have gone somewhat out of fashion in many homes, I think it's a lovely custom that works beautifully with candlelight recipes. Think of it somewhat like an invocation that welcomes the divine to your table to energize your magic even further.

Let me back up for a moment. I know that some Pagans and Wiccans feel a little uncomfortable about prayer because it reminds them of church. However, prayer need not be formalized or stagnant. In fact, it should be anything but that. And if we examine the thoughts on this subject by various theologians and philosophers (John Bunyan [1600s], Bishop Phillips Books [1800s], Victor Hugo, and R. W. Emerson—just to name a few) we discover something interesting. It seems that prayer is as much an attitude as it is an action—a demeanor of respect combined with focused will and anticipatory gratitude.

Even if you're not a deist, this time allows for a moment's pause to prepare your heart and mind for the energies you've created. The heart full of gratitude is one also ready to receive! If you do believe in god/dess, now's the opportunity to welcome him or her to your table. In either case, it's time well worth taking!

Now, don't get caught up in fancy words. Rather share what's in your heart. Focus on the goal of your candlelight recipe and direct the energy into your words and wishes. Visualize this like a circle of light surrounding everyone at the table and saturating every morsel of food. Then, at last, eat, drink, and let the magic manifest within and without.

So be it!

PART II

Gather Round the Fires

THE RECIPES

Keep up the fires of thought, and all will go well.

—HENRY DAVID THOREAU

Now it's time to get cooking! Part II is dedicated to candlelight recipes by theme. Before we begin, I would like to give you some helpful hints that should make using part II easier. First, when you think of the focus of your magical need, try to boil it down to one word. For example, if you wish to improve your finances, the key word might be *money* or *abundance*. See if that word is listed alphabetically in the table of contents for part II. If not, try synonyms. For example, if you were focusing on work, try themes like employment (under Providence Platters).

BTW, if you feel that more than one theme can help manifest your goal, use the ideas in each of those sections to mix, match, and plan your menu so it has just the right balance of vibrations to create the desired change. Make one dish or several and integrate them into your week to likewise integrate the energies each recipe creates! Trust your instincts and your taste buds! Magical food isn't much good if you can't eat it.

Second, if you are allergic to something in a recipe, or you know your family won't like a certain ingredient, try to find a meaningful substitute. Be careful not to eliminate necessary ingredients in the process, though. And don't forget that the beginning of each theme provides you with a list of potential candlelight recipe components that correspond to the magical intent of the spell. This list includes aromatics, types of candles, ingredients, decorative touches, and optional timing so that you can whip up your own original blends to incorporate the best of both worlds—your creativity and symbolic energy.

5

Dabbler's Dishes

THEY'RE NOT JUST FOR WITCHES ANYMORE

It would be remiss if I gave you the impression that candlelight recipes are only for witches. Throughout this book you'll hear me talk about members of my family who, as far as I know, were certainly not involved in the craft. Nonetheless, their attitude, outlooks, and passion for cooking instilled every bite they made with special energy. That means no matter what path you walk, you can use these recipes and cook up something really special. Just focus on your intention diligently, and get cooking!

What are some common things that nearly everyone desires? Well, beauty comes immediately to mind. Everyone likes to look and feel more attractive. If this is your goal, read the recipes under Appetizing Beauty and Attraction.

The second thing that people crave is good fortune. Luck may not solve everything, but it does make life a little more interesting and fun! If you're hoping to inspire more serendipity, turn to Luscious Luck recipes.

Finally, in this section, if you're coming up on an important business or personal commitment in your life that you really want to keep, we have foods for that too. The hectic nature of life combined with the pressures and nerves that often accompany commitments sometimes makes them hard to see through. Let magic help you. Whip up some Oath and Promise Provisions.

APPETIZING BEAUTY AND ATTRACTION

Beauty comes in all ages, colors, shapes, and forms.
God never makes junk.

—Kathy Ireland

It's perfectly natural to want to feel beautiful or handsome. In this case, we'll be making meals that help us shine from the inside out! As you're preparing these candlelight dishes remember to focus on your best attributes and bring them to the forefront. After all, attraction is, in part, a function of self-confidence and awareness. When you shine a light on those things that make you special, the small (and rather unimportant) flaws fade to the shadows where you can quietly work on them.

These dishes are ideal for those times when you feel a little frumpy, when you're going into important social situations, or when you just want to improve the way you feel about yourself.

Potential Abundance Components

- *Aromatics:* Rosemary, heather, lavender, tansy, ginseng, basil, catnip, nonedible lotus.
- *Candle types:* If you can find a candle designed like a white swan, that would be wonderful. Otherwise use a shape that's visually appealing to you.
- *Color:* Choose colors that bring out your best features (like your eyes) and that don't clash with your skin tone.
- *Candlelight recipe ingredients:* Beet, avocado, water, oats, egg, rosemary, tea, ham, apricot, pear, peanut oil, olive oil, cucumber, rosewater, honey.
- *Crystals, metals, stones:* Amber, cat's eye, amethyst.

- *Decorative touches:* Make sure these dishes *look* as good as they taste. Symbolically this creates sympathetic energy with your goal (i.e., to look good). Other items that accent your goal include willow wands, pearly items, soft lines in your tableware and decorations, swan imagery, and mirrors.
- *Timing:* Full moon, Leo or Virgo moon, May Day, Fridays.

APPETIZER

Alluring Avocado Gelatin

Makes 3 servings

Avocados are used as skin conditioners because they have natural moisturizing qualities. Symbolically speaking, the rough outer skin hides the inner lusciousness, which is exactly what you want to bring out in yourself to charm everyone you meet that day.

1 envelope lemon gelatin
½ cup plain yogurt
3 ounces avocado dip (store-bought is fine)
½ cup diced almonds

Magical preparations: Eyes are the window of the soul, and since this spell relies on your eyes to communicate a message (such as a come-hither look), it's important to treat them in a special manner. Lay a couple of cucumber slices or cool tea bags over them for about 15 minutes before creating this candlelight recipe. This reduces puffiness (which isn't very appealing anyway) and provides a fresh outlook for approaching your magic!

Candle types: Take a candle into the space where you'll be preparing this dish. Let that gentle light shine into your aura to spark the fires of confidence.

Prepare the gelatin as directed. Stir in the yogurt. Add avocado dip, beating until frothy (this increases the ambient energy for your spell). Stir in the nuts. As you do recite an incantation like:

Beauty within, confidence without,
Remove all fear, remove all doubt!

Refrigerate 2 hours until firm (this is kind of neat in that the firming process symbolically "firms up" anything saggy, baggy, and frumpy including attitudes). Serve with sliced avocados as garnish, or perhaps a hard boiled egg on the side (eggs are another beautifying food that continues to be used in salons for skin care).

As you eat, visualize yourself in the most positive way possible, then go out and meet the world head on! You'll be amazed to discover how many people comment on noticing something "different" about you!

Adaptations: Substitute strawberry gelatin for self-love, or orange gelatin for sex appeal. You can also use apricot gelatin instead of avocados. Apricots are said to make those who eat them as delectable and attractive as the fruit itself. Sounds good to me!

BEVERAGES

Perfectly Pleasing Pear Cocktail

Makes 1 serving

Pears are sacred to Hera who had a peacock as one of her sacred animals, an animal known for its beautiful feathers and seemingly unmatched confidence. This symbolizes the kind of self-pride we're looking to create. The shape of the pear may make this drink more suitable for women (men may wish to substitute apple liquor, which has stronger masculine energies).

1 teaspoon pear flavored liqueur
6 ounces champagne
1 fresh pear, sliced, for garnish

Magical preparations: Prepare yourself for this candlelight recipe by standing in front of a mirror and saying:

Mirror mirror, reflect to me
Of what I am, and what I can be
Mirror mirror, where magic abides
Inspire in me healthy self-pride!

Candle types: Pick out a personally pleasing color for your candle and bring it into the sacred kitchen.

Pour pear liqueur into a champagne glass. Swirl this so it coats the inside. Top with champagne and garnish with a pear slice. (Note: If you're feeling creative you can easily carve a symbol of pride or confidence into the pear slice too.)

Stunning Spiced Punch

Makes 2 servings

Most of the herbs in this zesty blend support your goal of attractiveness. Vanilla, for example, is a seedpod harvested from orchids. (A lovely flower!) It's said that the Aztec people wore vanilla flowers to attract people but to repel insects! Additionally it represents eternal happiness, in this case joy and confidence in yourself!

2¼ cups water
⅓ cup orange blossom honey
¼ cup (packed) light brown sugar
2 tablespoons chopped peeled fresh ginger
16 whole cloves
16 whole allspice
1 vanilla bean, chopped
1 Earl Grey tea bag
(750-ml) bottle dry red wine
¼ cup dark rum

Magical preparations: Use a little ginger, cloves, and allspice and simmer them on the stove to fill your kitchen with warm, eye-catching vibrations.

Candle types: Definitely use a vanilla candle, as the scent increases energy and improves your focus.

In a large saucepan, combine the first seven ingredients. Using medium heat, bring mixture to a boil. Stir to make sure the honey dissolves. Continue a low, rolling boil for 5 minutes. Turn off the heat and add the tea bag. Steep for 5 minutes. Remove, then add the wine and rum. Serve this warm (for stimulating warm reactions).

Temptation Tea

Makes 5 cups

Many botanists claim that the true fruit that tempted Eve was not an apple, but a golden apricot. When you want to be just as tempting, try this tea blend!

3 orange pekoe tea bags
5 cups water
3 cups apricot nectar, chilled
Sugar or honey to taste

Magical preparations: What tempts your mate? What are your date's greatest weaknesses when it comes to appetizers, snacks, etc.? Make sure to have some of these items scattered around the sacred space to begin the energy of enticement!

Candle types: Dab your favorite perfume on the candles and carve a symbol of the aspect of yourself that you want to be the most attractive (like an eye if you want people to notice your eyes more or your neck if you want to be nuzzled).

Put tea bags in a heatproof decanter. In a saucepan bring water just to a boil and pour over tea bags. Steep tea 5 minutes and remove tea bags. Cool tea and chill, about 1 hour. Add nectar and sweetener saying:

Tempt, coax, attract
With my magic react!

Drink just before going to a social situation.

MAIN DISHES

Gorgeous Ginger Noodles

Makes 2–4 servings

Ginger has often been considered a spice of paradise, and it was a common ingredient in perfumes and foods meant to attract attention and inspire passion. The Greeks even believed the phoenix built its nest in knowing that the aroma of this spice would help it fly. The aroma of ginger can also give flight to our sense of attractiveness and overall confidence.

VEGETABLES

2 tablespoons peanut oil
2 tablespoons minced fresh ginger
8 ounces broccoli, cut into florets
1 large carrot, peeled, cut into thin strips
1 celery stalk, thinly sliced
1 tablespoon diced garlic
8 green onions, chopped
1 medium zucchini, cut into ⅓-inch-thick slices
1 medium-size yellow squash, cut into ⅓-inch-thick slices
1 red bell pepper, cut into thin strips
2 tablespoons dry sherry
10 ounces extra-firm tofu, cut into ½-inch pieces
Salt and pepper to taste

NOODLES

12 ounces spaghetti, freshly cooked
Peanut sauce to taste (available at Asian and international stores)
1 cup lightly salted roasted peanuts

Magical preparations: Your working and serving space should be visually appealing for this dish (the more attractive it appears to you, the better the energy you're creating).

Candle types: Go with a fancy candle, perhaps the floating ones shaped like blossoming flowers.

☙ For the vegetables, pour the peanut oil in a wok or large nonstick skillet over medium-high heat. Be sure to move it around the pan clockwise to generate positive energy. Add ginger and stir 30 seconds. Add broccoli, carrot, and celery and sauté 5 minutes. This is a good time to use a verbal component like:

A little bit of glamour
Tossed into this mix
Sprinkled with the ginger
With magic, now affix!

Add the remaining ingredients except the tofu and sauté until vegetables are crisp-tender, about 3 minutes longer. Finally, toss in the tofu and heat through, about 2 minutes. Season with salt and pepper.

For the noodles, place spaghetti in a large bowl and toss it with the peanut sauce. Place this in a circle on a serving platter and put the vegetable mixture in the center. Sprinkle with peanuts just prior to serving.

Ham It Up!

Makes 4 servings

For this ham sandwich recipe we're depending on the saying "hamming it up" and the overall appearance of the dish to inspire self-confidence and a theatrical flair that concludes with a strong performance of which you can feel proud.

2 cups egg salad
6 ounces smoked ham, diced into ½-inch pieces
½ cup thinly sliced green onions
Dollop of mayonnaise
Salt and pepper to taste
4 hero rolls
1 red bell pepper, thinly sliced into rings
4 large romaine lettuce leaves

Magical preparations: You must look and feel your best for this spell recipe. Put on a piece of clothing or jewelry that makes you feel really special. As you don that item (or items) say:

Puttin' on the ritz, putting on the glitz
Inside my heart, beauty sits
Attractive without, attractive within
By my will, let this spell begin!

Candle types: This is all about what makes you feel good, so choose the color of candles and the aromatics accordingly.

Place your hands, palms down over your ingredients before you start blending them, and repeat your incantation three more times. Three is the number of body/mind/spirit in symmetry, something that also emphasizes the goal of beauty within and without!

Mix egg salad, smoked ham, and green onions in a medium bowl. Stir in mayonnaise. Season to taste with salt and pepper. This is enough for the four rolls you have, so divide the mixture accordingly adding pepper rings and lettuce into the bread's protective womb where the energy can grow and blossom.

SIDE DISHES

Beauty Beets!

Makes 2 servings

This side dish's energy is going to be directed at improving the attractiveness of your hair. If beets were good enough to maintain Aphrodite's beauty (the Greek goddess of passion), then they're certainly good enough for us mortals! The ginger in this recipe provides additional energy, while pear juice promotes improvements in your hair and complexion.

3 medium beets
6 cups water
Pinch of salt
Capful of vinegar
3 ounces pear nectar
½ teaspoon cornstarch
½ tablespoon honey
¼ teaspoon ground ginger

Preparing the cauldron: Since the focus of this spell is your hair, take the time beforehand to wash it well. Many spiritual traditions use baths and bathing as a means to clean away unwanted energy and prepare the aura to accept the magic more readily. As you wash, you can hum that old *South Pacific* tune "I'm Gonna Wash That Man Right Out of My Hair," with a few minor changes that direct the word-power toward your goals. For example:

Gonna wash that anger out of my hair
Gonna wash that sadness out of my hair
Gonna wash that self-doubt out of my hair
And send them on their way!

Candle types: Match the aroma of your candle to whatever hair product you use (for example, if you have a floral shampoo, use a floral-scented candle).

It was not unusual for ancient cultures to use vegetables and fruits as poppets, little dolls that represent people. In this case, your beet is your poppet and you will begin by cutting its "hair" off—namely the beat tops! Boil the beats in the water to which the pinch of salt and capful of vinegar have been placed (both salt and vinegar have purifying qualities). Boil the beets for 50 minutes until they are tender, then chill for about an hour in a container whose color matches that of your hair (roughly). This creates a sympathy between your goal and the food.

Meanwhile, blend pear nectar with cornstarch, honey, and ginger. Warm this over a low flame until it comes to a boil and thickens slightly. Symbolically speaking this promotes thick, luxurious hair. Remove the beets from the refrigerator, cutting off the skins and ends, and slice them thinly. If you want, you could certainly shape them at this juncture, like hearts (to inspire loving glances) or other symbols. Pour the ginger sauce over top to surround the beets with all that warm, good-hair energy, and enjoy!

Hint: After consuming this candlelight recipe, go to a professional hairstylist and let the magical energy within you inspire his or her work. Get a good trim, conditioning, and styling and just watch and see the amazing results in both your appearance and your outlooks!

Charming Cucumber Salad

Makes 4 servings

Beauty has a lot of dimensions from the drop-dead visual beauty to quiet internal loveliness, and let's not forget about how powerful cuteness can be (just look at the reaction puppies get!). When you'd like that rather innocent, "cute" appeal, this salad serves the energy up just right.

Cucumbers have been cultivated for over 3,000 years. They provide us with a cool head alchemically (being aligned with the Water element) and have been used in cosmetics for a long time as skin softeners/whiteners. On a personal note, my children must be awfully cute since I cannot keep any cucumbers in the house for more than moments at a time!

2 large cucumbers, English style, seedless
2 tablespoons salt
1/3 cup water
5 tablespoons red wine vinegar
1 tablespoon sugar
2 tablespoons minced dill
Salt and pepper to taste

Magical preparations: Don something white, the color of innocence. If the item is soft and cuddly, even better (there's something about cuteness that makes people more huggable!). Bless the item saying:

> _____ [type of clothing] *of white*
> *Of spirit's light*
> *Give to me an aura bright!*
> *Filled with innocence, and charm so fair*
> *For as long as this _____ I wear!*

Candle types: Stick with the colors of youth and innocence like white, pink, and basic pastels.

Now make the spell recipe!

Peel the cucumbers decoratively so that you have alternating strips of white and green all the way around. Magically this does two things. It provides a balance between earthy energy (green) and purity (white) so that you're wholly approachable. Second, peeling the cucumber helps "peel away" unwanted self-images.

Slice the cucumbers very thinly. Put these into a container and sprinkle salt over top (a purifier). Chill for 2 hours. Next, drain any excess liquid created from the salting, which also drains away any unwanted energies. Place the cucumbers in a bowl with all the remaining ingredients saying:

Sugar for sweetness
Dill for delight
Pleasing all day, enchanting all night!

Marinate in the refrigerator for an additional 2 hours, shaking or stirring regularly so the cucumbers absorb the energy. Serve with a sprig of dill for garnish and eat playfully with your fingers to help inspire the right attitude.

Adaptations: If you're hoping for physical appearances to inspire a bit of sexual attraction, toss 2 large stalks of celery (Romans ate celery to improve their sex drive) into this blend, diced, during the marination. A couple of sliced tomatoes as garnish will increase the effect, but with more loving overtones.

DESSERT

Charismatic Cookies

Makes 3 dozen

These oatmeal cookies will sweetly inspire your most charming attributes. Oats are ruled by the planet Venus and are often used in facial masks to improve the skin's shine and tightness. Here, we're making them into a sweet treat to nibble when you're feeling a little self-conscious or frumpy. It will transform and fluff up that limp energy, giving you an irresistible aura.

½ cup (1 stick) softened butter
⅔ cup packed brown sugar
1 egg, beaten
1 teaspoon vanilla
½ cup peanut butter
1 cup flour
½ teaspoon baking soda
½ teaspoon salt
1 cup rolled oats
Jelly, optional (your choice)

Magical preparations: Put on an item whose color is assuring and uplifting to you. For some people red works very well as a power color, but whatever your choice make sure it's vivid! You're trying to say "notice me" and "hey, I've got it together" and drab colors just don't portray those attitudes. Additionally, consider preparing this candlelight recipe on Sunday, a day that supports the qualities of leadership, assurance, and poise.

Candle types: The bigger and brighter the better! Banish any lingering gray clouds altogether!

Preheat the oven to 350 degrees F. Cream the butter and sugar together to smooth the way for personal change. Add the egg and vanilla, beating this well as you say:

Charm, charisma, appeal
In this blend, my magic seal!
Allure, magnetism, and enchantment shine
And as I mix, I make them mine!

Next, stir in the peanut butter by hand (peanut butter's sticky nature helps the magic "stick" to you). Continue stirring until smooth. (Again, you don't want the path to transformation to be bumpy!) To this add the remaining dry ingredients. Mix well.

Using a teaspoon, drop cookies onto a non-stick cookie sheet and make a dimple in the middle for your choice of jelly. Use strawberry jelly for self-confidence in a relationship, peach jelly for confidence in your wisdom, or orange jelly for confidence in managing finances. Fill, then bake for about 13 minutes.

Before you have to go out in public, eat one of these cookies, making a conscious effort to nibble away at any self-defeating attitudes you might be harboring.

Adaptations: Choose the flavor of the jelly so it represents your goals. If wanting some attention at work, for example, mint is a good choice since it represents prosperity and sweetens your breath! Apple improves your confidence for bringing peace to a touchy situation, or honey can be used to bring certainty in a health-related situation.

LUSCIOUS LUCK

Diligence is the mother of good luck.

—Benjamin Franklin

My life is such that it seems luck always comes to someone else. Perhaps Mom was right when she said we make our own luck, but I would like to think that magic can help in that arena, too, especially when nothing but bad luck comes our way. There are cycles like that in life, but the cycle can be broken by transforming the energy in and around yourself and directing magic toward more neutral ground. From there it's much easier to begin to generate a positive trend.

I don't look at luck as being evidenced by "big" things—rather, it's in the little moments and gentle smiles they bring. Finding a five-dollar bill when you need gas in the car is one example. Luck tilts the law of cause and effect just a tiny bit in our favor as long as we shape our recipe spells with *good* luck in mind. The universe has an odd way of teaching us about how important specifics are in our workings—and if you just ask for "luck" you could get good luck *or* bad luck, so be specific!

Potential Luck Components:

- *Aromatics:* Allspice, cinnamon, basil, nutmeg.
- *Candle notes:* Use your "lucky" number of candles, or choose those that are as close as possible to what you consider your fortunate color.
- *Color:* Red, white, rainbows (or a color that you associate with luck).
- *Candlelight recipe ingredients:* Fish, cabbage, champagne, bread, cherries, corn, apples, egg, heather, kiwi, nasturtium, onion, parsley, rabbit, Yule pudding, rice, black-eyed peas, coconut, kumquat, mincemeat, pear, red foods (like beets and pomegranates), bamboo shoots, orange, pineapple, wine, tea, sugarcane.
- *Crystals, metals, stones:* Jade, carnelian, tin, copper, cat's eye.
- *Decorative touches:* Decorate your serving space with items that have serendipity in their design—like a found coin, a dragonfly image, and rainbow hues. Flowers to consider include violets and primroses.
- *Timing:* Blue moon, Dawn, the season of spring, Virgo or Pisces moon.

APPETIZER

Providence Salad

Makes 6 servings

Greek legend tells us that the nasturtium sprang from a brave fallen warrior's blood. If such good things can come for him, we will trust in this plant's bravery to get us through hard times and make something good come of a bad situation. In particular nasturtium enlists the aid of fairy folks to help improve your luck.

1 cup olive oil
½ cup red wine vinegar
1 cup lemon balm, coarsely shredded
4 tablespoons fresh chopped parsley
1 teaspoon salt and pepper
2 cups multicolored nasturtium blossoms, whole (if you have them in your "lucky" color that would be best)
1 head iceberg lettuce, shredded
4 small tomatoes, thinly sliced
4 radishes, thinly sliced
4 eggs, boiled and halved

Magical preparations: Since you're hoping to attract some helpful fairy friends, leave out a small cup of sweet milk or mead and sweetbreads on your windowsill for them. Also, if you can work this recipe at dawn, noon, or dusk (in-between times) that will improve your chances of devic contact.

Candle types: Avoid red ones (this color is said to be disliked by fairies).

Combine olive oil, red wine vinegar, lemon balm, parsley, salt, and black pepper. Cover and chill half an hour until ingredients have blended flavors. Meanwhile, combine nasturtiums, lettuce, tomatoes, and radishes. Pour over dressing and toss to coat well. As you do, hum a happy tune (fairies like humans who have a playful side) and perhaps call them into your space with an invitation like:

Fairy friends of earth or wind, hearken as this spell begins
Fairy friends of water and fire, push the energy ever higher
And in this food I leave my wish
Good luck and fortune served with this dish!

Serve chilled, garnished with egg halves. This salad makes a colorful prelude to steak and chicken at summer barbecues.

BEVERAGES

Fortune in a Teacup

Makes 6 servings

If the flow of good luck could be easily poured into a glass, this beverage would be the perfect choice! It has all the right herbs and spices, along with some champagne to uplift the energy in the whole blend, and rum to protect your luck when it arrives.

2¼ cups water
⅓ cup sugar
¼ cup brown sugar
1 tablespoon chopped ginger
8 cloves
8 allspice berries
2 vanilla tea bags
2 orange tea bags
1 (750-ml) bottle dry champagne
¼ cup rum (optional)

Magical preparations: According to early American folklore, putting the tea and sugar into your pot before the water or milk insures good luck. Give this a try while adding an incantation like:

Sugar brings luck so very sweet,
My every need, this magic meets
Soon ill fortunes shall all abate
With tea to transform my future fate!

Candle types: Add a candle in your "lucky" color to the above spell by lighting it before you recite the incantation.

Boil the water. Meanwhile, place the sugar, spices, and tea into a kettle or pot, pouring the boiled water over top. Let this steep for 10 minutes until heady with aroma. Whisper your wishes into the steam so it rises to the four winds to express your need.

Strain this into a punch bowl (perhaps one that's your lucky color) and add the champagne and rum. Serve over crushed ice.

Adaptations: Play with a variety of tea bags to direct luck to the area where you most need it, like mint instead of orange for financial luck. Additionally you can use honey instead of sugar to stimulate more serendipity.

Kismet Kiwi Sangria

Makes 8 servings

The geranium in this recipe speaks of your hopes and dreams, while the kiwi bird (after whom the fruit receives its name) helps you sniff out fortunate opportunities where they lie. Kiwis are known for having a fantastic sense of smell!

8 cups water
8 wild-berry tea bags
2 cups sugar
4 (1-pint) baskets strawberries, hulled
2 (25.4-ounce) bottles chilled sparkling apple cider
6 kiwis, peeled, cut into ½-inch cubes
16 fresh rose geranium leaves, crushed slightly
¼ teaspoon rosewater
4 cups ice cubes

Magical preparations: If you grow geraniums it would be a nice touch to have a bouquet of them either in the working or serving space for this candlelight recipe. You can also dry some petals to use in luck-oriented charms. If not, look to some incense that will support the goal of both insight and luck (like lotus).

Candle types: Choose candles that best represent the area of your life where you want to apply this energy effectively.

Bring 4 cups of the water to boil in a large saucepan. Add tea bags; cover and let steep 10 minutes. This is a good opportunity to put your hands over the pot (palms down) and bless the blend with a prayer or incantation. If a prayer, direct it to your chosen pantry god or goddess. Remember to be specific.

Discard tea bags. Add sugar to hot tea; stir until dissolved. Stir in remaining 4 cups of the water. Chill tea until cold. Meanwhile, puree 2 baskets of strawberries. Slice remaining 2 baskets strawberries. Place pureed and sliced berries in large pitcher. Add tea and all the remaining ingredients. Stir and serve.

MAIN DISH

Coincidence Chicken

Makes 4 servings

Coincidence can be a fun thing, and it can also help guide you in a positive direction. The heather in this recipe inspires a change by opening a new path—an odd chain of events that brings you to a different place. It also protects you on the road to your newfound luck.

1 (4-pound) whole chicken
3 ounces olive oil
4 ounces heather honey
Salt and pepper
3 ounces Dijon mustard
1 teaspoon chopped garlic
Fresh heather flowers
¼ cup zinfandel

Magical preparations: Make yourself a lucky charm using heather (or a picture of a heather flower). Wrap it in a cloth of your favorite color and bless it saying:

A turn of events
An unexpected way
Where once a wall, an opening
Transform my luck today!

Candle types: I like to use spiral shaped candles for this spell because they spiral the energy outward and represent the "turning and changing" desired.

Preheat the oven to 375 degrees F. Put the chicken in a baking dish that can be covered. Mix all but the heather flowers and zinfandel together and rub this into the chicken's skin (if you have a flavor injector, inject half under the skin). Dip the heather flowers in the wine and place them inside the bird (this creates an amazing aroma but it's an optional step if you can't find the fresh, organic flowers).

Bake, covered, for nearly 2 hours, basting regularly. If you wish, you can repeat your verse for the luck charm during the basting process. Uncover for another 20 minutes or so until the chicken browns. Let sit at room temperature for about 10 minutes before carving. The remaining drippings make a tasty gravy that can support the magic already saturated into the meat.

Lucky Fish

Makes 2 servings

Need a fortunate windfall or a dramatic change in fate? This recipe produces the energy necessary to help that happen. According to an Arabian proverb, pitch a lucky man into the Nile and he will come up with a fish in his mouth! In this case we're one step ahead of the game because we already have the fish (and it doesn't have to be Friday)!

1 tablespoon chopped garlic
1 cup diced red and white onion
⅛ cup olive oil
Pinch oregano
¼ cup wine vinegar
¼ cup cooking wine
Pinch sugar
½ pound white fish fillet strips
¼ cup milk
Seasoned flour, for dredging
Salt and pepper

Magical preparations: It's fun to do a whole fishing motif for this candlelight recipe. Wear a fisherman's cap. Create a makeshift fishing line out of a wooden spoon and some thread. And on the end of that thread place an edible item that represents the area of your life in which more luck is needed. For example, if you need financial luck—use something green. Dip this periodically in the marinade to catch luck while saying:

Oil smoothes the way for change,
All my luck—rearrange
Here, surrounded in fine wine,
I claim my fate, good luck is mine

If the item you've chosen needs to be cooked, cook it with the fish. Otherwise, eat it before starting the spell recipe. This adjusts your aura to better accept the energies you're about to create.

Candle types: At the end of the candlelight recipe you can burn your fishing line in the fire of the candle to release your wishes to the winds.

☙ Sauté the garlic and onion in the olive oil, then move this into a marinating dish. Add the oregano, vinegar, your choice of cooking wine, and sugar. Let the fish marinate in this mixture for 2 to 3 hours. Drain.

Dip the fish in milk, which nurtures your magic, then dredge in flour seasoned with salt and pepper. Fry this in a nonstick pan until golden brown. Note that after the first turn you can etch an image into the surface of the fish to energize your focus further.

Drain on paper towels and serve with a hearty portion of rice (especially good for luck with money) or potatoes (which provide solid foundations in which your fortune can take root).

Adaptations: Use white wine in this recipe if you were born under the sign of Aries, if you want luck with friendship or need assistance with a difficult change. Use a red wine if you were born under Scorpio, if you need luck with health or a leadership matter.

Prospect Spaghetti

Makes 3 to 4 servings

Open Sesame! That's the key phrase for this dish. Make and consume this fortunate candlelight recipe, and like Aladdin watch the path to improved luck open before you with amazing ease.

1 tablespoon chopped garlic
1/8 cup sesame oil
1 1/2 tablespoons soy sauce
3/4 tablespoon rice vinegar
1/4 cup cashews, chopped
2 tablespoons sesame seeds
1/4 cup water
1/2 pound thin spaghetti
sesame sticks for garnish

Magical preparations: It was quite common in Arabic regions, especially among merchants, to have a special prayer rug that people took with them everywhere! In this case, if you have a small pretty rug around the house, bring it into your kitchen. Sit comfortably, take several deep breaths, and pray to spirit in whatever manner feels comfortable, especially a god or goddess under whose dominion luck and fate come! Express your needs and ask for a blessing on your candlelight recipe, then stand on the rug while you cook to keep that energy flowing!

Candle types: White, or a color that honors the deity toward whom you directed your prayer.

Sauté the garlic in sesame oil. Transfer this into a blender adding the soy sauce, vinegar, cashews, seeds, and water. Blend this until smooth saying:

Open Sesame!
Open the way
I need fast changes
Bring good luck, today!

Let this mixture sit at room temperature while you prepare the spaghetti to personally desired tenderness. Toss the drained spaghetti noodles with the sauce (to stir up good fortune) and garnish with sesame sticks.

Adaptations: Add some chicken marinated with soy and ginger to the blend for luck with your well-being, or pork for luck in the way people perceive you.

SIDE DISH

Auspicious Spinach

Makes 4 servings

In the Far East bamboo shoots represent strength, vitality, durability, and long life. In general, they're a lucky plant. When combined with the rich green of spinach, this dish makes formidable energy toward your fortunate goals.

1 pound fresh spinach
½ cup peanut oil
¼ cup shredded bamboo shoots
1 garlic clove, minced
Pinch lemon zest
1½ teaspoons salt
2 teaspoons sugar

Magical preparations: Get yourself a living piece of bamboo and tend it well. Each time you water it, thank the spirit of the plant for its lucky energies. If you're the black thumb type, you can instead simply dry a piece of bamboo shoot and carry it as a good luck charm.

Candle types: Use a lucky number of candles, perhaps in dark green especially if you're looking for luck with money.

Wash spinach leaves thoroughly under cold running water. Drain well. Heat the oil in a skillet. Using a medium-high flame, cook the bamboo shoots, garlic, and lemon in the oil for approximately 45 seconds, stirring constantly. With your movements add a verbal component like:

Fortune favors those who do not wait
I, for one, will not hesitate
When opportunity comes my way
I'll seize the moment
I'll seize the day!

Add spinach and stir until wilted. Add salt and sugar, and cook, stirring, 2 minutes longer.

Chance-It Coleslaw

Makes 2 servings

Ever catch yourself saying "if I only had the chance"? Well, let this dish implore the fates on your behalf! There are five main candlelight recipe ingredients in this dish, the number of the pentagram, which will also protect your luck once it arrives. (Usually within five days of making this dish!)

$1\frac{1}{4}$ cups green cabbage, shredded
$\frac{1}{4}$ cup shredded carrot
$\frac{1}{4}$ cup shredded red cabbage
$\frac{1}{2}$ cup baby peas or snow peas
$\frac{1}{4}$ cup springwater sprouts (optional)
2 teaspoons wine vinegar
$\frac{1}{2}$ teaspoon dry mustard
$\frac{1}{2}$ teaspoon ground ginger
2 tablespoons sesame oil
1 teaspoon soy sauce

Magical preparations: Chance is often as much a matter of luck as it is a matter of personal ingenuity. So if you can prepare this dish at noon for mental clarity and perception, all the better.

Candle types: Light a yellow candle in the area where you're working (for creativity) saying:

The light of hope, be with me
The light of awareness and insight, fill me
The light of protection, surround me
The light of luck, be mine

Place the first five ingredients in a large bowl and toss. This is a good time to repeat your incantation to reinforce the magic you began.

In a separate container, blend the remaining ingredients to create a zesty dressing that jumps with lucky energy. Make sure everything is well blended, then pour as much as you wish over the cabbage mixture. Eat with hope in your heart and watch what options open to you in the next few days, or even hours!

Adaptations: Increase the proportion of red cabbage for luck in love, or the amount of carrot for good fortune with fertility-related matters.

DESSERT

Fortune Tart

Makes 8 servings

Your fate isn't written in the stars, it's baked into these little lucky mandala tarts! When you want a change, or even just want things to keep going the way they have because all is well, the symbol of a circle moves and manifests the magic you want.

1 cup shredded, sweet coconut
8 small tart crusts
3 teaspoons instant coffee crystals
2 cups coconut pudding
Whipped cream for garnish

Magical preparations: Prebaked tart crusts are fairly sturdy. Get a toothpick and etch each one with a symbol that represents the area of your life where you require luck. For example, if you want luck finding a house, draw a simple image of a house gently in the inner bottom of the crust so that you can fill that image with magic, and then bake the energy into every crack!

Candle types: Mirror the pattern in your piecrust and carve that into your candle.

Sprinkle coconut evenly over the bottom of the tart crusts. Stir just a little warm water into the coffee crystals so they dissolve, then mix this into the coconut pudding (magically this gives you more power for manifestation). Stir clockwise saying:

See the wishes of my heart,
Put good luck within these tarts!
And when we go to take a bite,
Let the magic take to flight!

Put ¼ cup of filling into each tart and garnish with whipped cream. Repeat the second half of the incantation just before you dig in!

Adaptations: Flavor the whipped cream in various ways to accent your goals. Use vanilla extract for luck in the bedroom, add a pinch of allspice for even more luck, stir in a drop of almond flavoring for luck with money, or a dash of cinnamon with luck in your spiritual life.

Serendipity Sauce

Makes 1 cup

When you want a nice warm blend that brings out serendipity in a bold and zesty way, make this sauce and enjoy it over some vanilla ice cream . . . to saver sweet success!

½ cup mincemeat
⅓ cup sugar
½ cup orange juice
¼ cup ginger brandy
1 teaspoon cinnamon
2 tablespoons whipping cream

Magical preparations: Find a dish that's made in your lucky color to serve out this spell. If that's not possible put on a shirt or some other item of clothing that really energizes you. Remember, luck has a lot to do with your personal vibes—if you feel down, you tend to attract negativity instead of the good stuff you want.

Candle types: Consider dabbing them with cinnamon or orange oil in keeping with the recipe's ingredients.

In a medium saucepan, combine the first five ingredients saying:

Mincemeat to bless this lucky treat
Sugar to make the spell complete
Orange juice for healthy thoughts and ways
Brandy to protect me all my days
And last, a pinch of cinnamon flick
So that fortune starts to stick!

Warm this over a medium flame, stirring clockwise until the sugar is completely integrated. Slowly raise the temperature so the liquid boils, then simmer over a low flame until the sauce reduces and thickens to the consistency of maple syrup. Remove from the heat, adding cream, then chill and use as desired.

Adaptations: To make this sauce even more fortune bearing, serve it on Christmas Day. To direct the energy of the sauce into specific areas of your life, you can use numeric or flavor correspondences for the ice cream. For example, if you want luck in a partnership, serve the sauce over 2 small scoops of ice cream. Or, if you want luck with money, serve the sauce over a bit of orange sherbet.

OATH AND PROMISE PROVISIONS

An acre of performance is worth a whole world of promise.

—WILLIAM DEAN HOWELLS

The saying goes that the road to hell is paved with good intentions. While witches don't believe in hell, we know a lot about good intentions. Our hope is to always work with trust and love as a guide—but love and trust are earned. One way of earning both is to stick to our promises like glue. Unfortunately, life doesn't always make this easy to do, no matter how much we originally anticipated so doing. That's where a little magic can step in and help us, especially when we feel our resolve wavering.

Potential Promise Components

- *Aromatics:* Rose, bay, orange, lemon, nutmeg, basil.
- *Candle type:* Consider carving your chosen candles with the image of a knot, or something else that (to you) represents steadfast commitment. Place this image at the very bottom (the foundation) of the candle to symbolize your intention as stabilizing the magical energy.

- *Color:* For purity, white is a good choice.
- *Candlelight recipe ingredients:* Lemon, fig, sunflower seed, orange, honey, peanut butter, sticky foods, salt, wine, rosewater, onion, garlic, tea, plantain, mulberry, rye, licorice, cumin, lettuce, beans, vinegar, apple.
- *Crystals, metals, stones:* Carnelian, amethyst, agate.
- *Decorative touches:* If there's a way to serve your food from one common container, or beverage from one shared cup, it strengthens the symbolic value of unity. For flowers consider magnolia, which represents devotion in the language of flowers.
- *Timing:* Virgo, Libra, or Aries moon; Thursdays; when the sun is shining (so there's no shadow of doubt).

APPETIZER

Certainty Onion Salad

Makes 4 to 6 servings

Devotion implies a sense of safety and security—of knowing that what you've started will last. Both the lemons and onions in this candlelight recipe are perfect to this task, providing fresh ongoing preservative power and protection.

3 cups red onions, thinly sliced
½ cup parsley leaves
2 tablespoons olive oil
1 lemon
1 large garlic clove, minced
¼ teaspoon ground coriander
Salt to taste

Magical preparations: Consider the focus of your spell recipe, then choose, mix, and mingle the type of onions used in this dish for a variety of energy. For example, use white onions to manifest pure intentions, Spanish onions if you want your commitments to endure, and cooking onions for commitments having to do with domestic matters.

Candle types: Match your candle's color to intention and perhaps use four of them to create strong foundations.

☙ Take care in slicing the onions so you get unbroken rings. (This will help increase the protective power of this dish by surrounding your promise with a sacred circle.) Rinse the onions gently, then drain. Place these in a bowl with the remaining ingredients and chill for a half hour before serving. This will provide you with a clearer mind for whatever promise needs your attention. Just before serving you may wish to add an incantation like:

Within these sacred circles, drawn round
My personal commitment shall abound
Then when accepted, from without to within
So the magic shall begin.

Adaptations: Toss in some sliced green olives if you would like to feel at peace with a promise regarding money, or black olives for a promise relating to personal health and well-being.

Oathing Orange Breadsticks

Makes 16 large bread sticks

These breadsticks bind your magical desire and your promise into the dough as you twist them into shape! Then eating them releases the magic to where you need it most—within! They also make neat edible magic wands!

1 loaf frozen bread dough
2 tablespoons aniseed, crushed
1 tablespoon fennel seeds, crushed
2 tablespoons grated orange peel, powdered
Cornmeal
1 egg, beaten
Coarse salt (optional)

Magical Preparations: Make yourself a portable charm for commitment based on the idea for this candlelight recipe. In Arabia and other parts of the world, knots were often used to bind energy and keep it safe until needed. In this case, get some yarn or a small piece of sturdy cord and bind it into three knots, repeating this incantation thrice with each knot:

it is not the cord I bind, but my magic spell
heed my words and heed them well
commitment and devotion shall be found
when this knot is then unbound!

Carry this with you anywhere you wish, but only release a knot when you really need the energy. Never undo the third one. It should remain in place so you can re-use and recharge the charm.

Candle types: Following the pattern of your spell thus far, consider using three candles and allowing only two to burn out. Keep the other one safe for similar magical goals.

Defrost the bread dough according to the directions provided. Once it's completely defrosted, let the dough begin to rise for 30 minutes in a warm area covered by a cloth. Blend the aniseed, fennel seed, and orange peel evenly into the dough, then let it rise again for 1 hour. Remember that this process also "raises energy!"

Divide the dough into 16 equal portions. Sprinkle the cornmeal on a large nonstick surface like a cookie sheet. Roll each of the dough pieces into a long rope, then roll the rope into the cornmeal. Twist this into any magical shape you need (like a heart for love), or an equidistant cross that represents balance and symmetry. With the cross shape you can add a verbal component like this, touching each of the four quarter points as you speak:

I affirm my words will be true to my promise (air)
I affirm giving on-going energy to my promise (south)
I affirm my heart's desire to keep this promise (west)
I affirm my dedication to manifesting this promise (north)

Leave the twisted shapes to rise again for 45 minutes.

Preheat the oven to 375 degrees F. Brush the top of the bread twists with a little beaten egg, then sprinkle with salt. Bake for approximately 20 minutes until golden brown (they will sound hollow in the center if tapped lightly). Cool and enjoy!

Adaptations: If several people are involved in a promise, have each one help weave the breadsticks into a braid. Then eating the braid indicates each person's acceptance of the promise made, and his or her commitment to keeping it.

BEVERAGES

Guarantee Grapefruit and Orange Juice

Makes 6 cups

Making a blood pact has gone out of fashion for health reasons in modern times; however, it was not unusual even fifty years ago to see kids making themselves blood brothers and sisters. For this recipe we'll use blood oranges as a substitute for the "blood" pact, and grapefruit for clear intention.

3 cups fresh red grapefruit juice
3 cups fresh blood-orange juice
Ice

Note: If you cannot find blood oranges, pomegranate juice may be substituted here without changing the energy of the candlelight recipe.

Candle types: Go with red to stick with the color theme of the beverage.

Delightfully simple to assemble, just put everything in a blender adding as much ice as you wish for texture (this makes it more like a smoothie). As the beverage whips you can focus on your goal and add an incantation like:

My promises made with a cool head
May I always stand by what I've said
Like blood ties that run thick and deep
I only make promises I intend to keep.

Honeymoon Mead

Makes 1 liter

Mead is a honey-based wine that was often used to seal promises, especially those given in love throughout Europe. Also, according to Roman tradition, the honey in the mead will make your promises long lasting and incredibly eloquent and creative!

1 liter dry red wine
½ orange, peeled and sliced
1 cup honey
1 teaspoon rosewater (available at many international supermarkets and Asian shops)

Magical preparations: When you're slicing the orange for this candlelight recipe, get creative and shape the slices to look like hearts so they symbolize your intention. As you do, focus on the feelings you have in your heart and say:

> *Orange for fidelity*
> *Devotion and true love abide with me!*

Candle types: You could use orange scented candles, or pink/red ones to represent romance.

Using a nonaluminum pan, warm the wine gently over a low flame (love should be gentle and warm, unless you're looking for passion—then you might consider a low rolling boil, but this also changes the flavor). Along with the wine, warm the sliced oranges, while adding honey very slowly. The nice thing about honey is that it drizzles and you can actually write with it on the top of the liquid. So perhaps scribe your name and that of your beloved's, or more hearts with the honey as you pour it.

Taste the blend regularly during this process to make sure it doesn't get too sweet for you. Once the honey is thoroughly mixed in, add the rosewater. Serve warm to put a new spark into your commitment to a person or situation, or cold if you need to look at your promises with a cool head. As you take the cup to your lips, whisper your promise into the mead three times so you can honor it in body, mind, and spirit. Drink with pure motivations.

Adaptations: Add a bay leaf to improve your inner fortitude for promise keeping and nutmeg for loyalty.

MAIN DISH

On My Honor Hen

Makes 8 servings

Hens were domesticated by about 3000 B.C.E. and kept in sacred temples, especially those dedicated to Hercules. If you feel you need a little Herculean strength to keep your promises, try this dish!

8 (1½-pound) Cornish hens
2 cups olive oil
½ cup red wine vinegar
½ cup orange blossom honey
1 tablespoon ground cumin
1½ teaspoons aniseed
1 teaspoon ginger
¾ teaspoon ground cinnamon
Salt and pepper

Magical preparations: It would be nice to have an image of Hercules or items sacred to him in your sacred space. Such items include anything mirrored and apples.

Candle types: Take a piece of thread and tie it around the middle of the candle you've chosen and knot it, tying in your promises (you can say them out loud or in your mind). Knots were often used for such magic to "bind" the energy. Note: Do not let the candle burn off the knot unless you want to release yourself from this promise.

Preheat the oven to 400 degrees F. Rinse, pat dry, and place game hens in large roasting pan. In a heavy medium-size saucepan, combine olive oil, wine vinegar, honey, cumin, aniseed, ginger, and ground cinnamon. Simmer until mixture thickens slightly, stirring constantly, about 3 minutes. Remove glaze from heat. Brush some of the glaze evenly over game hens. Sprinkle game hens generously with salt and pepper. Roast about 1 hour until last drops of juices run clear when thighs are pierced. Baste every 10 minutes with glaze saying:

Keep my honor true
Keep my promise sure
Let neither my actions nor thoughts Abjure!

Serve after you've allowed the hens to set at room temperature for about 5 to 7 minutes.

Valiant Fig Chutney

Makes 1½ cups

In Islamic tradition Muhammad is said to have pledged an oath beneath a fig tree, making it a heavenly plant. There's no reason why we can't adapt this concept to make a sauce for our main dishes that helps us overcome our fears and fills our oaths with a strong sense of commitment and certainty.

1 cup dried figs, diced
1 tablespoon freshly grated orange peel
½ cup water
1 cup oranges, peeled and diced (any kind)
1 tablespoon honey
¼ teaspoon minced rosemary
½ teaspoon fresh lemon juice
¼ cup pine nuts

Magical preparations: Fear is a very strong obstacle to magic and life. To prepare for this candlelight recipe, I'd like you to try a brief visualization where you see fear as a dark shadow shaped roughly like a human form. Reach toward this shadow and turn it inside out! You'll discover it sparkles inside with conviction and knowingness (fear, reversed is strength and courage!). Take that positive energy and image into your kitchen.

Candle types: White for clarity.

Place the figs with the orange peel and water into a small saucepan (nonaluminum is best). Simmer them for about 10 minutes to tenderize the figs, evaporate most of the water, and likewise dissipate your misgivings.

Place this mixture into a mixing bowl, adding orange pieces, honey, rosemary, and lemon juice. Place in the refrigerator overnight, then toss with pine nuts saying:

Orange and lemon for citrus' zing!
Banish my fear and misgiving
Honey—my promises to make and keep
Conviction sown, conviction—reap!

Serve on chicken for a healthy commitment or on pork for a commitment into which you need to bring a dramatic flair, like when you're proposing.

Adaptations: To protect the commitment once it's made, add some diced onion, scallion, or shallots with the orange pieces.

SIDE DISH

Promise Me Herbed Potatoes

Serves 2 as a side dish

Potatoes tend to grow well in a variety of conditions, including harsh ones. Magically this provides the potato with the symbolism of staying power (in this case to keep our promises no matter how difficult the circumstances appear)!

2 medium-size sweet potatoes
1½ tablespoons olive oil
½ teaspoon ground cumin
¼ cup minced scallion

Magical preparations: Set up the eating area so that it reflects the goal of your candlelight recipe. For example, if you're supporting a promise you've made to a friend, use that friend's picture as a centerpiece. Since this dish is intended for two people, it's ideal for improving the devotion in a relationship.

Candle types: With this in mind, decorate with a red candle for love and two other candles that represent each person in the relationship. Each person should light his or her own candle and whisper their wishes for the relationship into the flame. Then, just prior to serving this dish, light the central candle together from your personal one, signaling the start of the magic and potently symbolizing your oneness of mind and spirit.

Peel and shred the sweet potatoes while focusing on your goal to get rid of anything that deters or divides your allegiance. Meanwhile, begin heating the olive oil in a frying pan. Add the shredded potatoes to sauté them with both the cumin and scallion. This is an ideal time to add an incantation to energize the blend like:

> *Promises to make, promises to hold*
> *Let our hearts be pure and our tongues be bold!*
> *A promise kept true, by this spell it's done*
> *By our will, the magic's begun!*

Stir until cooked through, about 4 or 5 minutes.

Adaptations: Use red potatoes for commitments having to do with love, purple potatoes for spiritual commitments, and new potatoes for dedication to new projects.

DESSERT

Loyalty Plantains

Makes 2 servings

Plantains are an ideal promissory food, having often been used in wedding rituals to ensure devotion. Additionally, many Shamans are said to have enjoyed this vegetable-like fruit, which symbolically provides us with extra wisdom for making and executing our promises.

2 plantains, very ripe
1/4 cup (1/2 stick) sweet butter
1 cup sugar
1/2 cup coconut milk
2 tablespoons rum
1/4 cup heavy cream
1/4 cup fresh ground coconut

Magical preparations: Think of a symbol that represents your goal and carve this into each plantain slice after you've peeled and cut them. Focus wholly on your goal as you etch the emblem so that the energy of that symbol cooks up with the rest of the candlelight recipe.

Candle types: Carve the same symbol into the candles that you used for the plantains.

Peel the plantains and slice them into 1/2-inch-thick slices (etch symbol(s) at this juncture). Using a nonstick frying pan, warm the butter over a low flame until its melted. Add the sliced plantain into this, coating thoroughly. Cook until the plantain is browned on each side. Remove from the pan and drain on paper towels.

To the remaining butter in the pan, add the sugar and cook until caramelized (the butter turns a light golden brown and thickens slightly). Blend the coconut milk with the rum, and add this into the sugar-butter. Whisk over a low flame until the sugar-butter is fully integrated with the coconut milk. Since the whisk literally whips up some energy, this is a nice time to add a prayer like:

Great spirit, I come to you
Keep my commitments sure, my promises true!

Add the plantains back into this mixture along with the cream, shaking the pan to mix the ingredients.

Serve topped with the fresh coconut sprinkled in a circle around the outside of the plantains to protect your magic.

Adaptations: Add 1/2 teaspoon of banana extract to improve the devotional energy in this dessert, 1/2 teaspoon of vanilla if it's aimed at a loving relationship, and/or 1/2 teaspoon of rum extract to safeguard a promise.

Stick to It Sweet Buns

Makes 2 dozen buns

Oaths and promises require "stick-to-it-iveness," and what better way to create that energy than the ultimate—sticky buns. Also, since these are lightly sweet it will make your commitment likewise sweet instead of difficult. The rose honey supports the promise of love.

DOUGH

1 cup warm water
4 teaspoons dry yeast
2/3 cup sugar
1/2 cup (1 stick) butter, room temperature
1/2 cup dry nonfat milk powder
1 1/4 teaspoons salt
2 large eggs
4 1/4 cups all-purpose flour

GLAZE

1 1/4 cups brown sugar (packed)
3/4 cup (1 1/2 sticks) unsalted butter, room temperature
1/4 cup rose honey
1/4 cup dark corn syrup
1/4 cup water
2 cups pecan halves, chopped
4 teaspoons sugar
4 teaspoons ground cinnamon
1 teaspoon ground ginger

Magical preparations: Rose honey may be difficult to find, but you can make it yourself adding some special energies along the way. Simply buy your favorite honey and 1 ounce of rose flavoring (available in international shops or Indian food stores) to 1 pound of honey. You can warm the honey minimally to incorporate the flavoring fully while saying:

Love and sweetness in roses fine
Dedication in this honey, bind.

Candle types: Dab a little rose oil on your candles while making the honey.

For the buns, mix 1/4 cup of the warm water, yeast, and a pinch of the sugar in a small bowl. Let stand until foamy. Using electric mixer, beat remaining sugar, butter, milk powder, and salt in large bowl until well blended. Beat in eggs one at a time. Mix in remaining 3/4 cup warm water and yeast mixture, then 3 cups of the flour, 1 cup at a time. Using rubber spatula, add the 1/4 cup of flour, scraping down sides of bowl frequently (dough will be soft and sticky). Sprinkle the remaining 1/4 cup flour onto work surface and knead until smooth and elastic, adding more flour if sticky. Set aside. Butter a large bowl. Add dough; turn to coat. Cover bowl with plastic wrap and let dough rise in warm area until doubled.

For the glaze, butter 2 (10-inch) round cake pans with 2-inch-high sides. Beat brown sugar, 1/2 cup of the butter, honey, corn syrup, and the 1/4 cup water in medium bowl to blend. Spread half of glaze in bottom of each prepared pan. Sprinkle 1 cup pecans over each.

Punch down dough and divide it in half. Roll each dough piece out on floured work surface to 12 by 9-inch rectangle. Brush any excess flour off dough. Spread remaining butter over dough rectangles, dividing equally. Mix the 4 teaspoons of sugar and cinnamon in small bowl. Sprinkle cinnamon sugar over rectangles, then roll them into logs. Cut each log into 12 rounds.

Place the rounds, cut side down, in each prepared pan, spacing evenly. Cover with plastic wrap. Let buns rise in warm area until almost doubled.

Preheat oven to 375 degrees F. Bake buns until deep golden brown, about 30 minutes. Run small knife around pan sides to loosen sticky buns. Turn hot buns out onto platter. Cool and serve.

6

Edible Alchemy

CRACKING DOWN AND CLEANING OUT, CHANGING AND REARRANGING

I have read some spiritual books that seem to send the wrong message. They portray spiritual living as easy where everything is rosy—no rainy days, no gray clouds, no problems. Now, I know my life isn't like that! Magic is a help-mate to life. It's there to give you a coping mechanism, something positive to do, when things go awry. Better still, it yields results!

This chapter focuses on candlelight recipes that deal with those not-so-perfect days. We begin with Cleansing and Banishing. Ever notice how bad things seem to come in cycles? Well, make these dishes and clean out that negativity, turn away the blues, and get things back on track.

Next there's Decision-Making Dinners. Every day we're faced with small and large choices. Some are minor, some are big, but they all matter in how positively our future plays out. Cook up these dishes to keep your path sure.

Third, turn to Tasty Transformation and Change. These recipes provide us with energy to maintain our wits about us even when change comes like a whirlwind. No matter what choices you make, and what situations come, trust these candlelight dishes to help you land on your feet.

Last, we'll take a look at Psychic Platefuls. After all, forewarned is forearmed!

CLEANSING AND BANISHING

Confront the dark parts of yourself, and work to banish them with illumination and forgiveness. Your willingness to wrestle with your demons will cause your angels to sing. Use the pain as fuel, as a reminder of your strength.

—AUGUST WILSON

Life definitely has its ups and downs, and negative energies have a way of coming home to roost at the worst possible time (not that there's ever a good time for bad things!). When you find that you're in a very bad head-space, or when the energies in and around your life all seem "down," consider making some of these transformational edibles. Cleansing meals help wipe away residual metaphysical messes (after all, clean as you go!).

Banishing is, in part, a matter of turning things around. Keep that symbolism in mind while preparing your meals. For example, turn your apron so that it's backward, or flip an egg while thinking about likewise flipping around the energy that's been hindering your life! Sensual cues like these two examples really help get you on track mentally for the magic you're creating.

We often overlook the stray energy we leave around, let alone those vibrations that come from places and people, like the friend who stops by and is overly stressed or just had a fight with his or her mate. All those bits of energy affect your aura daily, especially in busy city environments. So regular spiritual cleansing becomes very important to maintaining your well-being. That's the focus of cleansing and banishing dishes—to help us internalize what we need, and get rid of what we do not.

Potential Cleansing Components

- *Aromatics:* Lemon, bay, mint, sage, thyme, fennel, cinnamon, coconut, all citrus, clove; non-edible frankincense, myrrh, sandalwood, pine.
- *Candle types:* If you can carve the candle into the image of what you wish banished or cleansed, it will literally melt away before your eyes!
- *Color:* Black or brown for banishing, white for cleansing.
- *Candlelight recipe ingredients:* Vinegar, water, onions, beer or whiskey, all red foods, sage, grapefruits, pepper, hot peppers, horseradish, prune, lime, hot sauce, mustard, garlic, chicken, salt, tomato sauce.
- *Crystals, metals, stones:* Agate, chrysolite, onyx, calcite, aquamarine.
- *Decorative touches:* Because of the symbolism, it's very important that your work space be neat and clean for these candlelight recipes (this visually supports your goal).
- *Timing:* Waning moon (so negative energies shrink). Aries moon, Gemini moon, Sagittarius moon.

APPETIZERS

Unadulterated Onion Soup

Makes 6 servings

This recipe helps you internalize the purifying power of onions known readily by medical science. The juice of onions has been scientifically shown to cleans the blood, stimulate appetite, improve digestion, and disinfect—just to name a few! Egyptians considered the onion as a symbol of the universe, whereas sailors ate onions as one dietary supplement that prevented scurvy. Magically onions were, and are, sometimes used as poppets (dolls) that absorb negativity.

1 (10-ounce) can chicken stock
1 (10-ounce) can beef stock
½ tablespoon brown sugar
1 pound red onions
½ pound small Spanish onions
½ pound small cooking onions
1 bundle of green onions
2 tablespoons corn starch or flour
Salt and pepper to taste

Magical preparations: In keeping with the theme of this chapter, I suggest mopping your kitchen floor (or wiping the countertops) with a tea of sage or mint. This prepares the way for a "clean" flow of magic. Additionally, you can put small onions (in their skins) on your window ledges in the kitchen or other parts of the house to act as natural negativity magnets. Remember to replace these regularly.

Candle types: Since you're working with onions, it won't hurt to have another aromatic to balance things. Dab your candles with mint or lemon oil and burn them while you cook.

Preheat the oven to 325 degrees F, remembering that the hearth is the heart of your home, and preheating can be a magical prelude to your spellcraft if you approach it with a positive outlook. You can even consider blessing your stove by closing your eyes and placing your hands palms down on the surface while saying something like:

What comes from my hearth, comes from the heart
Here magic begins, with love from the start
______ (insert the name of a pantry protector)
Bless my stove, your power impart

Next, mix all but ½ cup of the chicken and beef broth with the brown sugar in a large ovensafe pot. Add the onions and cover saying:

Onions of cleansing, onions of power;
I claim purity, hour by hour

Through this dish of onions, warm;
All negativity will transform

Place this in the oven for 2 hours and remove.

Meanwhile, place the remaining stock over a low flame. Mix the cornstarch or flour with a little water to make a paste. Stir this into the stock counterclockwise (you want to banish any negativity or bad vibes) a little at a time until thickened. Add this to the onions and stock, blending well with salt and pepper. This time stir clockwise and repeat your incantation, perhaps three times for the body–mind–spirit connection.

Adaptations: Add some finely chopped red pepper (hot or sweet) for improved cleansing power. Note that the leftovers from this side dish can be mashed and blended into gravy or soup for a rich onion flavor. The more concentrated the onion flavor gets, the stronger the purifying energy.

Bane Banishing Peppers

Makes 4 servings

If you're feeling a little funny and think you might be coming down with a physical or psychic bug, use this purifying blend to clean out your system, even as the Incans did. Over thirty varieties of hot peppers were grown by the Incan people. Here, and in many other areas of the world, hot peppers are used medicinally as a natural decongestant and stomach cleanser.

24 large shrimp
1 garlic clove
6 ounces pickled jalapeño peppers, without liquid
2 tablespoons olive oil
24 large wooden skewers

Magical preparations: Physical and psychic dis-ease (hyphen purposeful) can be traced back to specific origins. If you're feeling physically ill, make sure you get some rest before creating this candlelight recipe. A weary body and mind can't focus on magic and get optimum results. Similarly, if your spiritual sensitivity seems "off," take the time to meditate and center before undertaking this formula.

Candle types: Pale green is a good color for renewal. White is nice to protect yourself, and if you're trying to actually banish something that's settled in, try black.

☙ Rinse the shrimp well in cold water and set aside. This step cleanses away any energy that would undermine your spell. Mash the garlic and 1 jalapeño pepper together, visualizing the "bug" in your system being likewise smashed apart. Blend this crushed mixture with the olive oil, which also symbolizes smooth transitions. Use this to marinate the shrimp for 1 hour in the refrigerator so it absorbs the energy you've created thus far. As you place the shrimp and marinade together add an incantation like:

By garlic and pepper marinade
Shrimp therein neatly laid
The spell's begun, the magic made
So my _____ problems quickly fade!
(fill in the blank with the type of difficulty
you're banishing)

Slice up the remaining peppers into 24 equal pieces (one slice to place on each skewer with each piece of shrimp). As with the mashing earlier, the act of slicing "cuts up" the negative energy of which you're trying to rid yourself. Place the shrimp and pepper on skewers.

Grill over a medium flame for 2 minutes on each side (shrimp should be pink). Visualize your problems being burned away. Savor, and within 24 to 48 hours you should be feeling much better.

Serving ideas: Serve out the shrimp on a white platter (for purification) or a green platter (the color of health).

Adaptations: Choose the type of hot pepper so it reflects your goal. Green ones might symbolize clearing out a financial problem.

Red ones can represent purging yourself of anger or negativity in a relationship, and yellow peppers inspire pure communications. Also, you can put one small red or white onion on each skewer for more cleansing power.

BEVERAGE

Lime Immunity

Makes 1 serving

Whip up this beverage when you want to clear out sickness and renew the immune system. Romans felt that lime juice counteracted poisons, and limes played a key role in Germanic lore as endowing invulnerability.

2 teaspoons lime juice, fresh if possible
8 ounces cold beer

Magical preparations: Since the focus here is renewing the body, take the extra time to treat your body properly for three days (a common number in healing modalities) before making this spell recipe. Namely, get plenty of rest, take vitamins, and exercise.

Candle types: Use black or brown to banish and ground out a malady, coupled with a bright green candle for renewal.

Place the lime juice and beer in a tall mug (Corona is a good choice as it has lovely golden color, like the sun). Mix them with a spoon (clockwise to create positive energy to support the body, counterclockwise to counter sickness) saying:

Immunity, grow in me
Good health, sow in me
When this passes through the lips
Gentle cleansing in each sip!

Adaptations: For those who do not wish to use alcohol, you can find a non-alcoholic version of beer, or make yourself a limeade mix instead.

MAIN DISHES

Purification Garlic Chicken

Makes 2 servings

This is an excellent dish to consume the day before you undertake any special religious functions like a healing circle, bearing in mind that your body is your temple. The ingredients herein purify both mind and spirit so you're in the best possible "space" for that undertaking.

In Christian tradition a white hen represents the purity of Christ. They were also regarded as suitable offerings for Athene and Demeter in Greece, Mercury in Rome, and Bride among the Celts. Garlic and "fire water" add to the symbolic cleansing value.

2 or 3-pound cooking chicken, cut into quarters
Salt, pepper, poultry seasoning to taste
½ head of garlic, peeled and separated
1 tablespoon olive oil
¼ cup bourbon or cognac
2 cups chicken stock
2 sprigs of fresh rosemary
¼ lemon
¼ cup light cream

Magical preparations: Since you're making yourself a sacred space, put a few of your magical tools on the kitchen countertop (making it into a functional altar) and invoke the Quarters using a wooden spoon for a wand. A suitable invocation goes like this:

Powers of the East come with the winds of transformation
Powers of the South, come with your magical cooking fires
Powers of the West, come with the waters of cleansing
Powers of the North, come with the food for this spell
So be it!

Remember to point to the appropriate direction with your spoon wand while invoking that element.

Candle types: Since you're creating a sacred space, you could put out four elementally colored candles around your kitchen while you're working and light them during the invocation.

☙ Preheat the oven to 300 degrees F. Rinse the chicken thoroughly under cold water and pat dry, bearing in mind that you're also rinsing away any unwanted energy from the main component of this dish. Rub the chicken inside and out with a blend of the salt, pepper, and poultry seasoning, and insert whole cloves of garlic evenly into the skin using a small knife to secure them. This process literally massages magic into the meat and instills cleansing power into the garlic. Note that you can use a symbolic number of garlic cloves to improve the effect here. For example, if the pure intention desired is within the bounds of a relationship, I'd suggest three cloves to represent you, your significant other, and the relationship as a whole.

When you're done instilling energy and spices into the chicken, place the pieces in a skillet with the olive oil for browning. Turn regularly, always flipping them counterclockwise so you're literally turning any unwanted energy around. Once all sides are browned, move the chicken to a casserole dish, adding the alcohol and chicken stock. Bake for 15 minutes.

Remove this briefly from the oven adding the rosemary and the juice from the lemon while saying:

In this meal, the power of change
In this meal, the magic of love
In this meal, the freshness of cleansing
All blessed by the god/dess above!

Put the dish back into the oven for about 25 minutes until the chicken is cooked through.

Remove this from the oven, and transfer the chicken to a separate platter. Place the cooking dish over a low flame on the stove, and slowly add the cream to create your sauce. Let this cook for about 8 minutes until thickened. Pour the sauce over the chicken, repeating your incantation one more time before serving. As you and your guests eat, watch as the tensions and negativity flow away with every magical bite. Serve this with plenty of water to keep the cleansing power flowing.

Adaptations: Serve this with a loaf of fresh French bread. Smash the baked garlic into the bread to manifest healthy foundations and pure motivations. Another alternative is to use crabmeat instead of chicken when you want to dispel a crabby situation.

Cool-Head Horseradish Sauce

Makes 2 to 3 cups

For cleaning out animosity (be it directed toward you or another person), this recipe will do the trick as a sauce for nearly any main dish meat. The horseradish purifies the negativity, while the frozen nature of the cream cools an overheated temper.

2 cups heavy cream
1 teaspoon sugar
1 teaspoon lemon vinegar
4 tablespoons horseradish, freshly grated
Salt and pepper to taste

Magical preparations: Consider the source of your anger (like a fight with your mate), then choose an item over which to serve this sauce according to that focus. For example, serve this over poultry if the anger has to do with relationship problems, over beef especially when the problem is money or stability oriented, over apples when innocence has been lost, or over pork when you're upset over a lack of productivity.

Candle types: In keeping with the "cool" theme, freeze your candles for a short time before using them. This also helps them burn longer!

Whip the heavy cream to soft peak stage. Slowly add the sugar and continue to beat until stiff. As you do, really release your anger into the beating process (if you have the patience, doing this by hand is great therapy!).

Hand-fold the lemon vinegar into the cream (you can make this by steeping $\frac{1}{4}$ lemon in 1 cup warm vinegar for 1 hour, squeezing, straining, then storing for use). Finally, stir in the horseradish and however much salt and pepper you desire. Place all of this in the freezer saying:

Quell my anger, my resentment wane
Cleanse my spirit, bring peace again!

Leave this in the freezer until it reaches a frappé-type consistency. Spoon out over your chosen dish remembering that applying the sauce acts like a salve on an open wound, soothing away the unwanted emotions and restoring balance.

Suggestions: Eat this just before going into a difficult confrontation. It is always best to serve the sauce cold so that you can keep a cool head no matter what happens.

Adaptations: Since this goes nicely with chicken, pork, and beef, consider making a sweet-hot sauce by using crushed fruit (applesauce works), a dollop of maple syrup, or a teaspoon or two of brown sugar. Magically this sweetens a sour disposition!

SIDE DISHES

Good As It Gets Garlic Oil and Garlic Bread

Makes 3 cups oil, 2 cups garlic

The ancients regularly used garlic as a tool to banish evil spirits or influences. Persians felt that garlic could drive away the devil, Italians wore it to negate the evil eye, and both Arab and Romanian people feel garlic repels vampires. Meanwhile in Greece it was offered to Hecate (the Goddess of magic) in order to ensure her help in curing maladies. This oil is great for frying up any of your savory cleansing dishes, and the leftover garlic goes great on bread or into pesto.

3 large heads garlic, cut horizontally in half
1 garlic clove, elephant ear, cut in half
3 cups virgin olive oil
4 sprigs thyme
1 teaspoon peppercorns, toasted

Magical preparations: Actually this is more of a post-recipe recommendation. You can use this oil to season iron pans and other good cookware. The beauty here is that the herbs cleanse away any negative energies the pots and pans may have absorbed. Just be aware that any food you cook in these pans will take on a mild garlic flavor.

Candle types: Since you're preparing this as a culinary aid, you need not decorate the eating space, but you can certainly bring a candle into the kitchen (near the stove) while you work.

⁂ Preheat the oven to 300 degrees F. Put the garlic heads cut side down in a small casserole dish. Pour the olive oil over them. Add the thyme and peppercorns evenly over top. (Note: If you want a more savory oil you can also put in sprigs of rosemary, marjoram, etc.) Cover with a lid or foil and bake adding an incantation like:

Pepper, garlic, and thyme,
Bind this magical rhyme
Warmth without, cleansing within,
By my words, this spell begins

Bake for 45 minutes to 1 hour, until the garlic is soft enough to mash.

Remove garlic and whole herbs from the oil and set aside. Strain the oil into a bowl and let cool, then pour into an airtight container. The oil will keep for at least a month. Now, the rest of the herbs can be used to make something akin to pesto with more flavors. Squeeze the cloves out of their husks into a bowl. This is a good time to focus on removing any barriers that stand between you and your goals.

Mash the roasted garlic with a fork. Break up the whole herbs into similar-size pieces (you can use a food processor or chopper for this). Spread some on rolls or a loaf of bread for your side dish, then store whatever's left over in an airtight container in the refrigerator for up to 1 month. Use in soups, sauces, stuffing and so forth.

Pure Salt Potatoes

Makes 4 to 6 servings

I love the simplicity of this dish. The salt and vinegar provide the cleansing, and the potatoes neatly ground out all the "dirt" that the salt and vinegar wash away! It's fast, easy, and functional—perfect for time-challenged kitchen witches!

3 pounds finger potatoes
Salted water, enough to cover
2½ tablespoons cider vinegar
Flaked sea salt or kosher salt to taste
1½ tablespoons extra-virgin olive oil

Magical preparations: Rinse your hands with a blend of vinegar and water before making this dish. This will clear away any residual energies that your hands may have picked up (such as when you shake hands with a person who is upset). As you wash, add an incantation like:

Away, away . . . wash negativity down the drain
By my will, purify, make clean again!

Candle types: In keeping with the grounding theme, perhaps put a sturdy pillar candle near the floor (or ground if you're cooking outdoors). This provides a stronger connection to the Earth element.

In a 4-quart pot, cover potatoes completely with salted cold water and simmer until just tender, about 10 minutes. Drain potatoes and rinse under cold water. While potatoes are still warm, gently toss with vinegar and salt. Cool potatoes to room temperature, stirring occasionally, and gently toss with oil.

Adaptations: To clean out issues in a relationship consider wine vinegar. Balsamic is also a very good grounding agent because of its earthy flavor.

DESSERT

In the Pink Grapefruit Sorbet

Makes 3 servings

This tasty sorbet inspires overall well-being and physical cleansing specifically so you'll literally be "in the pink" for the rest of the day. Pink is a healthful, welcoming hue. Additionally in the language of dreams, grapefruit represents a reordering of priorities—cleaning out the old and returning to balance in your personal life.

5 cups ready-made pink grapefruit juice (NOT cocktail)
1¼ cups sugar
¼ cup light corn syrup
¾ cup Spumante-style champagne

Magical preparations: Keeping with the overall theme of the spell, surround yourself with as many pink items as possible (tablecloth, napkin, plate, glass, toothpick). Pink has a very friendly, upbeat vibration that neatly chases away gloom.

Candle types: Yep, make those pink too!

In a large saucepan, place the juice, sugar, and corn syrup over a low flame. Warm slowly until the sugar is completely dissolved, envisioning whatever problems have plagued you likewise disappearing.

Remove this from the heat and stir in the Spumante. Note that champagne bubbles inspire giggling and symbolically uplift your sense of humor! Pour the blend into a large pan and place in the freezer until it's slushy and then turn it into a blender (note that symbolically freezing can also "freeze" negativity and sickness in its path). Whip until smooth and serve with a pink umbrella. (An umbrella's shape is that of the sun, which inspires blessings!)

Now, grab a pink shirt, socks, or something else of that color and wear it to symbolically put on "pink" energy. Consume the sorbet visualizing pink, bubbly light tickling your aura. You'll find yourself smiling and laughing soon thereafter!

Adaptations: Serve this over pink grapefruit, whose circular nature represents wholeness. For pure love, add a teaspoon of rosewater to the initial blend, garnishing with a rose petal.

DECISION-MAKING DINNERS

It is change, continuing change, inevitable change, that is the dominant factor in society today. No sensible decision can be made any longer without taking into account not only the world as it is, but the world as it will be.

—Isaac Asimov

Decision dinners for the most part focus on honing the conscious mind so you can think and see things clearly. While there's no question that our emotions and instincts play a role in making choices, it's very important to also use sound reasoning. Thus, in some of these menus, you'll find herbs like rosemary that augment memory, and candlelight recipe ingredients like coffee that keep us alert.

It's good if you can somehow reflect the part of your life to which the magic will be directed in the construction of your sacred space or serving table. For example, if the choice is between two job offers, you may want to have those business cards under the candles on your table, or on your refrigerator door where they can represent the matter at hand.

Potential Decision Components

- *Aromatics:* Dill, apple, vanilla, nutmeg, rosemary, marjoram.
- *Candle types:* Choose the color and shape of your candle according to the area of your life in which the decision lies, like a heart-shaped candle for matters of the heart, or a yellow candle if your job decisions entail a lot of communication skills. If you wish, use one candle to represent each option facing you.

- *Color:* Decision making combines instinct and rational thinking. Yellow is a good color for this—or perhaps two candles (one black, one white) might do.
- *Candlelight recipe ingredients:* Turkey, beans, celery, grapes, caraway, rosemary, mustard, brazil nuts, hazelnut, walnut, coffee, honey, raisins, tea, watercress, almond, parsley.
- *Crystals, metals, stones:* Calcite, bloodstone, hematite, fluorite, aventurine.
- *Decorative touches:* Make several of these dishes and serve them in a buffet. The variety in this layout maintains a continuity with the energy of decision making.
- *Timing:* When the sun is shining for clear vision. Cancer, Libra, or Scorpio moon. Tuesdays and Thursdays.

APPETIZER

Fork in the Road Buns

Makes 2 dozen

Here we're using the symbolism of hot cross buns to accent our coming to a crossroad in life. The traditional hot cross bun has for centuries been made during Easter, the time when the sun returns and offers us illumination of mind and soul.

1 loaf frozen bread dough
⅔ cup raisins
⅔ cup chopped hazelnuts
1 teaspoon lemon powder
2 teaspoons orange juice
1 teaspoon vanilla
½ cup sugar
1 cup honey

Magical preparations: Put on an item of gold clothing or jewelry, since this is the color of the conscious mind as well as the sun at its brightest. Add an incantation as you don this item like:

> *gold to concentrate, options to find,*
> *give me the focus, to make up my mind*

Candle types: Continue with your gold/yellow theme to support the conscious mind.

Follow the directions provided for defrosting and raising the bread dough, keeping your goal in mind all the while. Note that as the dough rises, so does your magical energy!

Preheat the oven to 375 degrees F. The first time the bread rises, knead in the next six ingredients, and when everything is evenly blended, add the honey. Let the dough rise again, then pinch off small biscuit-size balls and put them on a nonstick cooking pan. Bake for about 15 minutes until golden brown.

Meanwhile, warm the honey so it will drizzle easily. When the buns cool, pause for a moment and put your hands palms down over them, thinking of your choice. Take the honey in hand and draw an *X* on each bun, using the honey, continuing to focus your attention on the center where the two lines join. In this case, *X* really does mark the spot! Remember to be considering your decision as you eat the buns. Afterward I'd recommend writing up a pro and con list based on the two choices before you and see which one makes more sense!

Adaptations: Use strawberries in place of nuts when making a decision about a romantic relationship, or red currants for decisions related to health or finances.

BEVERAGE

Sweet Selection Liqueur

Makes 4 servings

This lovely beverage provides coffee to stimulate the conscious mind and coconut to tap your intuitive nature, thereby creating a heart-head balance in your decision.

¾ cup chilled whipping cream
6 tablespoons sugar
6 tablespoons unsweetened cocoa powder
½ cup water
3½ cups whole milk
12 tablespoons coffee liqueur
12 tablespoons coconut liqueur
Grated semisweet chocolate

Magical preparations: Bless the ingredients by the light of the sun and the moon to stress the conscious and intuitive nature equally.

Candle types: Likewise use one white/silver candle and one yellow/gold candle.

Beat cream in medium bowl until peaks form (this whips up energy that you can direct into the beverage). Set aside. Whisk sugar and cocoa powder in a saucepan to blend. Slowly add the water, whisking until smooth. Bring mixture to simmer over medium heat, whisking constantly. Simmer 1 minute. Gradually blend in milk and return to simmer. Divide hot chocolate among 6 mugs, stirring 2 tablespoons of each liqueur into each mug clockwise saying:

Choice of heart, choice of head
Listen well while this spell is said
Choice of head, choice of heart
By my will, a decision impart!

Top each with a dollop of the whipped cream, then sprinkle with grated chocolate.

SIDE DISH

Picking Nits . . . um . . . Nuts

Makes 1 cup

Prepare these sweet nuts to inspire your ability to apply knowledge wisely. European folklore tells us that hazelnuts provide that energy and also inspire a bit of humor as a coping mechanism.

1 cup water
1¼ cups sugar
½ cup hazelnuts
⅓ cup brazil nuts
1 tablespoon butter

Magical preparations: What area of your life is being affected by this decision? Write down some key words that describe it, then consider what other candlelight recipe ingredients might be added or substituted to this spell recipe to support that goal. For example, add almonds to the blend if your choice has to do with finances or health, coconut for spiritual matters, and pecans if the decision is employment related.

Candle types: Match the aroma of your candles to that of your pie filling for even more supportive energy.

Preheat the oven to 350 degrees F. Simmer the water with the sugar until it is dissolved. Stir the nuts into the sugar water, then transfer them to a nonstick baking pan using a slotted spoon. Bake for 15 minutes until brown.

Melt the butter and pour it over the nuts, making sure to turn and coat them evenly saying:

Nuts and butter, nuts and butter
Grant to me all the logic I can muster
Turn and change, remove all fear
By magic and will, my choice make clear!

Finally, put the nuts on waxed paper to cool (they get crisp upon cooling). Store in an airtight container to preserve the energy and crispness. Nibble as desired, especially when you want to consciously, logically, mull over several options.

Adaptations: These candied nuts taste really nice if you add dried fruit upon storing. Blend in apple slices for wisdom, pineapple for decisions regarding guests in your home, dates when you need to be firm in your choice, and papaya for love-related issues.

Watercress Fix-It Plan

Makes 8 servings

Watercress was often used for remedial purposes in Europe; in this case we're using it to remedy our indecisiveness. The frying energizes this vegetable to motivate action.

2 large garlic cloves, minced
3 tablespoons olive oil
16 cups of watercress, rinsed, coarse stems discarded

Magical preparations: You'll notice that there are 16 cups of watercress in this recipe—a strong earth-oriented number [being 4 × 4]. This provides foundations for your choices, so be focusing on your decision as you clean and prepare this vegetable.

Candle types: I'd suggest white or yellow to emphasize Spirit's guidance and instinct taking part in this process.

In a frying pan, sauté the garlic in the oil over moderately high heat for 30 seconds, or until it is fragrant. Add the watercress and stir the mixture until it is combined well. If you wish, add an incantation at this juncture like:

Wherever uncertainty and stagnation abide
Fix it with confidence, help me Decide

Sauté the watercress for 2 to 3 minutes, or until it is just wilted, and season it with salt and pepper.

Adaptations: Add ½ cup of chicken stock at the end for a watercress-style soup that supports making "healthy" choices.

MAIN DISHES

Resolution Raisin Toast

Makes 2 servings

When you're facing a hectic day filled with numerous choices, this breakfast is perfect! It provides you with energy, improved concentra-

tion, and all the right ingredients to make the best possible decisions all day long.

½ cup vanilla ice cream
2 eggs
¼ cup ground hazelnuts
1 tablespoon rum flavoring
⅛ teaspoon cinnamon
4 slices raisin bread
Butter and syrup for garnish

Magical preparations: Breakfast is the most important meal of the day, especially when there are difficult choices looming on the horizon. Look at your breakfast as a mini-ritual. Add a tall glass of orange juice for healthy outlooks, pouring a little out your window or door by way of an offering.

Candle types: Light a candle to light the way toward positive change, and consider saying a brief prayer as you do so that all the magic you're placing therein is released in the best possible way.

Melt the ice cream and mix it thoroughly with eggs, nuts, flavoring, and cinnamon. As you do, visualize any barriers between you and your final choice melting neatly away.

Dip the bread slices into this mixture so that they are evenly coated (this surrounds the bread with your magic) on both sides. Fry these gently over a low flame. After the first turn, use a toothpick or knife to etch a magical symbol on the sides, and let the remaining frying process heat up your magic. With each turn of the bread add an incantation like:

Bread for sound foundations
Cinnamon for energy
To make my choice, this spell is freed!

Serve with garnish.

Adaptations: Change the type of bread so it more closely resembles the question at hand. For example, wheat and corn bread relate well to money, sourdough bread can represent a decision that's somewhat distasteful to make, and white bread can symbolize a common, everyday choice that for whatever reason has you stumped.

Truth-Be-Told Turkey

Makes 1 serving

The turkey and mustard in this recipe help with fact finding so that you'll have the information and insight necessary to make a good choice. Turkey provides a foundation and the mustard spurs on progress with its energy. The maple syrup brings abundant joy and sense of comfort with that decision.

1 good-size turkey breast steak
¼ cup wine vinegar
¼ cup sesame oil
2 tablespoons soy sauce
1 teaspoon each salt, ginger, anise
2 tablespoons brown sugar
2 slices orange
¼ cup maple syrup
¼ cup white cooking wine
⅛ cup spicy mustard
Pat of butter

Magical preparations: Truth finding has both a conscious and an intuitive element to it. You need to look logically, but also trust your gut instincts to lead you in the right direction. Consequently, I'd suggest timing this spell recipe so you're putting the basic ingredients together at midnight, dawn, on New Year's, or any other date/time that's balanced on a hinge (midnight and dawn are between darkness and light, New Year's is between two years, etc.). Additionally, wear black and white clothing while you're preparing this recipe so that your final decision will be as clear as "black and white." One easy choice here would be one black and one white sock. Since these go on your feet, they also help represent a decision that has good foundations!

Candle types: Continue the theme of balance with equal numbers of black and white candles.

Pierce the turkey steak with a fork to pierce any misconceptions or illusions you have with regard to any aspect of this decision. Marinate it in a blend of the vinegar, oil, soy sauce, salt, ginger, anise, brown sugar, and the juice of the two orange slices. Leave the meat to soak for 6 hours in the refrigerator, turning it regularly saying:

Turkey and salt, uncertainty halt
Ginger and juice, my decision deduce!

Meanwhile, create the glaze by mixing the syrup, wine, mustard, and butter together in a saucepan. Set this aside and use it to brush on the turkey while grilling it. Generally speaking, it will take about a half hour to cook the turkey completely on a medium-heat grill, basting every 7 minutes for even coating. Garnish with additional orange wedges.

Don't be surprised if your mind starts rolling with fresh outlooks about the matter at hand shortly after dinner!

Flavoring hint: If you have the ability to smoke things on your grill, add hickory chips into the blend for an amazingly rich taste.

Adaptation: Substitute a little lemon juice for the orange in this recipe to improve mental clarity.

DESSERT

Fast-Action Hazelnut Piecrust

Makes 1 (9-inch) crust

Decisions are usually not something we want to make quickly; however, there are times when life gives us few alternatives. For this candlelight recipe we use brandy to help us choose swiftly, and hazelnuts are added for good luck!

7 honey graham crackers, crushed
½ cup hazelnuts
2 tablespoons brown sugar
¼ cup (½ stick) butter
2 tablespoons hazelnut brandy or liqueur

Magical preparations: Fill the piecrust with any type of filling that symbolizes the area of your life in which a decision is pending. For example, if you are thinking of moving you might make a pecan filling (pecan is associated with the Air element, and thus movement). Or to decide among what expenses to eliminate in your budget, fill the crust with quince (a fruit associated with the Earth element and happy outcomes). Apples would be an ideal filling for health-related choices, and berries are suited to relationship questions.

Candle types: Match the aroma of your candles to the pie filling for improved focus.

Preheat the oven to 350 degrees F. Grease a 9-inch pie pan lightly with vegetable oil. You can draw an image of the area of your life in the oil, too, if you wish (like drawing a house when you're trying to decide among several different houses on the market).

Place the graham crackers, hazelnuts, and brown sugar in a blender and grind them until mixed. This blends magical energy, whips up a little extra power, and breaks the barriers between your making a sound decision. Scrape the nuts out of the blender into a bowl, and add the butter and brandy by hand until evenly distributed. Press this evenly into the pie pan and bake for 10 minutes. Fill as desired.

As you slice this "life" pie, remember that the act of slicing opens and activates the flow of magic, so that would be an ideal time to add an incantation that empowers your effort like:

> *When opened with my kitchen knife, manifest a slice of life!*
> *To banish any reservation, I bite into this sweet sensation!*

Adaptations: Top your pie with candied hazelnuts or a hearty portion of whipping cream. The cream accents gentle acceptance of whatever choice you make.

Finale Grapes

Makes 4 servings

When you find yourself growing frustrated with a decision-making process, and simply want to settle everything, turn to this spell recipe for help. The circular/solar nature of grapes will help you narrow down your focus and refresh dwindling energy so you can make the right move, ending up with a great finale!

3 egg yolks
⅓ cup sugar
2 tablespoons cornstarch
2 tablespoons flour
1 cup light cream
2 teaspoons finely grated orange peel
1 teaspoon vanilla extract (not imitation)
1½ cups seedless grapes
¼ cup sliced almonds
¼ cup brown sugar

Magical preparations: Consider what type of decision you need to make, then choose the color of your grapes accordingly. For example, use red grapes when making a decision about a relationship, green grapes for financial or career-oriented decisions, and purple grapes for decisions regarding your spiritual path.

Candle types: The advice for the grape colors holds true with your candles too. The more sympathy and synchronicity you can obtain with your goal the better.

Beat the egg yolks till frothy to whip up creative energy. Slowly add the sugar so the outcome of your decision will be "sweet." Once the sugar is well integrated, add the cornstarch and flour a little at a time (magically this creates coherency).

Pour in the cream, continuing to beat the mix until smooth. Transfer this blend into a saucepan bringing it all to a low rolling boil. Stir clockwise constantly to bring about a positive change. Add orange rind (for accuracy), continuing to stir for another 3 or 4 minutes. Remove from the heat and fold in the vanilla. Strain this through a sieve and chill for at least 1 hour. As you put this in the refrigerator say:

Cool head, clear mind
A decision made, the magic here bind!

Meanwhile, preheat the oven to 425 degrees F. Place the grapes on the bottom of an ovenproof, nonstick dish. When the hour is up, turn the egg mixture over top of the grapes, garnishing with almonds and brown sugar. Place this in the oven until the top is bubbly. Serve warm when you need to make a fast decision or cold when you want to slow down the decision-making process.

Adaptations: Substitute hazelnuts or brazil nuts for the almonds in this recipe to increase the overall decision-making power. Substitute lemon peel for the orange when you need additional clarity in your thought processes.

TASTY TRANSFORMATION AND CHANGE

All change is a miracle to contemplate; but it is a miracle which is taking place every second.
—Henry David Thoreau

It has often been said that change is the one constant on which we can depend. The times change, our outlooks grow and change, the earth itself changes. That doesn't make keeping up with all this ongoing activity easy. There are days when people feel overwhelmed, as if standing in a whirlwind with too many choices and too much responsibility. Alchemical foods are those that help us cope with the hustle and bustle by granting firm foundations and inspiring an adaptable nature.

Potential Transformation Components

- *Aromatics:* Mint, fennel, citrus, vanilla, rosemary, lavender, ginger, oregano.

- *Candle types:* Candles are a beautiful medium for transformation magic since they too change size as they burn. If you can find candles that have different layers of color, that strengthens the symbolism!
- *Color:* In-between hues (yellow-green, orange-red, etc.).
- *Candlelight recipe ingredients:* Oranges, lemons, limes. All foods that change shape or whose preparation process creates variations in structure such as frozen food, microwaved food, fermented foods, blended or food-processed items, and bread or cake (which rise). Vinegar, cheese, beets, asparagus, beans, celery, saffron, pepper.
- *Crystals, metals, stones:* Shells and water-worn stones.
- *Decorative touches:* Look for items that represent the change you wish to make. For example, if you're suffering financial constraints, fancy up your house and cook in some of your best clothing (both of which tie into a feeling of being wealthy). Also consider any images of the phoenix—one of the most long-lived emblems for positive transformation even out of the worst circumstances.
- *Timing:* Work during in-between times like dawn, dusk, midnight, and New Year's. Pisces or Scorpio moon.

APPETIZER

Genesis Ground Soup

Makes 4 servings

My mother used to make this with leftovers from a roast; the vegetables and meat are broken into smaller pieces. Likewise, this soup will help you break down the barriers that hold back change, especially at the outset of a new lifestyle or project. Additionally, this soup has a very earthy nature that helps provide strong foundations on which to build once change occurs.

1½ pounds cooked roast beef, sliced
4 medium carrots, quartered
4 medium potatoes, peeled and quartered
4 stalks celery, with leaves
2 medium onions, quartered
2 cups beef bouillon
1 teaspoon chopped garlic
1 bay leaf
Salt and pepper to taste

Magical preparations: Take one small peel from one of the potatoes, rinse and dry it thoroughly. Place this in your shoe before going into the kitchen saying:

Here beneath my feet
Make foundations firm
The wheel of life changes
And with it, I too shall turn

Candle types: Building on the previous incantation, light your chosen candles saying:

The wheel of life changes
And with it, candles burn
Energy ever-turning
With lessons to be learned.

Using a food processor or food grinder, grind up the beef and vegetables into minced proportions. (Don't forget to crank your food grinder clockwise for blessings, or counterclockwise to banish whatever holds you back!)

Place the resulting material in a large soup pot (preferably non-aluminum) with the bouillon, garlic, bay leaf, salt, and pepper. If the bouillon does not cover the vegetables, add a little extra water. Bring everything to a low rolling boil, then turn down to simmer for 3 hours, stirring periodically.

This is more flavorful if you let it sit overnight in the refrigerator, then warm up the next day. Focus on the area of your life where you need changes, patterning the grounds of the soup into a symbol that matches that goal. Then eat the pattern of the magic you've created!

Adaptations: To ease changes occurring in a relationship add a pinch of basil, chili pepper, marjoram, or thyme. To adjust more readily to increasing psychic power add celery seed, an extra bay leaf, or a strand of saffron.

Modification Spinach Salad

Makes 6 servings

The energy of this recipe comes primarily from the citrus fruit, a common feast-day fruit in many ancient Jewish temples. In ritual, the gift of an orange in particular became a way to extend the wish for a smooth change from one lifestyle to another (such as in marriage). It's interesting that orange trees are a type of evergreen, meaning their energy can continue to blossom in your life as needed.

6 cups spinach
3 cups grapefruit sections
2 cups orange sections
2 cups chopped cooked turkey
1/4 cup orange juice
1 teaspoon honey
1/2 teaspoon dry mustard
1/2 teaspoon paprika
1/4 teaspoon garlic powder
1/2 teaspoon poppy seed
1/8 teaspoon ground ginger
1/4 cup mayonnaise

Magical preparations: Think celebration—and decorate your sacred space accordingly. This helps welcome the energy of change rather than fighting against it.

Candle types: Try citrus-scented or dress your candles with a citrus-scented oil.

Arrange torn spinach on four salad plates. Arrange grapefruit and orange sections alternately in a spoke-wheel fashion on the spinach. This represents the wheel of life, that ever turns and brings with it the times of change! As you fashion this add a verbal element like:

The wheel goes round and round
Toward change, I'm ever bound

But with the citrus in this dish
Refreshed awareness is my wish

Place cooked, chopped turkey in center of each fruit wheel. In a small bowl, combine orange juice, honey, dry mustard, paprika, garlic powder, poppy seed, ginger, and mayonnaise; mix thoroughly. Drizzle over the salad.

BEVERAGE

Trade-It-Out Limeade

Makes 4 servings

Limes are sacred to Hermes the god of traders, roads, and travel, so this tree's boughs can watch over the twists and turns in your life too. Additionally, limes played a role in Scythian divination (Ukraine region), meaning you can have some sense of where things are going to shake out.

3 cups water
½ cup honey
½ cup sugar
¼ cup minced peeled fresh ginger
1¼ cups fresh lime juice
Ice cubes
Lime and ginger slices for garnish (optional)

Magical preparations: Limes can be used as poppets. Carve the image of the type of change you're attempting to make in the lime, then stud it with cloves for a healthy and clear vision of how this change will affect you. As you prepare the poppet add an incantation like:

Let me see clearly
Let me know the path's way
Let me accept change bravely
By dark or by day.

Leave this in a bowl of potpourri as it will give off a very nice aroma for quite a while.

Candle types: Rub the wax of the candles with a little fresh lime juice.

In a heavy medium-size saucepan, bring 1 cup of the water, honey, sugar, and ginger to boil over high heat, stirring until sugar dissolves. Boil 5 minutes. Cool. Transfer this into pitcher, straining out the ginger. Mix in lime juice and the remaining 2 cups of water. Fill pitcher with ice. Let stand 5 minutes. Fill 4 to 6 tall glasses with ice; add limeade. Garnish if you wish with lime and ginger slices.

Adaptations: If you need to cool off a bit about all the chaotic energy that surrounds you, try a dollop of vanilla ice cream or frozen yogurt in your limeade.

MAIN DISH

Feisty Amendment Hen

Makes 1 serving

One of the ways of coping with change is approaching it in a playful or humorous way rather than allowing pressures or expectations to overwhelm you. This dish is designed to bring out a positive, competitive spirit that allows you to meet change head on with a strong will in one hand and humor in the other.

1 (1½-pound) Cornish game hen
Salt and pepper to taste
¼ fresh lemon
1 large rosemary sprig
1 tablespoon olive oil
6 garlic cloves, peeled
⅓ cup white wine
⅓ cup chicken broth
1 teaspoon Worcestershire sauce

Magical preparations: To improve your disposition even before starting this spell recipe, find a feather. Hold this in your strong hand and dust it over your auric field saying:

Laughter is good soul food
For helping me with change
By this spell shall rearrange,
Uplift my gloomy mood!

Candle types: Keep the spirit light in your choice of candle shapes and colors. A little levity can often be a great helpmate in magic.

Preheat the oven to 350 degrees F. Rinse the cornish hen completely and dry it. Rub the hen's cavity with salt and pepper, then put the lemon and rosemary inside saying:

Salt purifies; pepper energize!
Lemon for clarity and composure
Rosemary—give me closure!

Next, rub the exterior of the hen with oil. Make six slits in the skin and insert the garlic cloves underneath (be sure these are evenly distributed around the hen).

Put this in an ovenproof pan pouring the wine, chicken broth, and Worcestershire sauce in the bottom. Cover with aluminum foil. Bake for 45 minutes to 1 hour, basting regularly, until the hen is tender and cooked through.

Eat with your fingers—it's more fun!

Adaptations: Make a thematic stuffing for your hen in place of the lemon and rosemary. A simple sage stuffing accents wisdom, celery stuffing provides a sense of peace when change is happening quickly, and fruit stuffing provides happiness with the results of change.

Renovation Ravioli

Makes 4 servings

We talked about using foods that themselves change in the process of making them. These ravioli are perfect—not only do they go from frozen to deep-fried, but this is also a very unique and clever way of preparing them (providing you with similar creativity when it comes to making positive change). The cheese inspires self-love and confidence.

Vegetable oil for frying
2 eggs, beaten
2 tablespoons milk
Salt and freshly ground pepper to taste
1 (16-ounce) package frozen cheese ravioli, thawed
Medium chicken wing sauce
Chunky blue cheese dressing
Carrot and celery sticks

Magical preparations: Take small but meaningful actions that represent change, like turn your socks inside out, or move through your morning routine in a completely different way.

Candle types: In keeping with self-support, use a pink candle, saying something like this when you light it:

Magic is to turn and bend
And with it loving energies, lend
By my will this spell, send
Into this dish my path amend.

Heat oil in deep-fat fryer to 300 degrees F. Beat the eggs with the milk, season with salt and pepper. Dip ravioli into egg mixture. Fry about 4 to 6 ravioli at a time. Drain on paper towels. Toss with chicken wing sauce (use the proportion for 1 pound of chicken wings as directed on the label). Serve with blue cheese dressing for dipping and a side of carrots and celery.

Variation Vinegar

Makes 6 cups

Use this vinegar as part of a marinade for a personally created meat main dish for peaceful resolutions. In the language of flowers, lavender represents calm acknowledgment. In this case you are accepting change and being willing to go with the flow. In particular, this recipe encourages a highly restless situation to slowly settle down into an even keel.

6 cups white vinegar
3 cups freshly picked lavender (or dry organic)

Magical preparations: Change brings a lot of tension in its wake. To rid your home of the negative vibrations that result from anxiety, sprinkle some extra dry lavender around your home moving counterclockwise through each room. Add an incantation like:

Negativity, away, away
Where this lavender falls, only good energy stays

Move through the house clockwise now and vacuum up the lavender (which neatly cleans up the unwanted energies too).

Candle types: Consider blue, for peace and inner knowingness.

☙ In a nonaluminum pan, warm the vinegar slightly on the stove and steep the lavender therein. It is vital that this not boil or it will taste and smell terrible. While it steeps is the perfect time to envision rainbow-colored light filling the liquid (the rainbow represents hope, and the variety of colors symbolizes possibilities).

Once the lavender petals turn translucent, strain. The straining process magically saturates the vinegar with lavender's peaceful powers. Refrigerate, using as you wish for salads or marinades (marinate ham when you need to make a dramatic change, marinate beef for financial transformations, and chicken for changes in the way you handle personal health matters).

Adaptations: Many flowers are edible and make for lovely vinegars. Carnations, for example, make a piquant vinegar suited to inspiring personal changes that manifest inner beauty.

SIDE DISH

Adjustment Asparagus

Makes 4 servings

Magic is to bend and change energy, and ultimately WE are the magic. We are altered and transformed by everything we do. This candlelight recipe builds on that idea, allowing your magic to become the medium through which change occurs more naturally, and less stressfully.

2 pounds thin asparagus spears
1 tablespoon salt
4 tablespoons butter
2 teaspoons olive oil, chilled
2 teaspoons orange juice, chilled
½ cup freshly grated Parmesan-Romano cheese (or other of your choice)
Pepper to taste

Magical preparations: Take a ½-inch wide, 3-inch long piece of paper. Write on it the area of your life where you're facing difficult adjustments. Twist the paper once in the middle and glue the ends together to make a Möbius strip. As you glue the two ends together add an incantation like:

Turn and change, turn and change
Gently now, rearrange
Bring to me, by magic be freed,
Effortless versatility

Hang this somewhere in your magical pantry to support the candlelight recipe.

Candle types: Your choice, but if you'd like to release your wish at the end of this spell, burn your Möbius paper in the flame of the candle (put it in a fireproof dish as soon as it ignites).

Using an oriental-style bamboo steamer, steam the asparagus whole until tender. Meanwhile, melt the butter. Add the olive oil, salt and orange juice to it, and place the asparagus spears in a single layer into the frying pan saying:

The magic is me, the magic is free!

Continue to repeat this or the previous incantation as you cook the spears to tender. Be careful not to break them as this symbolically breaks the path of the magic.

Remove the asparagus and put the spears on a vegetable plate, shaping them into the form of a sacred circle (to keep the cycles moving). Sprinkle the cheese and pepper as a garnish.

Adaptations: This recipe is very serviceable for mushrooms of any kind (in place of the asparagus).

Flexibility Bread

Makes 5 servings

The beauty of this candlelight recipe is its dependability, and the fact that it can be altered to suit your goals easily (see adaptations). No matter what change you have to undertake, there's an ingredient you can add or substitute to symbolize successful achievement of that goal.

1 loaf frozen bread dough (defrosted and risen once)
2 tablespoons butter
1 tablespoon minced garlic
1 cup grated cheese
2 tablespoons powdered Parmesan cheese

Magical preparations: Since you're going to be working with bread dough, you have a malleable medium to shape into the form you want. For changes at home, for example, shape the dough so it looks roughly like a house. For a change of heart, shape it like a heart!

Candle types: Keep your patterns consistent in the carving of your candles.

Prepare the bread dough. Gently sauté the garlic in the butter until golden brown. Knead this along with the grated and powdered cheeses into the dough. As you knead, visualize the changes ahead, and the most successful outcome to them. Pour that positive energy into the bread (the magic expands as the dough rises!), remembering to shape the dough or mark it somehow when you're done integrating the ingredients.

Set aside and allow the dough to rise again before baking according to the directions provided on the wrapper. Remember that the heat in your oven activates the magical energy, so when you check on the bread's progress bless it by saying:

Rise with power, rise with hope
Help me change, help me cope

Adaptations: Feel like you need some serious strength to handle the changes in your life? Add minced spinach. For spiritual changes, add olives.

Revolutionary Raisin Couscous

Makes 4 servings

Enjoy this couscous when you know change is coming and you want to be prepared, but also remain patient. Slow change is often far more long-lasting. With this in mind, saffron becomes a keynote herb having been part of many rituals that honor life's changes (like marriage), and also representing patience according to Pliny the Elder (A.D. 77). Meanwhile, the raisins in this recipe help whatever changes come to be long-lasting, while mint provides clarity.

2 cups water
½ teaspoon saffron threads
1 teaspoon extra-virgin olive oil
½ teaspoon salt
2 cups (10 ounces) couscous
¼ cup raisins
3 tablespoons fresh mint, chopped

Magical preparations: Take time to seriously think about the changes you feel you want (revolution can be wonderful or terrible, so don't skip this step). Once you're sure, bless your ingredients saying:

Change is on the horizon
It will not come as a storm
But rather a gentle river
That my life accepts, transform!

Candle types: It would be nice if you used a slow-burning candle that has more than one layer of color so the visual impact is of slow, steady transformation from one stage to the next.

In a saucepan, bring the water to a boil and add the saffron. Let this stand off the heat for 30 minutes. Return the pan to the heat, bring to a boil, and mix in the olive oil, salt, couscous, and raisins. Remove from the heat, sprinkle fresh mint on top, and serve.

DESSERT

Conversion Cookies

Makes 4 dozen cookies

Ginger is a high-energy spice that will help you have enough inner resources for handling change, especially those that require fast adaptation.

1 cup light brown sugar, firmly packed
3/4 cup dark molasses
3/4 cup shortening
1 egg
2 cups flour
2 teaspoons baking soda
1 teaspoon each cinnamon and ginger
1/4 cup sugar, plus extra for garnish
1/4 teaspoon salt

Magical preparations: Fast change requires that we're clear headed enough to think and act on our feet. So, the night before preparing this spell recipe be sure to get a decent night's sleep. In the morning get up and make a good breakfast with juice (to get those juices flowing), take your vitamins, and nibble on a piece of candied ginger so that your words will match your wits!

Candle types: See if you can find golden colored candles and scent them with a dab of ginger extract.

Mix together the first four ingredients, slowly adding flour, baking soda, spices, and sugar until everything is well integrated. While you're stirring the cookie batter add an incantation like:

My magic in this batter's wrapped,
All forthcoming changes will be a snap!
Now, give me the power to adapt!

When you say the word snap, remember to snap your fingers. Chill for 2 hours.

Preheat the oven to 375 degrees F. Shape the dough into teaspoon-size balls and place them on a non-stick cookie sheet.

Bake for about 10 minutes until set (Caution: Overcooking will make them hard).

Adaptations: Instead of shaping these into balls, make a poppet out of the dough (e.g., a gingerbread person) that can represent changes taking place within you!

PSYCHIC PLATEFULS

> ***Imagination is the outreaching of mind . . . the bombardment of the conscious mind with ideas, impulses, images and every sort of psychic phenomena welling up from the preconscious. It is the capacity to dream dreams and see visions . . .***
>
> —Rollo May

One of the reasons for having candlelight recipes is to open ourselves to integrating magical energy in new ways every day. We want to wake up our spiritual nature and keep it alert to both the seen and unseen energies in and around our lives. This awareness, in turn, can help us intuitively avoid potential problems and spot elusive opportunities (both really good things!).

Psychism is not simply about our tomorrows. It is also about our todays and all the vibrations that dance around us from moment to moment. It's about seeing magical doorways as they open to us and about being more sensitive to the people in and around our lives. These plentiful platefuls are designed to help with that by opening the third eye and keeping its sights tuned in!

Potential Psychic-Enhancing Components

- *Aromatics:* Bay, cinnamon, thyme, nutmeg, mint, rose, lemon.
- *Candle types:* You might carve an eye image into your candles, or find ones shaped like a star to symbolize the pentagram.

- *Color:* Yellow (pale), white, purple.
- *Candlelight recipe ingredients:* Carrots, potatoes, lettuce, grapes, cucumbers, cauliflower, all lunar-aligned foods, citron, mace, fish, onions, sprouts, tofu, mushrooms, celery, coconut, bamboo shoots, water chestnuts.
- *Crystals, metals, stones:* Lapis.
- *Decorative touches:* Use a bouquet of roses, honeysuckle, and marigolds to emphasize the psychic self.
- *Timing:* Waxing to full moon, Cancer or Pisces moon, November.

APPETIZER

Seer Fish Soup

Serves 6 as an appetizer

All of the ingredients placed into this soup pot open your third eye wide (a psychic center located mid-forehead) to the spiritual energies around you every day. The slow cooking brings the ingredients' energies into harmony so you can accept new awareness at a pace that's wholly right for you.

1 pound orange roughy
2 tablespoons lemon juice
Chives
2 onions, diced
2 stalks celery, chopped
1 pat butter
1 block tofu, cubed
1 cup fresh mushrooms, sliced
4 cups chicken stock
½ teaspoon salt, basil, and celery seed

Magical preparations: There's no reason not to have a little fun with this project, so why not dress for the role? Toss on a gypsy-styled bandanna, pull out your crystal ball and use it as a decoration in your kitchen, and play lively music that lifts the energy and helps to move it where you want it to go.

Candles types: Stick with your decorating theme and use a variety of candles all around the space.

Slice the orange roughy into 1-inch pieces. Rinse these gently under cold water, then sprinkle with lemon juice to purify the energy. Meanwhile, into a large pan place the chives (to taste), onions, and celery. Sauté these in the butter until the onions are tender. Add the tofu, mushrooms, stock, and seasonings. Bring this to a low rolling boil, cooking for 20 minutes. Finally add the fish, simmering for 10 minutes until the fish is cooked, stirring clockwise, saying:

I claim the power around me
I claim the power within me
Open my senses and my inner sight
Raise my awareness to new heights!

Serve in white bowls (representing the moon) and eat with an open mind! Afterward, why not try practicing with that crystal ball you brought into the sacred space at the outset? Make sure to take notes of the results!

Adaptations: To keep your visionary sense clear of preconceived notions, add purifying herbs or vegetables to this blend (like garlic or other varieties of onions).

BEVERAGE

Devic Honeysuckle Wine

Makes 7 pints

Honeysuckle is among the flowers thought to improve our inner vision and open spiritual doorways to other realms, like those of the fairy.

6 cups honeysuckle flower petals
1 lemon
1 orange
7 ½ pints water
2 ½ pounds cane sugar
1 crushed Campden tablet
1 orange tea bag
Champagne wine yeast

Magical preparations: Get up early in the morning (dawn is best as it's an in-between time). Gather the honeysuckles as they just open. You want only petals, no greenery. Pack these lightly for measuring (and note that like roses you can put them in a ziploc bag and freeze them just as they are once they're rinsed and patted dry). Don't forget to thank the plant spirit for its gift.

Candle types: Since this spell recipe is somewhat tied into the wee folk, why not a "wee" candle like a birthday candle? Set this with some cream or thyme for your fairy friends to enjoy.

Since this spell does encourage visits by the fey, you may wish to set a sacred space that only welcomes good-hearted spirits. Stand in the center of your kitchen and direct your energy to each quarter saying:

From the East, only playful loving sylphs
From the South, only gentle sprites
From the West, softly flowing undines
From the North, loyal gnomes
Only those with good intent
Only those who wish to share this sacred space.

Rinse fresh flowers under cold water to remove dust, insects, etc. Drain. Thinly peel citrus, retaining peel and juicing fruit.

Put flowers and citrus in a covered saucepan, adding 1 quart of the water and bringing it to a simmer. Once to full simmer, turn off the heat and steep the flowers for 3 hours.

Meanwhile, in another non-reactive pan, bring remainder of water to boil and stir in sugar until dissolved. Cool. Strain flower water into the sugar water only after it's cooled to room temperature. Add citrus juice and all remaining ingredients except yeast, stirring until Campden powder is dissolved. If you wish you can put aside a little of this nectar at this juncture as a fairy offering.

Add yeast that's been suspended in warm water for about 15 minutes. Cover the pot with a heavy towel. Stir daily for 4 days. Rack into a secondary container like a glass bottle with balloon for a lid. After 30 days, rack into smaller corked bottles. Set aside in dark, cool region for 3 months. Strain off the clear liquid once again, then bottle and store for another 3 months and repeat once more. Taste at this juncture and adjust sweetness, then put it away to age for 6 more months before drinking.

MAIN DISH

Mystic Steamed Fish

Makes 4 servings

Ancient tales are swimming with magical fish. Ra was guided through the underworld by fish, Chinese lore uses fish as an emblem of freedom, and in Victorian America fish was eaten to inspire prophetic dreams! All this makes a pretty strong foundation for using fish as part of our divinatory and spiritual diets.

3 to 4 dried mushrooms
2 slices bacon
1 small can bamboo shoots
2 scallions
3 slices fresh ginger
1 tablespoon sherry
1½ pounds red snapper fillet
1 teaspoon salt

Magical preparations: Consider the area of your life to which you need to apply a little more mystical insight, then change the fish in this recipe to match. For example, the snapper might be an excellent helpmate for those conversations where you'd like to be a little ahead of the game and ready with a snappy comeback! Whitefish of any sort has lunar overtones, and shellfish implies protecting yourself from unwanted psychic input.

Candle types: Match your candles to the same goal as you did with the fish choice.

Soak the mushrooms for 30 minutes until softened, then dice fine. Similarly dice the bacon (cooked), bamboo shoots, scallions, and ginger, mixing these with the mushrooms and sherry. Make tiny cuts along the fish to allow flavoring to get inside. Salt the fish lightly and put it onto a heat-safe plate that will fit into a steamer. Pour the mushroom blend over top saying something like:

> *Steamy fortunes, rising thick,*
> *Tell me true and tell me quick,*
> *What will happen by 'n' by?*
> *Tell me where my future lies!*

Steam for 15 minutes until the fillets are flaky. Eat just prior to using your favorite divination tool.

Adaptations: Many varieties of mushrooms and herbs can be substituted into this dish. Determine the area of your life where you want to focus for a forthcoming divination effort. For example, a hint of rosewater in the blend would aid in love or relationship questions, whereas garlic (protective energy) added to the blend might help you uncover the cause of a magical or psychic attack.

Tranquillity Tofu Burgers

Makes 4 servings

One of the ultimate goals of kitchen magic is to transcend ho-hum dishes and transform them into magical menus. This recipe uses a blend of vegetarian delights to purify the spirit and open the pathway for visions.

1 (12-ounce) package firm tofu
½ cup grated carrot
½ cup grated green onions
2 teaspoons minced ginger
1 garlic clove, minced
½ cup almonds, finely chopped
1 large egg, beaten to blend
4 teaspoons soy sauce
Tomato slices and alfalfa sprouts for garnish

Magical and candle preparations: Use this as an opportunity to pause for a moment and take proper care of your personal divination tools. Pull out your divination candles, runes, tarot cards, or crystal ball and cleanse them by passing each through a purgative incense like myrrh. Afterward, recharge the set by placing each in the light of the sun (for mental keenness) and the moon (for the intuitive nature). Finally find a special housing for your tools so they won't be tampered with by unwanted hands or paws when not in use. Keep these items with you in the sacred kitchen while you prepare this candlelight recipe to improve its connection with your personal energy, and bless it with the magic you're creating.

Use a food grinder or food processor to grate the tofu into very fine granules and drain completely. (This may require allowing the tofu to sit on paper towels for about an hour beforehand. The additional magical benefit here is twofold: breaking down the barriers that you may have within to truly accepting your magical gifts and draining away any unwanted energies that the food may have picked up at the supermarket.)

Blend the drained tofu with the remaining ingredients as you might to make a meat loaf. Add bread crumbs and/or water as needed to get a good patty consistency.

Separate the blend into four sections, making a hearty-size tofu burger out of each (four is also the number that puts foundations under your visions). Grill these on low for about 15 minutes, then on a medium heat for about 3 more minutes until each side is golden brown. Note that you can add any favorite sauce during the last turn along with an incantation like:

> *Renew my spirit, let me trust in my gifts*
> *Remove the veil, all doubts—lift*
> *Psychic talents are a heritage true*
> *In me awakened again, by this magical brew*

Serve on a fresh bun with sliced tomatoes and sprouts so your magical insights likewise sprout to the forefront.

Adaptations: The beauty of this burger is that one may substitute all kinds of vegetables in place of carrots simply by changing the spices slightly. Eliminate the ginger and use chopped broccoli, for example. This new blend will protect you from any unwanted influences during divinatory or psychic endeavors, whereas adding spinach improves your insight with questions pertaining to personal resources (both physical and financial).

SIDE DISH

Fortune-Telling Potatoes

Makes 4 servings

It's very likely that even the earliest humans ate potatoes. And as a vegetable with so many "eyes," it is ideal for our psychic platters! To this we add cauliflower, to represent lunar intuitiveness, and dill for alertness.

2 pounds potatoes
1 (2-pound) head cauliflower
1 cup milk
1 tablespoon butter
2 tablespoons sour cream
1 tablespoon dill
Salt and pepper to taste

Magical preparations: To my thinking, psychism is as much a matter of preparedness as it is awareness. In this case, you want to prepare yourself for a shift in mental attitude. One great way to do this is by meditating quietly before entering the space of your kitchen. Breathe deeply, clear your mind, get rid of all your tension and worries, and approach the whole task with a fresh, hopeful outlook.

Candle types: Pick out a candle that can help you with your meditative process and then maintain that centered energy while you cook.

Peel the potatoes and cut each into seven pieces (a lunar number). Put these into a large (4–5 quart) kettle of water with a pinch of salt, then simmer for 20 minutes. Meanwhile, rinse the cauliflower and break off the florets. Add these to the potatoes and continue cooking in a low rolling boil for about 10 minutes or until both vegetables are tender. Drain and mash together with milk, butter, and sour cream, then stir in the dill by hand saying:

Awareness, come quick, my magic here bind
Awake in me an open mind!

Continue repeating the incantation until everything is well blended. Season with salt and pepper.

Adaptations: Decrease the cauliflower to 1 pound and add a pound of carrots to improve your inner "sight"! Or, add 2 beaten eggs with the milk, butter, and sour cream. Place in the oven at 350 degrees F until fluffy (about 20 to 30 minutes) to manifest a fertile imagination!

Full Moon Cauliflower Puff

Makes 4 to 6 servings

Cauliflower is a lunar food filled with all the best energies for strengthening your inner psychic. Additionally, this dish looks like a full moon when it's baked up perfectly.

1 (10-ounce) package frozen cauliflower, cooked and drained
2 large eggs
2 tablespoons milk
½ teaspoon salt
Pepper to taste
2 tablespoons finely chopped scallion
1 cup grated cheddar cheese
2 tablespoons butter, melted
2 tablespoons grated Parmesan cheese
2 tablespoons sour cream

Magical preparations: Since you're focusing on lunar energies, burn some lunar incense like sandalwood, lotus, or jasmine. If it's possible it might be nice to pre-prepare the cauliflower the night before while the moon is shining.

Candle types: Bless and dress your candles the night before when you're making the cauliflower (think white and silver for the moon).

Preheat the oven to 375 degrees F. In an electric blender whirl until smooth the cauliflower, egg yolks, milk, salt, and pepper. Say something like:

Whip up sensitivity
From the bright moonlight
Grant me vision—grant me the site!

Fold in the cauliflower mixture, scallion, cheddar cheese and sour cream. Spread over the bottom of a round, buttered 9-inch pan such as a pie plate. Drizzle with butter; sprinkle with the Parmesan cheese. Bake until golden brown and set, approximately 20 minutes.

Adaptation: Decrease the cauliflower and add steamed carrots to the blend for improved "vision."

DESSERT

ESP Carrot Ring

Makes 6 to 8 servings

Speaking of carrots, this root vegetable famed for improving one's eyesight among mothers everywhere also gives your inner vision a solid foundation (helps keep one foot on the ground).

2 cups all-purpose flour
1 teaspoon baking soda
¾ teaspoon salt
¾ teaspoon ground cinnamon
½ teaspoon ground allspice
½ teaspoon ginger
1 cup golden brown sugar, packed
1 cup (2 sticks) unsalted margarine, room temperature
4 large eggs
2 cups coarsely grated peeled carrots, packed
3 tablespoons fresh lemon or orange juice
2 teaspoons grated lemon or orange peel

Magical preparations: Whether you use lemon or orange in this dish depends on your goal. Lemon adds clarity to your vision and a sense of confidence in what you're learning. Orange provides more conscious awareness as to when you're getting those subtle nudges.

Candle types: Choose candles whose color or aroma matches the area where you wish to apply your intuitiveness and sensitivity.

Preheat the oven to 350 degrees F. Butter and flour a 12-cup Bundt-style pan. Draw an image of your goal in this surface (for example, you could draw the image of an eye for improved "site"). Sprinkle a little more flour where you drew your goal.

Place first six ingredients into a bowl. Using electric mixer, beat sugar and margarine in another mixing bowl until well blended. Beat in eggs. Add sifted dry ingredients; beat until blended. Stir in carrots. Beat in lemon or orange juice and peel. Transfer batter to prepared pan.

Bake carrot ring about 40 minutes (a toothpick should come out clean as with a cake). Cool on rack 15 minutes before turning onto platter.

A Medium's Marigolds

Makes 3 to 4 servings

Pot marigold was a Greek symbol for fond memories and gratitude, and among Germanic women the petals were considered a love charm. This makes a nice combination where you can bring spiritual sensitivity to intimate moments so they're fully enjoyed and remembered with thankfulness.

4 tablespoons organic marigold petals
3 eggs, separated
3 ounces cottage cheese
1 ounce of icing sugar
Pinch of salt
Pinch of nutmeg
1 baked piecrust

Magical preparations: I like fresh flowers in the house, so if you're getting some for the recipe, why not some for your magical space too? Set these in a moonlit window to saturate them with more supportive energy the night before.

Candle types: If you have a candle you like to use for scrying (observing the movements of the flame) that would be appropriate, as would a candle that represents the relationship to which you wish to bring more spiritual insight.

Preheat the oven to 325 degrees F. Bring petals to boil in about half a pint of water. Drain immediately. Mix the egg yolks with the petals. Sieve the cottage cheese and add the sugar, salt, and nutmeg. Add the petal mixture to the cottage cheese mix. Whisk the egg whites and fold into mixture saying:

Let me know my love
Within without; below above
Let me sense their need
And respond in word and deed

Pour into baked pastry case and bake for about 25 minutes or until pie feels firm to the touch. Cool and chill.

Paranormal Coconut Pastry

Makes 6 to 8 servings

The moon is among the most powerful symbols used repeatedly in magical traditions. This recipe helps you internalize all that symbolic power and awareness, having come to us from China. Here, people prepare these little cakes during the moon festival that takes place in the middle of the eighth lunar month, which is also thought to be the moon's birthday.

1 package piecrust mix
½ cup chopped dates
1 cup diced apricots
1 cup sweet coconut
1 cup raisins
1 cup walnuts, finely chopped
¼ cup grated lemon rind (optional)
¼ cup sugar

Magical preparations: I strongly suggest waiting for a full moon to create this spell recipe, as it will empower your magic. Additionally, dress in silver or white (which honors the moon) and leave an offering (perhaps some white bread that the birds can enjoy, and white is a lunar color) to the moon on your rooftop saying:

> *Lady Moon with silvery light,*
> *Hear my wishes on this night*
> *And bring to me inner-sight*

Candle types: Honor the moon with a silver or white candle.

Preheat the oven to 375 degrees F. Prepare the piecrust according to the directions. Once you roll it out, separate it into 26 triangular sections into which you can carve the image of an eye using a toothpick to represent "vision."

Blend the fruits and nuts together and divide it up equally on 13 of the triangles, one for each moon of the year. Put the other triangle on top, dampening the edges so that the two sides stick together and pinching firmly.

Bend the edges of the cakes so they're slightly curved to look like the moon. Sprinkle a mixture of lemon rind and sugar on top, then bake them for about 25 minutes until golden brown. Makes a baker's dozen.

Let them sit in lunar light to charge them up thoroughly before eating.

Adaptation: Add a little vanilla to the fruit mixture to bring "perfect love" (and/or good intentions) into all your psychic endeavors.

7

Lessons for Life

A WHOLE NEW SPIRITUAL LEARNING CURVE

My husband has often said that the proverbial meaning of life is that you're "not dead yet." The more I think about it, the more I realize he's right. That means grabbing onto every moment with renewed zeal, and an openness to learning all the things Spirit has to teach. Think of this as a karmic investment plan. Everything you learn now is less to tackle in the next incarnation!

So it is that we come to three types of food fare. First comes the Creativity Cuisine. Now you don't need to be an artist to use these. Creativity can be expressed in the way you live, not just what you do! And after all that transformation food, it won't hurt to have a little inventiveness in your back pocket.

Second in keeping with the theme is Education Edibles. Now, as with creativity, you don't have to be in "school" to use these. Life is an ongoing learning process. Let's make the most of it and these candlelight recipes.

Last, we have the Happiness Hot Plate. This comes under the heading of emotional education. Being happy is something that for whatever reason comes hard to many people. It's time to let go, and let god/dess!

CREATIVITY CUISINE

Creativity comes from trust. Trust your instincts.
And never hope more than you work.

—RITA MAE BROWN

There are moments and situations in which a little extra creativity would be welcome, like when you're faced with a new project and have no idea where to begin. On those days when you're tired, or it seems like your mind just can't access that inventiveness gene, it's time to cook up some creativity cuisine! The goal of creativity cuisine is to reactivate inventive energy in our lives either for one specific project, or for a certain amount of time during which you feel those vibrations are most needed. The best part is that once you get those creative juices flowing again, you will find your candlelight recipes becoming more and more innovative!

Potential Creativity Components

- *Aromatics:* Allspice, rosemary; non-edible—lotus, lilac.
- *Candle type:* Artistic (flowing).
- *Color:* Bright green and yellow.
- *Candlelight recipe ingredients:* Eggs, honey, mead, water, wine, pomegranates, celery, mustard, grapes, ham, pork, carrots, mushroom, milk, fig, tea, grapes.
- *Crystals, metals, stones:* Green quartz, any yellow stones.
- *Decorative touches:* Serving items in a cup or cauldron (a symbol of the god/dess and intuitive energy). Any inventive layout for the food and/or table.
- *Timing:* Cancer or Aquarian moon, Wednesdays, waxing to full moon.

APPETIZER

Invention Lettuce Salad with Discovery Dressing

Makes 4 servings

For those wishing to make a reasonable profit from their artistic abilities, this recipe is ideal. It blends together the prosperous energies of lettuce, fertile peanuts, and zesty pepper with a wine vinaigrette for guaranteed success!

4 cups mixed romaine, radicchio, Bibb lettuce, curly endive
¼ cup peanuts
½ cup olive oil
½ cup red wine vinegar
½ teaspoon dry mustard
¼ teaspoon cayenne, or to taste
1 tablespoon parsley, finely chopped
Salt and pepper to taste

Magical preparations: Take a 3 by 3-inch square of yellow and green fabric. Yellow represents the creative self, while green symbolizes money-making. Into this, place 4 peanuts (the number of earth and financial foundations), a pinch of mustard and pepper, and a little parsley—all of which you have for your spell recipe. Bless this saying:

From my vision, from my heart
From my work, wondrous art
From my vision, from my heart
Fortune flows, prosperity impart!

Candle types: Carve the candles with the image of an eye to help you keep your eyes open (within and without) for that best, right opportunity.

Rinse the lettuce to remove any unwanted energy and gently tear it (according to folklore you should never cut lettuce at it will cut off your prosperity). Put this in a large yellow or green bowl with the nuts so the color of the container surrounds the lettuce with supportive energy.

In another container mix the oil, vinegar, and spices. Shake well to "shake up" the energy therein. Chill this and shake vigorously again before pouring over the lettuce. Serve as a side dish suited to any ingenious feast.

Once you're done eating, get on the Internet and write up an ad for your work, enroll for a grant, or design a proposal and send it off. Money should follow soon thereafter.

Adaptations: Delete the mustard and cayenne, and substitute rosemary, basil, and oregano to create a good memory for working with your arts and crafts, or a strong devotion toward them.

For a nuttier flavor use sesame oil instead of the olive, and replace the peanuts with sesame nuts. Magically this opens the creative flow just like Aladdin did by using the power words "Open Sesame!"

Resourceful Celery Soup

Makes 5 servings

Celery is a classic symbol of victory as it often crowned the winners of various championships in the ancient world. In the language of flowers it represents applied knowledge. So, enjoy this dish to awaken your mind and re-inspire your creative spirit successfully.

2 tablespoons (¼ stick) butter
5 cups celery, chopped
2 medium onions, chopped
1 pound celery root, peeled and cut into 1-inch pieces
1 large russet potato, peeled, cut into 1½-inch pieces
2 garlic cloves, peeled
1 teaspoon celery salt
2 (14½-ounce) cans chicken broth
1 cup whipping cream

Magical preparations: It might be fun to set up some fresh, leafy stalks of celery in a flower container. Add some ferns and perhaps some yellow flowers (like daffodil) for a meaningful and pretty centerpiece.

Candle types: Find a green hue that complements the celery soup.

☙ In a large saucepan, melt butter over medium heat. Add celery and onions. Cook until tender, stirring regularly. Stir in celery root, potato, garlic, and celery salt. This is the perfect opportunity to add an incantation like:

Potatoes let my magic take root
Celery that creativity grows
Garlic to clear the way
Let the magic start today!

Add broth; cover and simmer until all vegetables are very tender, about 30 minutes. Puree in blender in batches, pouring the soup back into the saucepan after blended. Add cream, swirling it into the blend to create a clockwise spiral (excellent symbolism); simmer, stirring regularly. Season to taste with salt and pepper.

BEVERAGE

Muse Mead

Makes 4 to 6 servings

Enjoy a sip of this light-hearted mead whenever you need a quick boost of inventiveness, especially with your words. Mead is a honey wine that was very popular in Europe, especially among the Celts as part of nearly every social occasion. Honeyed wine also commonly appeared on altars as offerings in the ancient world, being considered a gift from the gods themselves.

1 liter of white grape-based wine (dry)
3 allspice berries (for body/mind/spirit connection)
1 cup of honey

Magical preparations: According to farming lore, you should pick grapes off the bundle from the top downward for taste, pleasure, and positive energy. This recipe skips that step and starts with a prepared grape wine for people who have pressing schedules that don't allow for pressing grapes! However, if you have a bundle of grapes handy, it wouldn't hurt to honor this bit of lore in your candlelight recipe by nibbling on them (from the top down) while you cook!

Candle types: Stick with the grape theme (which also implies a fertile imagination) and get grape-colored or -scented candles for this candlelight recipe.

Warm the wine over a very low flame with the allspice berries to begin generating positive energy. Slowly add the honey, tasting regularly to make sure it's not becoming too sweet for you to enjoy. By the way, if you can find heather honey it's a delightful touch, as heather is a fortunate flower (I've often found that a little luck helps creativity a lot!).

Rebottle and chill, drinking a cup any time you need an inspiring nudge. As you quaff this beverage release the magic you've placed therein by using an incantation as your toast. Here's one example:

Grapes so pure, from off the vine,
Let your creativity in me shine!
Honey sweet, with nectar blessed
Bring to me inventiveness!

Serving hints: Follow with Celtic tradition and pass the bottle of mead to the right when pouring it out. This invokes blessings and unity.

Adaptations: Grape juice may be substituted for those who do not imbibe. Substitute apple wine or juice for wise and creative ways of handling relationships.

MAIN DISH

Productive Pomegranate Chicken

Makes 4 servings

Many ancient civilizations revered pomegranates because they produced so many rich, red seeds. In some regions like Morocco pomegranate juice was poured on fields to ensure a plentiful crop. Add walnut for conscious awareness and we have a lovely productivity dish.

3/4 cup chopped walnuts
1/2 cup all-purpose flour
4 skinless boneless chicken breast halves
1 egg, beaten to blend
2 tablespoons (1/4 stick) butter
1 tablespoon vegetable oil
1/4 cup dry white wine
1 tablespoon chopped shallots
1 tablespoon chopped garlic
1/2 cup chicken broth
1/2 cup pomegranate juice
1 1/2 teaspoons molasses
1 teaspoon honey
Salt and pepper to taste
2 tablespoons chopped chives or green onion

Magical preparations: In order to stress putting creativity to work for you, warm up physically a bit before embarking on this candlelight recipe. Take a brisk walk or some other activity that gets your juices literally flowing.

Candle types: Light your candles before you do your physical activity so they're "on" from the get-go too!

Finely chop walnuts with flour in a food processor. Transfer to a plate. Pound chicken between sheets of waxed paper to 1/4-inch thickness. Dip these into the beaten egg, then into the walnut mixture. Coat evenly.

In a large frying pan, melt 1 tablespoon of the butter with 1 tablespoon oil over high heat. Add chicken and cook until golden and cooked through, about 3 minutes per side. Transfer to plate and cover with aluminum foil while you make the sauce.

In a heavy small saucepan, boil wine, shallots, and garlic until most of the wine has evaporated, about 2 minutes. This is a type of reduction, so if you wish it's a good time to likewise "reduce" any creative angst with an incantation like:

Uncertainty and tension wane
Creativity will flow freely again!

Add broth, pomegranate juice, molasses, and honey. Boil until reduced to ¾ cup, about 5 minutes. Whisk in the remaining 1 tablespoon of butter. Season with salt and pepper. Spoon over chicken. Sprinkle with chives and serve.

Adaptation: Use a turkey cutlet instead of chicken, especially if the creativity you wish to engender has to do with community service.

Quick Comeback Snapper

Makes 4 servings

I've designed this dish so that it accents ingenuity in your communications, especially with know-it-alls, wise-acres, and people who are quick to jump into conversations without really having anything worthwhile to say! The yellow tones of the parsnip, carrots, and pepper harmonize with the goal of good oratory skills.

2 medium carrots
2 medium parsnips
1 large yellow pepper
2 tablespoons butter
2 cups sliced cabbage
1 tablespoon white vinegar
¾ cup soy sauce
4 (4–5 ounces) red snapper fillets
¾ pound sweet potato, peeled and cooked tender

Magical preparations: Since this spell recipe focuses on verbalizing yourself in the most effective way possible, we'll begin by either gargling with mint mouthwash or nibbling on a mint leaf. Magically speaking, mint acts as an overall spiritual tonic and it's also protective so you can "watch your words." Note that you can also follow this suggestion after consuming your spell to increase the effect (not to mention keeping your breath fresh).

Candle types: Use yellow-toned candles dabbed with mint.

Cut carrots, parsnips, and yellow pepper into thin strips. As you do, focus on anything that you feel is hindering your creative progress and likewise cut that away. The visual effect of this activity is improved if you can use a carrot peeler and slice the strips in a motion moving out from yourself.

In a large frying pan, place the butter, carrots, pepper, and parsnips to fry. As you notice the carrots and parsnips getting tender, add the cabbage into the fray, along with the vinegar and soy sauce. Coat vegetables evenly (you want the magic to flow evenly into all the candlelight recipe ingredients) while saying:

Parsnips nip criticism at the source
Carrots and cabbage add magical force
This spiritual sauce with butter, dipped
Ingenious words flow through my lips!

When the vegetables are close to being fully cooked, place a little cooking oil in another frying pan and gently sauté the red snapper fillets. If you wish, you can carve a symbol into the fillet using a knife or a toothpick (a pair of lips would be ideal). Brown the fillets evenly until cooked, which also evenly warms and energizes the symbolic representation (about 5 minutes depending on thickness).

To serve, lay out a layer of sweet potatoes, covered with the vegetables, and the fish laid neatly on top. The potatoes create the firm foundations for your spell, while the vegetables inspire, and the fish makes sure you're never at a loss for words! Drizzle a little of the excess soy/vinegar sauce over all as a finishing touch (remember that the sauce contains your magical energy too!).

Hint: Since this meal is aimed at creative communication, eat very slowly, letting the energy of each bite linger on your tongue. Now, stand up and give a toast, go talk to someone with whom you've been shy, or whatever. You'll be amazed when your words become as snappy as the snapper!

Adaptations: A black bean salad on the side inspires creativity in your divinatory efforts so you can foresee the outcome of your conversations! To make this, blend cooked black beans, sweet corn, diced tomatoes, and a bit of red onion with vinegar, oil, and ground coriander to taste. This is great for people on-the-go. After all, having a sense of what's ahead helps us avoid a lot of trouble.

Trinity Ingenuity Mustard Spread

Makes 1½ cups

Add this spread to any main dish sandwich or meat (like chicken) to "spread" a little creative energy around. The Hebrews used the phrase "grain of a mustard" to imply something that's very tiny as having very great potential. Creativity is often like that—born in a very small spark that grows into an all-consuming fire.

1 cup mayonnaise
1½ tablespoons coarse grained mustard
1 tablespoon English-style mustard
2 teaspoons Dijon-style mustard
2 teaspoons fresh lemon juice
1 teaspoon honey
Pepper to taste

Magical preparations: If you have any actual mustard grains, put a small portion on your altar or windowsill as an offering. Release them to the winds after you prepare your candlelight recipe so that wish is moved throughout creation.

Candle types: Try to find one that's mustard yellow in color. If not, use a color that corresponds to the area of your life in which you need creativity.

In a bowl stir together the mayonnaise, the mustards, the lemon juice, the honey, and pepper. This can be applied to chicken, basted on a baked bologna, or used as a sandwich spread. I like using it on bread because that creates a womb in which your creative magical energy can be nourished. If you carve a symbol into the bread and toast it, you can also internalize more supportive energy. And remember, you can choose your meat so it represents the area of your life to which you want to bring that creativity (like ham when you're looking for a more dramatic flair).

SIDE DISH

Puny Potatoes

Makes 4 servings

Looking for a way for your inventive nature to begin taking root and manifesting in reality, especially in your words? The potatoes in this recipe provide all the right foundations for just that, celery adds creativity, and carrots open your inner vision to capture something truly unique. Additionally, the spices help you take those good ideas on the "road" so you're thinking on your feet while juggling other tasks.

- **½ pound peeled potatoes, cooked and mashed**
- **½ pound peeled carrots, cooked and mashed**
- **½ cup diced celery, sautéed**
- **½ teaspoon celery salt**
- **Salt and pepper to taste**
- **Ginger to taste (optional)**
- **Pinch sugar**
- **1 to 2 tablespoons butter, melted**
- **Oil**

Magical preparations: Take 2 tablespoons of corn starch and blend it with one teaspoonful of powdered ginger. Bless this by saying: *Creativity and Energy, today and always walk with me!* Sprinkle this in your shoes and put them on before you prepare the candlelight recipe so the magic walks with you.

Candle types: Continue the theme and rub your candles with a bit of ginger oil (if you can't find oil you can use a little ginger paste, just rub it into the candle and gently remove any chunks).

☙ Put all the candlelight recipe ingredients except the oil in a large bowl (a yellow bowl is best as yellow is the traditional color of creativity). Stir clockwise, visualizing the area of your life where you most need resourcefulness.

When everything is well blended, oil a skillet lightly. Press the entire mixture into the skillet so as to make a large cake. Into the top of this potato cake etch a magical image that represents an art, craft, or whatever else symbolizes your specific goal. The outer circle of the potato cake then becomes a sacred mandala within which your magical energy will be warmed to perfection.

Place this over a medium heat so it browns. Shake the pan every couple of minutes so the cake stays loose, cooking for 10 minutes in all. Flip the potato cake over carefully. Try not to break it as a whole cake is better symbolically to your working. Brown the other side for another 5 minutes. Do not cut until just before you plan to eat this dish so that you release the energy desired just prior to consumption. Afterward go back to the drawing board and see what wonders happen!

Adaptations: To be more creative in your relationship with another person, add 1 or 2 cups of grated cheese before baking the dish. To be more imaginative in your dealings with children, serve with sour cream. This accents maternal instincts.

Wild Side Mushrooms

Makes 2 to 3 servings

Feel like an adventure, but the rational self keeps getting in the way? Well, put that logic aside momentarily to enjoy some wistful, inventive, and wild living by way of this rice dish.

Nero considered mushrooms as food fit for the gods. In Mexico these represent the ongoing growth process, risk taking, and inner innovativeness necessary to obtain enlightenment.

1 pound wild mushrooms (your choice)
1 small onion, chopped
Handful pearl onions, peeled
2 garlic cloves, minced
1 tablespoon thyme, fresh diced
1¼ cup dry red wine
1 tablespoon olive oil
Salt and pepper to taste
2 cups wild rice, cooked and warm

Preparing the cauldron: Walking on the wild side is as much a state of mind as it is actions. Look at the sacred space of your kitchen for a moment and think: What would be something really "wild" to have here, or do here, that you wouldn't normally consider? Purposefully move that object into your view, or do that thing, to prepare the ambient energy in this space for radical transformation!

Candle types: Think outside the box in your choices here—remember this is all about letting go, and letting it flow!

Rinse the mushrooms, drain, and cut them into bite-size pieces so you can take a real bite out of complacency. Place these with the onions, garlic, thyme, wine, oil, and salt and pepper to taste in an ovenproof dish and cover it with aluminum. The aluminum here serves two functions—practically it keeps the dish from getting burned or dry. Metaphysically it creates a sphere of protection and nurturing in which your magic will warm to perfection. Let the mushrooms marinate at room temperature for 30 minutes.

Preheat the oven to 375 degrees F. Roast (stirring once every 10 minutes) for about 45 minutes until golden brown. Remove the aluminum foil and continue cooking for another half hour so the liquid is reduced by half. This is a good point to add an incantation like:

Mushrooms and herbs, from nature's grace
Open to me that "wild" place
The spirit within dreams and believes
Into this dish, my magic weave!

Serve over a heaping portion of rice, and let the wonderful flavors take you to the wild side of self.

Adaptation: For inventiveness with cash, serve the mushrooms with a crisp salad.

DESSERT

Genesis Grapes

Makes 2 servings

When you want to find a creative way of coping with difficult issues, try this treat and nibble away at some calm resourcefulness, and perhaps the chance to get a fresh start. As an ancient emblem of fertility and the mind, the walnuts in this recipe accent your ability to think clearly.

3 ounces cream cheese, softened
1 tablespoon crystallized ginger, finely chopped
15 to 20 large seedless grapes
¼ cup walnuts, finely chopped

Magical preparations: Take a piece of paper and write a short sentence on it describing the situation that's at the root of your anger. Light it aflame using the candle you've brought into your work space, then let it burn out in a fire-safe container while you cook.

Candle types: I recommend using a white candle for clarity or a yellow one for inventiveness.

Blend the cream cheese with the ginger using a hand blender to "whip up" the energy. Roll each of the grapes in this mixture, turning them clockwise to coat them evenly saying:

Like the cream around these grapes now wrapped
Show me how to astutely adapt!
Confusion be gone, my frustration wane
A creative solution is what I will gain!

Chill these in the freezer for 10 minutes. Meanwhile, pour the walnuts onto a piece of waxed paper. Roll the grapes into this powder again so they're evenly coated. Chill to likewise calm your emotions! Note that you can also wrap up the candle and put it in the refrigerator to halt any negative energy that could be deterring your creative flair.

Eat these slowly, allowing yourself to internalize the resourceful, clever energy. Think about the situation at hand.

EDUCATION EDIBLES

> ***Cultivate the habit of attention and try to gain opportunities to hear wise men and women talk. Indifference and inattention are the two most dangerous monsters that you'll ever meet. Interest and attention will insure to you an education.***
>
> —Robert Millikan

As you might expect, there's a relationship between decision dishes and education edibles because of the focus on the conscious, rational mind. Learning is truly a lifelong process. Spiritually speaking, it's also often a surprising process that reveals much about self and deity. On a mundane level, we're often put in positions where our learning curve is challenged to the maximum, especially when trying to apply transferable skills or adapt to a new social or professional environment. Those are the times to look to these foods to help give your brain cells and body the boost they need.

Potential Education Components

- *Aromatics:* Rosemary, apple, dill, citrus (all), nutmeg, mint, vanilla, lilac.
- *Candle types:* Square candles are a good choice for learning as they provide a strong substructure on which to build your energy.

- *Color:* Yellow and gold (or a color that represents the part of your life to which you're applying this energy).
- *Candlelight recipe ingredients:* Apples, coffee, beans, seeds, walnut, fig, caraway, savory, tea, mustard, cherry, grapes, fiery foods, meat (for grounding), carrots, parsnip, beet, orange, lemon, lime, grapefruit.
- *Crystals, metals, stones:* Aventurine, fluorite, beryl.
- *Decorative touches:* Put some pansies on your table.
- *Timing:* Best prepared during daylight hours to accent the awakened mind. Tuesdays. Scorpio, Leo, or Aries moon. Months of May and October.

APPETIZER

Silence Beet Salad

Makes 2 servings

Hollowed out beets lit the way in many homes on Samhain for protection in Scotland and neighboring lands. They also guided spirits who crossed the veil safely to their homes. We'll adapt this symbolism to guide you in your studies with the least amount of interruption.

1 (16-ounce) jar pickled beets
4 large lettuce leaves (romaine, preferably)
2 tablespoons orange juice
1 tablespoon wine vinegar
1 tablespoon cider vinegar
2 tablespoons olive oil
¼ teaspoon seasoned salt
⅛ teaspoon dill weed

Magical preparations: Since part of your goal here is to keep out unwanted distractions, you may wish to create a semiformal sacred space in your kitchen. Call in the elements with a little invocation like:

Air, awaken me
Fire, motivate me
Water, guide me

Earth, ground me
By air and earth, fire and sea,
The circle is cast, so mote it be.

Candle types: To match your calling, have four elemental colored candles that you can light during the invocation.

Chill beets; drain and arrange on 4 lettuce-lined salad plates. In jar with tight-fitting lid, shake together the orange juice, vinegars, olive oil, salt, and dill weed. Drizzle with dressing, moving clockwise over the beets in a spiraling circle while focusing on your goal.

BEVERAGE

Tea Time

Makes 6 cups

Buddha once said that many things in life, including perfect knowledge, depend on staying awake. For that, monks often used tea, so why shouldn't we follow the example?

1 cup fresh mint, washed and chopped
½ cup sugar
6 cups water
7 bags black tea
½ cup orange juice
¼ cup lemon juice
2 tablespoons grated lemon peel
Mint sprigs for garnish

Magical preparations: If you're feeling even a bit sleepy or groggy before making this, take a quick, cool shower to "wake up." As you stand in the water consider saying something like:

Wash away the weariness
Wake up my sleeping mind
Wash away distraction
By these words, my purpose bind.

Candle types: Go with bright, cheery colors to support the alert mood.

In a 2-quart ceramic bowl, mix together the chopped mint and sugar, and let stand for half an hour. Meanwhile, bring 6 cups of water to a boil. Put the tea or tea bags into a teapot, pour over the water, and allow to steep for 3 to 5 minutes.

Next, add the fruit juices and lemon peel to the bowl with the mint and sugar, and mix well. Strain the hot tea into the bowl. Let this rest for 10 minutes, then strain into a serving pitcher. Pour into tea glasses over ice, for cool clarity, garnished with a sprig of mint.

MAIN DISH

Concentration Meatballs

Makes 4 to 5 servings

When you find your mind straying and your ability to focus completely blown by other matters, these meatballs bring you firmly back down to Earth—get grounded in ground round! These also make a nice post-ritual feast that inspires a firm reconnection to the temporal realm.

½ cup herbed bread crumbs
⅔ cup milk
1 small onion, finely diced
1½ cups ground round
½ cup ground pork
1 egg
1 teaspoon garlic and onion powder
1 teaspoon Worcestershire sauce
Pinch nutmeg
Salt and pepper to taste
Olive oil, for frying

Magical preparations: The best place to eat these meatballs is on the ground for foundations, so set up a picnic-style eating spot either outdoors or somewhere in the house on the floor. Sit here for a few minutes before preparing the recipe to center and focus your will (which also helps support the goal of the spell). Take three deep breaths (for body/mind/spirit working in symmetry), then go into the kitchen being fully connected to the Earth element, which encourages foundations.

Candle types: Since you're sitting, put a secure pillar candle in front of you to help you direct your focus more effectively from the get-go of this candlelight recipe. If it's safe to leave the candle there while you work, all the better.

Preheat the oven to 300 degrees F. Mix all ingredients together thoroughly except oil. Form nice-size meatballs using a tablespoon. Remember to keep your goal in mind while you shape the meatballs into circles (which is the symbol of completion!).

Gently fry the meatballs in olive oil until golden brown saying an incantation like this three times, again to stress the body/mind/spirit connection:

Mind, wander no more
Come! Focus and Aim
By this spell, solid foundations I claim!

Transfer the energized meatballs to an ovenproof dish and place in the oven for about 25 minutes. This has the additional benefit of letting excess fat drip out of the meat. Serve with noodles, or as an appetizer by themselves.

Adaptations: Put a slice of garlic into the center of each meatball to safeguard your knowledge. This can be eaten with the meatball or placed inside warm bread with butter as a side dish. Another alternative is to shape the meatballs like an eye, which represents knowledge, wisdom, and insight.

Note to vegetarians: Use an equal quantity of finely ground and drained tofu instead of meat in this dish. I'd suggest also grinding up a bit of carrot with it (a root vegetable) for the foundational energy desired.

Cram for Exams Chops

Makes 4 servings

Chinese medicine places parsnips under the rule of Mercury and Saturn, which oversee the mind and mouth, making this vegetable an ideal choice for when you have to learn something in great detail, and then prove that knowledge verbally (like in a stand-up presentation).

4 (1-inch thick) pork loin chops
Salt to taste
2 tablespoons butter
2 cups shredded parsnips
1 cup shredded carrot
½ cup sliced green onion
½ teaspoon tarragon, crushed
¼ teaspoon salt
¼ teaspoon black pepper

Magical preparations: In this case, they're also your mundane preparations. As with any spell, you need to work toward this goal by keeping up with your studies before making this dish, then hitting the books afterward in preparation for the test.

Candle types: I think I'd stick with plain white unless you want to change the hue to reflect the topic of your studies.

Coat a skillet with a little olive oil. Brown chops over medium heat for 16 to 18 minutes, turning once until just slightly pink in center. Sprinkle lightly with salt if desired. Remove chops; keep warm.

Melt butter in skillet. Toss together the parsnips, carrot, green onion, tarragon, salt, and pepper. Add parsnip mixture to skillet; toss to coat well while saying:

Carrots—to see what I need to know
Parsnips so that knowledge can grow
Tossed with heat and spices combine
In this dish, my magic I bind.

Cover and cook 2 to 3 minutes, stirring once. Cook until vegetables are just crisp-tender. Arrange these in a circle on a serving platter and the meat in the center to surround your chops with your magic.

Grains of Knowledge

Makes 2 to 3 servings

The symbolism in this dish is designed to help you internalize tidbits of knowledge that, like well-tended seeds, will eventually grow and bear fruit in reality.

1 cup sweet corn, drained
1 cup baby peas, drained
1 cup black-eyed peas, precooked
1 teaspoon sesame seeds
1 tablespoon sunflower seeds
1 tablespoon olive oil
6 soft shell tacos
Sour cream for garnish
Chili powder or other hot spices to taste

Magical preparations: Take a moment and consider exactly what type of learning you're attempting. Change the type of seed or bean (or add one) to better suit your goal. For example, use yellow beans to learn how to communicate better, or all white beans when you're learning about spiritual matters. Black eyed peas might be used for learning psychic arts (e.g. to "see" better), green beans for learning how to balance the budget, red beans when you need to be more informed about a relationship, and black beans when you need to put down solid foundations for your education.

Candle types: Stay consistent and match your candle colors to the beans you've chosen for the dish.

In a small pan, warm the corn, peas, and seeds together with half the olive oil over a low flame. Meanwhile, use the remaining olive oil to lightly oil the tacos, then place them on a flat top grill to warm. You can make these crunchy if you prefer, but I like them soft for wrapping around the ingredients so that it creates a symbolic "womb" in which to nurture the magical energy you're creating.

Paint the sour cream onto the taco shell in a design that represents your goal. Add an incantation while you sprinkle the seeds and beans mixture with whatever Mexican-style spices you enjoy. Something like:

Within this shell the magic burns
Help me in my quest to learn!

Note that if you don't overstuff the taco shells, these make a great study food that you can snack on while accomplishing your goal!

Adaptations: Add grape tomatoes when you need more enthusiasm for learning, onions to keep distractions at bay and to increase your physical energy and attentiveness, or refried beans to better comprehend something you've already learned. You can also add other herbs or vegetables into this blend for sympathetic energy and flavorful changes. In particular, thyme inspires balance in the learning process (whatever you put in is what you'll get back), marjoram inspires a sense of peace about learning a new subject, dill provides mental focus, and chopped beefsteak tomatoes brings positive learning experiences your way.

SIDE DISH

Fig Fulfillment

Makes 4 to 6 servings

Speaking of figs, the Ancients used figs as an important source of nourishment even sometimes replacing bread. In Greece the fig is sacred to Hermes, the messenger, and in Egypt it was the tree of knowledge. So, let this dish convey your wishes to the universe and nourish your mind!

2 tablespoons butter
1 pound fresh figs, chopped
4 to 5 tablespoons red wine
¼ cup brown sugar, packed
1 package wonton wrappers
2 cups vegetable oil for frying
12 ounces blue cheese
½ cup whole walnuts
Fig jam

Magical preparations: Our minds cannot work when the body is weary, so make sure you're well-rested before preparing this spell recipe.

Candle types: The fig is a fairly simple fruit, so you might wish to carve an image of it in your chosen candles.

In a large pan over medium-low heat, melt butter. Add figs and sauté 1 to 2 minutes. Raise heat to a full medium and add red wine and sugar. Cook until liquid is absorbed. Figs will be softened. Remove from heat and set aside.

Lay one wonton wrapper on a clean dry surface. Place a tablespoon of fig mixture in center of the wrapper. Moisten outside edges of wrapper. Put a second wrapper on top and press edges together to seal (this looks a bit like a dumpling). Continue until the entire filling is used.

Using a large frying pan for which you have a cover, pour in a coating of oil. Place 4 wontons at a time therein (for foundation). Fry until they're golden brown on the bottom. This gives you time for an incantation like:

Figs of knowledge, figs so fine,
Strengthen and empower my conscious mind.

Pour about ½ cup of water into the frying pan and finish cooking the dumplings with steam. They will appear to be nearly translucent when done. Serve these with crumbled blue cheese, walnuts, and a bit of fig jam over the top.

Zeal Ziti

Makes 4 servings

When you find your enthusiasm for education waning, or are just down-right apathetic about the idea of learning something new, this dish will perk up your zeal. The spices and peppers offer tons of gusto to offset that indifference.

2 medium yellow bell peppers, chopped
1 small onion, chopped
1 teaspoon diced garlic
1 tablespoon virgin olive oil
1 cup heavy cream
1 small red bell pepper
1 small orange bell pepper
1 bundle small green onions
1 pound sliced mushrooms (your choice)
½ pound ziti
1 cup grated Asiago, Romano, and Parmesan cheese, mixed

Magical preparations: The best way to get yourself ready for this candlelight recipe is to undertake a little physical activity. Take a brisk walk, stretch, get your blood moving! Good physical exertion helps get your magical and mental juices flowing. As you're working out, consider adding a chant or incantation like:

Move and motivate
Move and motivate
Apathy, my magic abates!

Candle types: To me, zeal's color is bright, vibrant red; however, if you connect this energy with another color—use that.

Mix together the yellow peppers, onion, and garlic with half the olive oil and cook it over a low heat for a half hour. Stir in the cream, turning your spoon clockwise to motivate improved energy (or if you prefer, stir counterclockwise to banish indifference). Cool, then pour this into your blender mixing until smooth. This is an excellent time to repeat the previous incantation again since blending "whips up" more energy for the process (better still, set the blender to *whip*!).

Slice the red and orange peppers, and dice the green onions including the tops. As you do, think about cutting up any negativity or passiveness you're harboring. Put these vegetables with the mushrooms and remaining olive oil in a large frying pan. Cook 8 to 10 minutes until the peppers are soft.

At the same time, boil the ziti until tender and warm the pepper sauce. Toss the ziti with the pepper sauce, fresh browned peppers, mushroom, and serve topped with the grated mixed cheeses. Alternatively, mix the cheese in and brown the pasta in the oven for about 15 minutes. The smooth, creamy nature of the cheese here smoothes over any rough energy and blends it into harmony.

After you've eaten and your stomach's settled (this lets the energy settle too) try approaching your studies again. You'll find that while your stomach is filled, your hunger for knowledge has grown!

Adaptations: Change the type of noodle to better reflect your goals. For example, go with spinach noodles so your learning results in financial abundance, or carrot noodles for learning that has an instinctual/insightful dimension like religious studies? Match the noodle's color with your choice of peppers!

DESSERT

Clarity Citrus

Makes 2 to 3 servings

When you're tired of hitting the books, and your eyes feel ready to fall out of your head, the aroma and flavor of citrus fruit in this dish will refresh your tired mind. Additionally, the preserved nature of these treats help you confidently retain what you learn and compartmentalize it for later when needed.

1 large pink grapefruit
1 large orange
1½ cups water
⅔ cup sugar
2 tablespoons light corn syrup
½ teaspoon vanilla extract

Magical preparations: Take a clean washcloth and soak it in cool water into which you've placed a drop or two of citrus oil (grapefruit is one that maintains continuity with this spell and the recipe). Dab this gently counterclockwise on your face saying:

Weariness away,
Heed the words that I say
Exhaustion bind,
Refresh my mind

Candle types: Go with simple white candles, as crisp and clean looking as possible.

Remove the peels from the grapefruit and orange very carefully (think of this as if you were removing weariness from your shoulders). Cut the peels into ½-inch strips. Get as much of the white pith off as possible, then boil the strips in water for 10 minutes until tender. Drain.

In another large sauce pan bring the 1½ cups water, sugar, corn syrup, and vanilla to a boil. Stir clockwise often so that the sugar is completely dissolved as you invoke increased energy with an incantation like:

Oranges of earth, with grapefruit bind,
Bring to me a crystal-clear mind!

Place the citrus strips into this syrup and continue simmering for 20 to 25 minutes until the citrus is somewhat see-through and the syrup is very thick. Lay the strips on a piece of waxed paper to cool and dry. Store in an airtight container in the refrigerator for the longest shelf life.

Once completely cooled, take out and smell it. Enjoy a tiny bite and breathe deeply. Let your weariness fall away, and claim clear mindedness!

Adaptations: As the strips are cooling, sprinkle them with a mixture of sugar and cinnamon or ginger, both of which add extra energy to your magic. Stack one orange strip on top of one grapefruit strip for a very nice visual appeal. Serve as a snack when studying or an after-dinner treat before you hit the books.

Study Apple Munchies

Makes 1 serving

Sometimes simple is better, especially when you need to direct your attention to the work at hand. For this easy recipe I've turned to crunchy food to keep one foot on the ground, your energy high, and your resolution sure. By the way, in various traditions apples were regarded as the tree of knowledge.

¼ cup apple, finely diced
½ teaspoon rosemary, finely chopped
¼ cup cream cheese, softened
Celery stalks

Magical preparations: Steep 2 pinches of fresh rosemary in 2 tablespoons of good olive oil. Warm this until it smells heavily of the rosemary. Dab this on the items you'll be using to study saying:

In this oil my magic burns
Help me in my quest to learn!

Note: If you have leftover oil, it can be stored for up to six months in a dark, airtight container. Use it on your pulse points or books any time you want to improve your memory.

Candle types: Consider yellow or gold colored candles to represent the conscious mind. Alternatively green might be a good color (growth of knowledge).

Mix the apple and rosemary with the softened cream cheese and fill or dip the celery stalks into it. Nibble while you're studying! You'll find the crunching and the magic keeps you from getting distracted.

Adaptations: Eliminate the apple and rosemary, adding dill to the cream cheese with a little salt instead. The results are the same, but the flavor is dramatically different. Or chop up fig instead of apple, as it was under a fig tree where Buddha achieved enlightenment.

HAPPINESS HOT PLATE

A good cook is like a sorceress who dispenses happiness.

—ELSA SCHIAPARELLI

Even the best kitchen witch has "off" days when the gray clouds seem to hover just overhead and rain only on you! This is the ideal time to reach into your pantry of goodies, and grab hold of some joy and contentment. If it helps lift your mood, dance around the kitchen with your wooden spoon (which is now a magic wand) and jiggle up the energy of delight! Kitchen magic should be fun, and a little laughter might be the soul food you most need.

In choosing your happiness hot plates, please bear in mind that they should be foods you actually enjoy. You're not going to generate a lot of happiness if you can't stomach the energies you've created! Also look to comfort foods as another means of easing the blues. Perhaps even snack on those while you whip up your blissful meal.

Potential Happiness Components

- *Aromatics:* Apple, lemon, marjoram, oregano, mint, basil, rose, thyme, vanilla. Non-edible: lotus, pine.
- *Candle types:* Find something whimsical that brings a smile to your face.
- *Color:* Bright and lively hues, especially blue and yellow.
- *Candlelight recipe ingredients:* Peach, olive, cumin, raspberry, apricot, celery, chocolate, honey, dill, milk, wine, beer, cucumbers, cherries, saffron, lettuce, quince, gelatin, soda pop, champagne, barley.
- *Crystals, metals, stones:* Amethyst, agate, chrysoprase.
- *Decorative touches:* Morning glory, chrysanthemum, daisy, and hyacinth are two flowers suggested for improving one's spirits. Also balloons and other fun touches.

- *Timing:* Aquarius or Virgo moon; the season of spring, dawn (and most times when the sun is shining).

APPETIZERS

Good Spirits Soup

Makes 2 servings

Happiness has a lot of dimensions, including a playful, mischievous one. So when you'd like a little sassy, bold jubilation make this light soup and watch your whimsical nature awaken. Saffron has long been considered an excellent spice to help with this goal, especially in the area of spiritual joy.

2 tablespoons olive oil
2 large garlic cloves, minced
1 cup trimmed Russian rye bread cubes
¼ cup dry cooking wine
2 cups canned low-salt chicken broth
1 pinch saffron threads
Salt to taste

Magical preparations: Get a swatch of soft cloth approximately 3 by 3-inch square. Inside of it place a small feather and a pinch of saffron. Focus on your goal saying:

Magic to hold, for a personality BOLD
Filled with humor and cheer
A little sassiness, HERE!

Tie up the bundle with a thread or piece of yarn and keep it with you both while enacting the spell, and afterward as a portable charm that inspires sassy, silly, unbridled joy.

Candle types: Try to find something playful in its design, or perhaps tinker in your kitchen and make your own candle for this candlelight recipe.

In a frying pan, place the olive oil with the garlic. Sauté for 2 or 3 minutes, then add the bread cubes continuing to stir regularly until the bread is golden on all sides (note that the square shape of the cubes provides solid foundations in which your magic will grow).

Add the remaining ingredients and turn the heat up so the blend comes to a low rolling boil (as bubbly as you want to be after eating it!). Decrease the heat to a low flame and continue cooking for a half hour. This may be consumed as it is, but is even better if pureed so you can whip up some extra positive energy before serving.

Adaptations: This is quite tasty with melted cheese on top. The cheese adds love (especially self-love) into the magical equation. You could also change the type of bread cubes to alter the focus of this meal a bit. For example, use sourdough bread when you've been feeling particularly sour and want to transform that attitude.

High Spirit Cucumber Sandwiches

Makes 15 small sandwiches

In China, cucumbers come under the faithful patronage of the melon fairy (I'm not kidding), while in Japan they're a protective food that keeps away evil spirits. In this case I think we'll look to the protective nature to banish the dark spirits of sadness.

- **1 large seedless cucumber, sliced thin**
- **½ teaspoon kosher salt**
- **2 tablespoons white vinegar**
- **1 cup (2 sticks) butter, softened**
- **¼ cup minced fresh tarragon**
- **¼ cup minced fresh chervil**
- **30 slices bread (your choice), cut in 2 by 4-inch rectangles**

Magical preparations: It might be fun to honor the melon fairy by having a melon in the sacred space while you prepare these sandwiches (hey, you can even slice it in pieces to look like a smile served on the side!).

Candle types: A melon scented candle is one idea, or one into which you've carved a smiling face.

Put cucumber slices in large bowl. Sprinkle with the salt and vinegar. Toss to mix well. Let stand 1 hour. Drain any accumulated moisture. In another bowl mix the butter with the herbs, spreading this on each piece of bread as you say:

Smooth sailing, smooth the way
Sadness be gone, joy is born today!

Add the slices of cucumber and top with another rectangle of bread. Eat happily!

Adaptations: Use a vegetable flavored cream cheese instead of butter with a hint of horseradish to put a fire under your goal.

BEVERAGE

Cloud Nine Cherry Shake

Makes 1 serving

There are various mythological stories of how the cherry tree may blossom in the middle of winter. Typically such an event heralds good news or a propitious day. With or without the flowers, however, this light, cool beverage is wonderful for lifting your spirits to cloud nine, no matter the season.

2 ounces cherry brandy
¼ teaspoon curaçao
¼ teaspoon grenadine
¼ teaspoon lemon juice
Ice

Magical preparations: In keeping with the idea of blossoming happiness, bring in some fresh budding flowers to adorn the sacred space.

Candle types: Place bright candles on each side of the flowers and light them saying:

With the warmth of your glow, happiness bestow
As this spell is spoken, and the flowers open
Joy within and without, above and below

☙ Combine ingredients in a cocktail shaker and mix. Strain into a cocktail glass.

MAIN DISH

Bless Me Beef Brisket

Makes 4 to 5 servings

Need just a little blessing to make everything better? This dish does the trick! The honey and apple juice in this candlelight recipe both evoke healthy joy. Ginger energizes everything, while garlic protects your happiness, and vanilla inspires love.

1 (2½-pound) beef brisket, lean
1 cup honey
½ cup apple juice
1 teaspoon powdered ginger
1 teaspoon vanilla extract
1 teaspoon garlic, finely chopped

Magical preparations: Early in the day (dawn is ideal as the time of hope) put the brisket in a large pot and cover it with salted water. Bring this to a low rolling boil and leave it there for 5 hours, adding water as necessary to keep the meat covered. Each hour, turn the brisket adding an incantation to get the magic moving like:

Beef bubble and turn,
The magic burns
Within my heart and soul
Water to cleanse
Joy to impart
Make my spirit whole!

Candle types: If you start at dawn, a yellow candle would be ideal to represent the blessings of the sun.

☙ Check the brisket to make sure the meat is flaky (magically speaking this breaks apart negativity and lets the magical baste saturate the meat). Transfer the brisket into a baking pan and score the top of the brisket with X marks (or any other symbols that represent your goal).

Preheat the oven to 300 degrees F. In a small saucepan, warm the honey, apple juice, and spices together until the honey is completely mixed in. Pour this over the brisket, making sure it gets into the cracks, focusing on your goal and saying:

Honey so fine
With happiness shine
Here, magic bind
True joy be mine!

Transfer to an ovenproof pan and cover with aluminum foil. Bake for 30 to 45 minutes so that the honey makes a glaze. You may want to turn the brisket once during this process so the bottom doesn't burn, and so the meat on that side also receives some of the magical glaze. Slice thinly and serve. Watch your mood improve with each bite!

Adaptations: Change the fruit juice in this recipe to mirror your goals. To be happy in a relationship, for example, you might choose orange juice for devotion. Pineapple juice, on the other hand, will manifest the happiness that comes from feeling welcome wherever you go.

By the way, if you're a corned beef and cabbage fan, there's no reason not to cook up some cabbage with the beef—this represents luck!

Blissful Barley Soup

Makes 5 servings

This is great comfort food, making everyone who eats it feel warm, happy, and cozy. It's interesting to note that barley was often included in Indian wedding rights because of its joy-conferring quality and associations with fertility.

2 tablespoons (¼ stick) butter
1 cup red onions, chopped
½ cup cauliflower florets
½ cup broccoli florets
½ cup potatoes, chopped and peeled
½ cup celery, chopped
½ cup carrots, diced
5 cups beef stock
5 cups chicken stock
2 cups pearl barley
1½ tablespoons fresh thyme, chopped
1½ tablespoons fresh oregano, chopped
Pinch marjoram

Magical preparations: It's hard to follow your bliss if you don't know for sure where it lies. Consequently, I recommend taking the time to meditate for a few minutes every day, several days before preparing this recipe. Think about the things that make you truly happy (and recognize the things that do not). This will help you better direct the energy of the spell.

Candle types: Consider choosing bright, cheery colors or ones that match the area of your life to which you wish to apply the joy you're creating.

In a large soup pot, melt the butter (this melts away the barriers between you and true happiness). Add the vegetables and sauté lightly for 15 minutes over a medium-low flame. Add the remaining ingredients and cook for 30 to 45 minutes until the barley is tender. As it cooks, focus on your goal, close your eyes (this improves focus for many people) and say:

Barley, sealed with magic's kiss,
Renew in me a sense of bliss
Joy to my mind
Joy to my heart
Here I claim, the magic impart!

Non-vegetarians can add some finely diced beef too, which would magically manifest some good financial news that brings a lot of happiness with its timely arrival.

Adaptations: For truly sweet joy, add sweet potatoes. For happiness that has rich foundations in which to grow, add more root vegetables.

SIDE DISH

Relief Apple Rings

Makes 6 as a side dish or dessert servings

The circle is the perfect symbol of completion and protection. This dish uses that symbolism to reestablish a safe haven in our hearts. Here, our happiness will continue to abide like a light that constantly chases away the shadows.

1 cup dark beer
1 cup all-purpose flour
4 large apples (your choice)
½ cup fresh lemon juice
½ teaspoon cinnamon
2 tablespoons brown sugar, firmly packed
Vegetable oil for deep-frying

Magical preparations: The circle is the predominant symbol used in this spell, so why not build on that by casing a circle and making your kitchen into a sacred space? Pick up a wooden spoon (that doubles as a wand) and walk in a clockwise circle around your kitchen saying:

I welcome the fire, I welcome the sea
Powers of earth and air I call you to me
So mote it be!

Repeat the incantation four times, once at each of the four points of the compass (note: Fire is South, Sea is West, Earth is North, and Air is East).

Candle types: Light elementally colored candles as you're reciting the incantation.

☙ Place the beer and flour together in a bowl and mix thoroughly. Let this stand at room temperature for at least an hour. Meanwhile, slice the apples so they create rings about ¼-inch thick. Lay these on a nonstick cookie sheet, and if you wish etch into them a symbol of what kind of happiness you're trying to manifest.

Mix the lemon juice with cinnamon and brown sugar and pour this evenly over the apples. Let this sit for an hour as well, then remove from the flavoring. Finally, heat some frying oil in a deep skillet or pan. Dip the apple slices into the batter so they're covered completely and fry until golden brown (4 to 5 minutes). Drain on paper towels, garnishing with a sprinkling of sugar if desired (this will make your joy all the more sweet!).

Adaptation: This works quite nicely with firm pears. Symbolically this maintains happiness for a long time.

Happiness to me, happiness to me
The magic's stired, so mote it be!

Sunshine Mixed Lettuce Salad

Makes 3 servings

Take a walk on the sunny side of the street with this healthy and joy-producing salad. Better still, if you've had trouble sleeping because of stress or other negativity, lore tells us that lettuce will calm your mind and manifest a restful night.

¼ head of radicchio
½ head of Bibb lettuce
¼ head any other favorite lettuce
½ cup scallions, thinly sliced
½ cup olives, sliced
2 tablespoons red wine vinegar
⅓ cup olive oil
½ teaspoon each garlic and onion powder
Salt and pepper to taste

Magical preparations: The sunny side salad should be prepared in a similarly sunny location for best results. Take your candlelight recipe ingredients to a window that's receiving natural light (if the sun is shining the results will improve dramatically). Let the ingredients sit there for a few moments and absorb all the warmth and blessings of the sun as you visualize your goal. When the exterior of the lettuce has gotten just slightly warm it is then energized for your candlelight recipe.

Candle types: Again a yellow or gold candle would be ideal and maintain the theme here. You may want to carve it with a happy-face image.

Gently tear the lettuce (cutting it cuts off the magic) and put it in a large bowl with the scallions and olives. In another small container beat the vinegar, oil, powders, and salt and pepper until well blended. Toss this with the lettuce, visualizing your mood lifting just like the salad! If you wish, this is an excellent opportunity to add an incantation like

Worries and sadness, take to flight
My mood will lift with every bite!

Adaptations: Salads offer a lot of options for personal innovation. If you want to feel happy about what you have, add croutons (providence). For joy in more intuitive matters go with a lunar addition like sliced cucumbers that look like full moons, and for delight in a relationship add tomatoes, the love apple!

DESSERT

Cheer up Chocolate Fondue

Makes 4 servings

Chocolate lovers—there is nothing like this rich fondue for a quick pick-me-up! Make it for yourself or share it with friends who have been feeling a bit blue!

6 tablespoons whipping cream
3 tablespoons honey
7 ounces bittersweet chocolate or 7 ounces semisweet chocolate, chopped
1 tablespoon cherry or orange brandy
¼ teaspoon almond extract
Assorted fresh fruit (e.g., whole strawberries, banana slices, pear wedges, and orange segments)

Magical preparations: Bring as much light as possible into your work space. Dim lighting symbolizes low energy levels and often a similar "low" mood. If you're using lightbulbs, dab them with a light hearted oil and turn on the magic!

Candle types: The more the merrier here. Also if you're serving this to friends, have one candle per person that they can take home with them and light when feeling sad.

In a heavy medium-size saucepan, bring cream and honey to simmer. Add chocolate; whisk until melted. This is a good time to add your incantation as whipping provides in-dwelling energy that you can tap:

Whip up our mood, whip up some fun
By these words, this spell's begun!

Remove from heat. Whisk in brandy and extract. Pour fondue into bowl; place on platter. Surround with fruit. Serve with forks, long toothpicks, or skewers.

Contentment Apricot Tarts

Makes 36 servings

Just when wanderlust or seven-year itches begin to take hold, or you find that everything annoys you, make these cookies and rediscover contentment with life just as it is. In Persia apricots are called sun apples, which may be why they became associated with joy. The shining of the sun on special occasions is considered a sign of divine favor.

3/4 cup dried apricots
1/4 cup brown sugar
1 cup water
1/2 cup heavy cream
2 tablespoons apple brandy
2 tablespoons powdered sugar
36 shortbread shells (or other pastry shell of choice)

Magical preparations: What area of your life needs a little more peace or joy? Etch a symbol of this into the bottom of the shells (like a heart for contentment in a relationship).

Candle types: Before making this dish take a few minutes to meditate before your chosen candles. Still your mind and spirit so that you don't take anxiety into the kitchen—that won't produce contentment in the least! During your meditation, visualize the bright candlelight filling every cell of your body, collecting any lingering negativity, and transporting it away.

In a saucepan, place the apricots, brown sugar, and water and simmer for 15 minutes, until tender (this also tenderizes an apathetic or hardened heart). Transfer these to a blender or food processor and puree completely. Set this aside.

Whip the heavy cream to gentle peak stage. Fold in the brandy and powdered sugar saying:

Happiness to me, contentment to me
The magic's stirred, so mote it be!

Use this along with the apricot puree to fill the pastry shells with altering layers of cream and apricots. Chill for a half hour before serving.

Adaptations: You can use any fruit as the puree for this by simply changing the type of brandy you add to complement the flavors. How about raspberries and berry brandy for abundant joy, oranges and orange brandy for a happy relationship, or pears with brandy for long-lasting joy?

8

Providence Platters

A HEARTY SERVING OF PLENTY AND PROSPERITY

The philosophy among many neo-pagan practitioners is that we should use our magic only for those things we need, not those things we "want." I agree in part. Spirituality shouldn't be a grabby "mine, mine, mine" venture. On the other hand, I don't see any reason not to ask for a little more than you need, especially if you're willing to share! Sharing spreads the joy, and the Universe would not answer such a request if it wasn't a good thing!

Balancing those two—needs and wants—we enter into Abundance Allocations. Now, abundance doesn't just have to do with money. It can apply to any area of your life that you find wanting.

Next we move to candlelight recipes for Employment: Let's Do Lunch. There's no mistaking that our jobs affect our bottom line. When you want to turn that red lettering to black, whip up these dishes and stir up some significant, positive changes in the work environment.

And last, but not least, cold hard cash cooking! Money Meals focus on either saving or sustaining what you have, or improving the income flow. The idea isn't necessarily wealth, but maintaining an even keel even in the worst of times.

ABUNDANCE ALLOCATIONS

As we become curators of our own contentment on the Simple Abundance path. we learn to savor the small with a grateful heart.

—SARAH BAN BREATHNACH

To what in your life do you wish to bring abundant energy? Are you hoping for a plentiful garden? A copious financial flow? Numerous friends? Abundance has many facets, so remember to have a clear vision of the area of your life to which you wish to apply the energy of these recipes.

Potential Abundance Components

- *Aromatics:* Ginger, cinnamon, saffron, basil, vanilla, mint; Non-edible—sandalwood.
- *Candle types:* Try using a square candle for foundations. A square represents earth energy (for grounding).
- *Color:* Sprout green, emerald, silver, gold.
- *Candlelight recipe ingredients:* Grilled foods, corn, frog legs, kiwi, oats, orange, baby lettuce, alfalfa, honey, rosewater, nuts, berries, salt, pepper, beef, harvest vegetables, bread, apple, milk, peaches, olives, rice, coconut, carrot, fig, mustard.
- *Crystals, metals, stones:* Magnets (lodestone), lava stone; gold, silver and green colored stones, quartz.
- *Decorative touches:* Primrose, poppies, daffodil, potted plants, horn of plenty, chalice or cauldron.
- *Timing:* Waxing to full moon, blue moon. Taurus, Cancer, Virgo, and Pisces moon. The season of spring. Noon (especially if dealing with the conscious mind, such as wanting to generate energy for abundant logical awareness).

APPETIZER

Surplus Orange and Lettuce Salad

Makes 6 to 8 servings

This butter lettuce salad is an ideal color to help keep your abundance growing. Egyptians trusted in the fertile quality of lettuce, and often associated this vegetable with the vegetation god Min whose sacred animal—a white bull—represented potency. In Greece lettuce was often sown at harvest festivals and it grew very quickly—it became a symbol for fast manifestation!

¾ cup olive oil
¼ cup champagne vinegar
2 teaspoons grated orange peel
1½ teaspoons frozen orange juice concentrate, thawed
Salt and pepper to taste
½ red onion, very thinly sliced
1 head of butter lettuce, leaves coarsely torn (about 8 cups)
2 large oranges, peeled and thinly sliced into rounds

Magical preparations: If you can find an image of a bull to honor Min in your pantry sacred space that would be a nice touch.

Candle types: Lettuce green is a good choice in color.

This is a delightfully easy recipe that goes together quickly. Whisk oil, vinegar, orange peel, and juice concentrate in medium bowl. Season with salt and pepper. Add onion; marinate 30 minutes, stirring often. Divide lettuce among 4 plates. As you do add this incantation:

Bless me with bounty
Abundance come to pass
Bless me with bounty
By my will this spell is cast!

Top with orange slices. Ladle dressing with onion over.

Adaptation: Change the kind of lettuce you use to reflect slightly different goals. For example you might use a red leaf blend for abundant passion.

BEVERAGES

Fortune-Teller's Currant Tea

Makes 6 servings

Looking for a change in fate? Black currant is an excellent helpmate in that it banishes the fear of financial constraints and helps intuition. Rather than blaming yourself, you can now get past that issue and start focusing on how to fix things!

6 cups water
12 black currant tea bags
2 (3-inch-long) cinnamon sticks, broken in half
1 tablespoon fresh ginger, minced and peeled
6 tablespoons frozen raspberry-cranberry juice concentrate
¼ cup sugar
Ice cubes
8 crystallized ginger rounds

Magical preparations: Because this dish is aimed at bolstering your instincts and shifting perspectives, anoint your third-eye area with an enhancing oil like lotus or sandalwood.

Candle types: The same oil you used on yourself can also be used on the candles you choose for your table. That way, as they burn the aromatics bless everyone present.

In a large saucepan, bring the 6 cups water to a boil. Add tea bags, broken cinnamon sticks, and fresh ginger. Remove from heat. Cover; steep 10 minutes. Mix in juice concentrate and sugar. Chill until cold. Strain tea mixture into pitcher. Pour into a glass with ice cubes and a piece of crystallized ginger each.

Pineapple Plenty Juice

Makes 1 serving

Pineapples are associated with fertility, plenty, and welcoming energy, especially in Polynesia. This beverage is particularly suited to encouraging an abundance of friends. It can also be used to restore the flow of well-earned rewards.

1½ cups packed fresh mint leaves
1 cup sugar
1 cup water
3 tablespoons dark rum
½ cup unsweetened pineapple juice
Mint sprigs for garnish

Magical preparations: If you enjoy pineapple, get a whole one and have a slice every day over four days before enjoying this beverage. That will set the tone for this candlelight recipe by adding more internalized energy from the pineapple to the process. Also, if you use a sharp knife you can carve a symbol of your need into the center of the pineapple slices.

Candle types: Keep the theme going—find a pineapple scented or shaped candle to use in decorating your sacred space.

Chop mint. In a saucepan, bring sugar, water, and mint to a boil, stirring until sugar is dissolved. Simmer syrup, undisturbed, 2 minutes. Pour syrup through a fine sieve, pressing hard on solids, and cool. Take 2 tablespoons full of this and mix it with the rum and juice. Garnish with a mint leaf.

Note that the remaining mint sauce can be used in tea, on toast, and as a glaze for lamb. It keeps refrigerated for about 2 weeks.

MAIN DISHES

Almond Abundance Tofu Burgers

Makes 4 servings

Make these great veggie burgers when you want to create a strong foundation in which your abundance can grow. The mythology of almonds in Greece is tied directly to goddesses of fertility and gods of plenty. Among the Hebrews an almond branch was said to give the bearer vigilance in Hebrew tradition. The Hebrew word for almond (shaqad) *roughly translates as "to watch for," so eat these—and keep watch for a change of fortunes!*

1 (12-ounce) package firm tofu, drained, patted dry, cut into 1-inch-thick slices
Nonstick vegetable oil spray
½ cup grated carrot
½ cup green onions, thinly sliced
2 teaspoons ginger, minced and peeled
1 garlic clove, minced
½ cup almonds, toasted, finely chopped
1 large egg white, beaten to blend
4 teaspoons soy sauce
1 teaspoon oriental sesame oil
4 sesame seed buns, toasted
1 cup alfalfa sprouts
4 tomato slices

Magical preparations: Burgers make me think of picnic fare, so this might be a good opportunity to create a green side salad with plentiful baby greens and a zesty dressing for supportive energy.

Candle types: Anoint your chosen candles with a bit of almond oil (available in supermarkets) to increase the overall power with which you have to work.

Drain tofu completely by wrapping it in a clean dish towel and putting a wooden cutting board on top for about an hour. Get as much liquid as possible out of the tofu. Put this into a mixing bowl and mash into tiny pieces. As you do, focus on those negative cycles that you want to likewise break.

Spray a frying pan with the nonstick spray (or use olive oil).

Fry the carrot, onions, ginger, and garlic lightly for about 3 minutes. Cool. Add these to the tofu along with the almonds, egg white, soy sauce, sesame oil, and seeds. Add a personally pleasing amount of salt and pepper. Shape the mixture into four patties about ½-inch thick. On the surface of each one, etch a symbol of your need using a toothpick (such as a dollar sign if you need abundant money) so that direct heat is applied to that goal.

Fry these in a large pan treated with the spray or oil. It only takes about 5 or 6 minutes to cook thoroughly (3 minutes on each side). As you turn the patties, you can add an incantation like:

Turn and change, Turn and change
Good luck and fortune, now arrange!

Put the burgers on the buns with a nest of sprouts and a healthy slice of tomato.

Adaptations: You could easily substitute ground turkey or beef for tofu in this dish. Turkey would promote the energy of being able to share your abundance with others, and beef promotes both prosperity and firm foundations so abundance continues to take root and grow.

Feta and Olive Plenty Pitas

Makes 6 to 12 servings

Among Mediterranean people, the olive was considered a precious and plentiful gift, provided by the goddess Athena. The flavorful pita bread in this recipe provides a warm, cornucopia-type womb and combines olives and sprouts.

1 lemon
1 teaspoon chopped garlic
1 teaspoon rosemary
1 teaspoon thyme
2 whole bay leaves
Pinch of salt
Pepper, freshly ground
⅓ cup fine-quality olive oil
1 cup olives (your choice)
1 dozen greek pitas (6-inch size)
1 cup sprouts (your choice)
1 pound herbed feta cheese

Magical preparations: Before enacting this spell, consider what kind of plenty you most need, then choose the color or type of olives according to that need. For example, use green olives for financial abundance, black olives if you want abundant and secure ground on which to build and secure your dreams, or Greek olives to preserve your abundance once it arrives. Or, better still, blend all three together for a combined effect!

Candle types: If you can't wait for the timing suggested in this recipe to create this meal, bless your chosen candles during those auspicious times.

Begin by slicing the lemon into four wedges (four is the number representing solid groundwork) saying:

By the winds seeds are borne
By the sun they are nurtured
By the waters, nourished
By the earth, given roots
So too, give foundation to my magic

Place these slices with the garlic, rosemary, thyme, bay leaves, salt, pepper, olive oil, and olives into a large container. Cover and refrigerate the olives over the 3 days of a full moon (if possible, if not a waxing moon will suffice). Each day at dawn (the time of hope), shake the olive mixture saying:

By the light of a new day
I claim my plenty and give magic its way!

On the third day (any time), heat a ridged frying pan on the stove. Brush each pita with a little of the olive oil mixture from the olives and warm them for 1 minute on each side. Make a nest of sprouts into which you crumble some of the feta cheese on each pita, and place a heaping tablespoonful of olives with a little liquid thereon. Pattern this filling with a dollar sign to receive money, a heart for love, and so forth. Finally, gently wrap the bread, which protects and nurtures your abundance, around the mixture and consume expectantly! You should see some significant change in your situation fairly soon.

Adaptations: Grill some marinated chicken with the pitas and dice it up fine, mixing it with the olives and cheese. Magically this creates energy for an abundance of health.

Wealthy Barbeque Pork Ribs

Makes 3 to 4 servings

Prepare these sticky ribs and watch all the money that comes into your hands stay there!! In Celtic tradition those that enter paradise partake of pig meat in unending supply. In this region it is also sacred to Keridwen, who represents abundance and fertility. Next add honey for sweetness, ginger for power, and orange and mustard to round off the flavor on the grill.

2 sides baby back pork ribs
½ cup soy sauce
1 cup orange juice
⅓ cup cider vinegar
½ cup apple juice
¼ cup honey
1 teaspoon powdered ginger
1 teaspoon powdered mustard
½ cup minced chives or green onions
2 tablespoons minced garlic

Magical preparations: In the United States we often equate money with the color green, so put a green shirt on before you begin this recipe (so you literally have a "green back"). Also surround your cooking space with rich things—gourmet coffee, a decadent type of chocolate, or anything else you associate with being really flush to support the wealthy vibrations you're creating.

Candle types: Go with four gold or green candles since you're focusing on prosperity. Four is a foundational number, being associated with Earth and grounding that encourages success.

☙ Think about any obstacles standing between you and financial success. When you have those things clearly in mind, begin removing the membrane from the underside of the ribs (this helps remove those obstacles even as you're removing the membranes and make the meat more tender). In another pan, combine all the remaining ingredients and stir over low flame so the honey is evenly mixed in. Stir this clockwise saying:

Honey make my fortunes sweet
Ginger make this spell complete
Apple and orange for financial health
Come to me, good luck and wealth!

Cut the ribs partially in between each bone. Place these in a large green or gold colored pan if you have one (you can sometimes find these at culinary stores). Alternatively use a bowl, pouring the marinade over top. Put this in the refrigerator covered for a while (at least 3 hours) so they absorb the spell and the flavor. I prefer to leave them overnight.

Next, remove the ribs from the marinade letting excess drip off. Wrap the ribs completely with plastic wrap. Sheath this bundle yet again with aluminum foil so the rack is covered tightly. Put this in a low-heat oven (200 degrees F) for 2 to 3 hours until the meat begins to retract from the bones (this also symbolizes "shrinking or decreasing difficulties"). They're now ready for the grill.

Brush the grill with a little cooking oil so the ribs don't stick. To continue the energy you created with the marinade, add an incantation while you prepare the fire like:

Bless these ribs, and the sacred flame
Prosperity grows and scarcity wanes!

Wait until the grill has a nice medium flame (about 320 degrees F). Cook the ribs, turning them every 10 minutes. Every other turn lavish with leftover marinade. (I often add more honey to this for really sticky ribs!) Approximate cooking time: 20 minutes. You'll know they're done as the meat starts falling off the bones! A windfall should come your way soon after enjoying these! This good fortune will not disappear as fast as it came, but "stick" with you a long time.

SIDE DISH

Bounty Beans

Makes about 8 servings

This bean blend makes a tasty side dish that supports your abundance fare thanks to their symbolic value. Ever try to play count the beans as a child? You'd stand in front of the jar of beans and there always seemed to be more than you could possibly guess. This is one reason why they make perfect plenty foods!

The most famous Roman families were named after beans because this was such an important crop in their culture They signify abundance because of the numbers that grow from one plant. (There's the bounty!) They're also associated with providence in a variety of settings because beans were often a staple in times of famine. There are over 500 varieties of beans known, and they come in many shapes and colors—as diverse as you wish your blessings and bounty to be!

2 cups long grain rice, cooked
1 cup sweet corn
1 tablespoon lemon juice
2 green onions, minced
Salt and pepper
1 pound precooked mixed beans (red, black, white, black-eyed)
1 large tomato, chopped
½ cup sliced olives
1 green pepper, sliced
1 tablespoon balsamic vinegar
2 tablespoons olive oil

Magical preparations: To what part of your life do you want to apply this spell? Bring a representation of that into the kitchen while you're preparing this dish and try to pick your beans according to that focus. For example, if you want a prolific green thumb I'd consider using green beans or peas to encourage sympathy with all "green" things. For physical "fertility" you might want to use yellow beans (the color of creative power) and bring a statue of a pregnant goddess into the kitchen. If you want money, consider green beans.

Candle types: Choose the color of your candles according to need (yellow for creativity, green for money, etc., even as you did the decorative accents). Use lots of them (this illustrates bounty).

After preparing the rice, keep it in its pan so its as steamy and warm as is your spell! To this add all the remaining ingredients and toss gently (you don't want to stir up any unwanted energy). During the mixing process try an incantation like:

For money

Constraints shall wane
Within these beans, financial gain
Money to me, magic fly free
Today I claim prosperity!

Repeat a money incantation four times. Four is an earth-oriented number associated with creating strong foundations. Serve the beans on a bed of lettuce as it looks quite pretty and adds to the symbolic value for the financial spell. Prepare this dish when you want your "hill of beans" to pile up faster than you can eat or spend them!

For the garden

Green for sowing, energy's flowing
From within to without
My garden's magic is growing!

After you eat this dish, turn a teaspoon or two into the garden to transfer some of the good magic right into the soil.

For physical fertility

Feed my womb with energy; let life begin within
Born of love and bounty beans
The magic now begins!

Consume this with your significant other while it's still steamy then retire to a night of passionate lovemaking.

Adaptations: Think about the kind of rice you choose too! Brown rice, for example, has strong earth energy. You can also use any type of grain instead of rice, if you prefer. In this case the mixture can be served cold with sweet peas as a garnish, to generate "cold hard cash."

DESSERT

Kiwi Prospects

Makes 6 servings

Tired of waiting for opportunity's door to open? Make this dish whenever a lack of development or progress impedes the path to abundant living. The Greeks considered orange trees a symbol of abundance because they were a kind of evergreen. Better still, the spices in this dish add support with more energy (cinnamon). The lush green color of the kiwi magically emphasizes steady progress toward your goal.

¾ cup water
⅓ cup brown sugar
Pinch allspice
1 teaspoon cinnamon
½ teaspoon vanilla extract
3 large seedless oranges
3 large kiwi
2 tablespoons chopped walnuts

Magical preparations: Have a special small bowl or cup into which you can put a dollop of the mixture for the actual spell casting. You may choose this container for its symbolic value too! For example, a silver container might represent abundant insight and psychic ability, and a deep red container might reflect the wish for plentiful passion.

Candle types: Carve your chosen candles with a symbol of the area of your life to which you want to apply this energy (like a heart for abundant love). Light the candle as you begin to prepare the food and let it burn until the image has melted completely—releasing your intent.

In a saucepan, place the water, sugar, spices, and vanilla and let warm over a low flame. If you'd like to add a drop or two of symbolic food coloring to this blend, this is a good juncture at which to do it. Green food coloring brings growth, a drop of yellow adds creativity, or a drop of orange stresses "harvesting" or "reaping" the rewards of your magical efforts.

Meanwhile, peel the oranges and kiwi visualizing any hindrances between you and success likewise being peeled away or barriers broken down. Cut the fruit cross-wise to 1/3-inch pieces. (Note this creates a natural mandala-circle with outward pointing spokes on the orange, and dots on the kiwi, neatly keeping your energy moving forward!)

Check the water now and see if it's become thicker, if not continue stirring until it has a syrup-like consistency (remember you want your success to stick to you like the syrup to the fruit!). Add the oranges and kiwi, tossing until well coated saying:

Orange for plentiful devotion and health
Kiwi for profuse love and wealth
Bound together with vision and sauce
And with a heaping dose of magic, toss!

Pour into a decorative dish, sprinkling the walnuts on top. Take about 1/4 cup of this blend in a measuring cup, and chill the rest for about 2 hours before serving. Carry your cup of the reserved blend outside any door in the house saying:

I open the door, I open the way
Let opportunity's knock come today!

Knock on the door, open it to welcome the energy, and eat the small portion you've brought with you to internalize that transformation.

Adaptations: Substitute peaches for the oranges. Magically this accentuates the wise use of your abundance once any difficulties are overcome. This is also tasty when drizzled with a bit of warm honey, which makes your success all the more pleasant and inspiring!

EMPLOYMENT: LET'S DO LUNCH

The crowning fortune of a man is to be born to some pursuit which finds him employment and happiness, whether it be to make baskets, or broadswords, or canals, or statues, or songs.

—RALPH WALDO EMERSON

When you need energy for work, when you're hoping to improve the skill or aptitude with which you work, or when you're looking for a new way to apply your career-oriented abilities, turn to these candlelight recipes. Mind you, not all of them are lunches per se (but, hey, there's always leftovers for the lunch box!).

I do issue some caution when it comes to the following menus. More often than not, when you're trying to cook up a raise, you also cook up more work by which to earn that raise! That's just checks and balances working. The universe rarely just "gives" anything to anyone. Hard work is still good magic in my book!

Potential Employment Components

- *Aromatics:* Cinnamon, almond, mint, ginger, basil, clove, dill, nutmeg, bay. Non-edible: pine.
- *Candle types:* Candles come in all sizes and shapes these days, so one representative of your career would be ideal. Otherwise, use color aroma and/or carvings to indicate your goals.
- *Color:* Green, gold, orange (harvest hues), or a specific color that's associated with your job (or desired employment). For example, if you wish to work for the Red Cross the color would be red.
- *Candlelight recipe ingredients:* Wheat, flour, bacon, meat, maple syrup, oats, cashew, grapes, berries, pineapple, orange, pomegranate, pecan, chamomile, radish, salt, pepper, alfalfa, barbecue, corn, rabbit, fish, rice, peas, pretzels (also crackers and other long-lasting or preserved foods like jerky).

- *Crystals, metals, stones:* Amber, silver, and bloodstone for success. Tin for luck.
- *Decorative touches:* Use primrose in your space for productivity.
- *Timing:* If you're looking for work, it makes sense to prepare these dishes on the day when the main want ads appear (here that's Sunday). Otherwise, prepare these dishes near the noon hour, on Sundays, or when the moon is in Virgo.

APPETIZER

Application Radishes

Makes 3/4 cup dipping sauce

Nibble on these zesty snacks while you're preparing to apply for new jobs, or updating your résumé. Before you know it, you'll be offered that dream job (and it will be a "hot" one!).

1/4 cup sour cream
1/4 cup salad dressing (any)
1/4 cup cream cheese, softened
1 tablespoon minced fresh chives
1 tbs. dill
1/4 teaspoon hot sauce
1/4 teaspoon Worcestershire sauce
1 bag radishes, cleaned

Magical preparations: I believe that honest effort is one of the greatest magics in the world. So, before creating this dish, collect several newspapers that carry employment listings. Have these ready to peruse while you eat or just shortly thereafter, send out those résumés, and follow up on each diligently!

Candle types: The color of the candle should correspond to the type of job for which you are applying. After the application, put the business card for your potential boss under the candle's base (if it turns out to be something you think you'd really like to do).

Place all the ingredients but for the radishes in a mixing bowl and blend liberally while saying:

The magic begins with résumés, sent
Bring to me secure employment!

You can repeat the incantation as many times as you wish, but four is a good number for establishing foundations. Pour this into a dipping dish (perhaps a green one for prosperity) and dip in radishes as desired (just don't get the gook on your résumé!). Store excess in an airtight container, which also preserves your magic.

Now go get some ads and intuitively mail out your résumé. Eat a couple of snacks just before these go in the mail. Your phone will be ringing off the hook within two weeks.

Adaptations: This makes a tasty dip for bread and vegetables. Combine it with carrots to improve instincts in your interviews, celery for a better self-image, or broccoli and cauliflower to protect the jobs you're most interested in until you get the chance to at least present yourself.

Alternatively, choose the type of salad dressing you use so it corresponds with your employment goals. A cucumber dressing, for example, might represent a health-related profession, whereas a cumin-flavored dressing might symbolize a safety-oriented profession like that of police officer because of its protective power.

Fortuna's Shrimp

Makes 4 servings

Shellfish symbolize profuseness, in this case financial abundance. Shrimp also keeps your psychic self honed so you recognize good opportunities where and when they avail themselves. Clove promotes a sense of rapport with coworkers, bosses, or those people with whom you have interviews.

$2\frac{1}{2}$ cups water
$\frac{3}{4}$ cup white wine
$\frac{1}{4}$ lemon
$\frac{1}{4}$ orange
$\frac{1}{2}$ tablespoon salt
1 bay leaf
$\frac{1}{4}$-inch ginger root, pounded
1 teaspoon flaked red pepper (optional)
1 bundle green onions, chopped
2 pounds large shrimp
$\frac{3}{4}$ tablespoon white wine vinegar
1 tablespoon lemon juice
2 tablespoons orange juice
$\frac{1}{2}$ teaspoon ginger
$\frac{1}{4}$ cup olive oil
1 teaspoon diced garlic
Sugar, salt, pepper to taste

Magical preparations: Dress for success! Put on something that represents a personal victory in whatever employment matter is at hand. For example, if you're going for a promotion and you'd use or wear something different in your new job, get that item or don those clothes before beginning your spell recipe. What we wear changes the way we feel, which in turn improves the outcome of our magic!

Candle types: Choose candles in the sacred colors of Fortuna to honor her (green, gold, or silver).

Using a large soup kettle (symbolically a cauldron), boil the water with the next eight ingredients for 10 minutes. Turn down the water to a low rolling boil. Add the shrimp and cook for 4 to 8 minutes until pink. This is a good time to add an incantation like:

With the water's motion
I claim promotion!

Strain the shrimp. If you wish, you can retain the stock in the refrigerator as the base for a precharged financial fish soup (use within 48 hours). Otherwise, discard.

Next, in a large food storage container, mix together the vinegar, juices, oil, ginger, and garlic, remembering to stir clockwise to engender positive energy. Sprinkle with a pinch of sugar, salt, and pepper to bring out the richness of these flavors. Soak the shrimp in this mixture for 12 hours in the refrigerator. Strain again and serve cold so that you will keep a cool head no matter what employment opportunities come your way. Eat just before going into an important meeting, prior to a review, or on the day of an interview (note to follow with a breath mint to keep communications fresh!).

Adaptations: If you're going for a really "hot" job, warm the shrimp up on a grill skewered together with orange pieces, pineapple, or onion and pepper slices.

If you think there might be some kind of deception going on at the workplace, or in the interview process, use crab in this recipe instead of shrimp (crab symbolizes dishonesty, which you overcome by eating it!).

Substitute clams for shrimp in instances where you're hoping to illustrate strong written and verbal skills. In shamanic lore, clams were assistants to Spider Woman, who invented the alphabet.

BEVERAGE

Prosperous Pomegranate Cocktail

Makes 8 servings

When you want your work environment to be both prosperous and healthy, enjoy this drink and visualize success. Pomegranate seeds support abundance while the orange encourages inner well-being.

½ cup pomegranate juice (in the refrigerator section of the supermarket)
¼ cup sugar
1 teaspoon orange flower water
2 tablespoons pomegranate seeds
8 tablespoons orange juice
2 (750-milliliter) bottles champagne

Magical preparations: Take the pomegranate seeds and put them in a bag in the freezer (this preserves their prosperous energy until you release them to the beverage). Add an incantation like:

Prosperity within, this spell begins
Held by the cold, until the magic unfolds
Released to the glass, let prosperity last!

Candle types: Green or gold for prosperity.

In a small, nonaluminum saucepan, bring the juice and sugar to boil. Stir until the sugar dissolves. Reduce heat and simmer until the mixture thickens and reduces down to 1/4 cup. Cool and add the flower water. Place in the refrigerator for 1 hour.

Remove the pomegranate seeds, putting a few into each champagne glass. Add one tablespoon full of orange juice in each glass along with 1 1/2 teaspoons of the pomegranate syrup. Top off with champagne. Toast to your own anticipated success!

MAIN DISH

Bring Home the Bacon Pie

Makes 6 to 8 servings

The phrase "bring home the bacon" means to maintain steady employment and support one's family, which is exactly the energy we want in this dish. The expression likely ties into the use of the word bacon as meaning "prize" for several centuries because bacon was often awarded in county fair competitions and the like.

12 bacon strips
1 cup shredded Swiss cheese
1/3 cup onion, chopped
1 heaping teaspoon crushed garlic
1 1/2 cups milk
3 large eggs
3/4 cup biscuit baking mix
1/8 teaspoon pepper

Magical preparations: To help stay in tune with the recipe, go out and buy your bacon just prior to making this (so you've just literally brought it home).

Candle types: I might suggest brown candles for this spell to inspire the firm foundations of the Earth element.

Preheat the oven to 350 degrees F. Cook bacon in a skillet. Crumble into a well-greased 9-inch pie pan. As you do, focus on anything that seems to be standing between you and success and break it apart too! Add the shredded Swiss cheese, chopped onion, and garlic.

In a separate bowl, beat milk, eggs, biscuit baking mix, and pepper with an electric mixer until smooth. This whips up energy that you can direct into your goal, and during which you might add a verbal component like:

I'm tired of the pennies I'm makin'
It's time to bring home the bacon!

Pour into the pie pan and bake for 35 to 40 minutes, or until the center is set. Cool for 5 minutes before cutting.

Promotion Pita

Makes 1 serving

This is one of my favorite sandwiches to consume just prior to an important business meeting, interview, or promotional review. It's got a rich flavor (as rich as you'd like to be!) and provides plenty of positive, conscious energy.

1 large wheat pita
2 thin slices gouda cheese
Handful alfalfa or bean sprouts
Cucumber dill dressing (1/8 cup approximately)

Magical preparations: Before creating this spell recipe, make yourself a work charm that will be further energized by the spell (and that will carry the energy afterward). The ingredients for the charm are a pinch of coffee (for alertness on the job), chamomile or rosemary (for success), a primrose petal (for productivity), and tea for awareness. Bind these together in a swatch of cloth with a white piece of string (for protection) saying:

Coffee, so I will stay awake
Chamomile for victory's sake
Primrose and tea herein laid
To keep me secure in my trade!

Keep this charm with you while making the candlelight recipe, then carry it with you to work thereafter.

Candle type: Gold for success.

Carefully slice open the pita pocket and lay the gouda cheese inside. This makes a warm, secure place in which to nurture your magic. On top of this, nestle the sprouts, then pour the salad dressing evenly over top of all. Eat expectantly just before you go into an important business meeting and see how quickly your expertise is appreciated!

Adaptations: Alter the types of cheese, sprouts, and salad dressing to better represent your circumstances. For example, if you tend to be "mousy" when you receive a review, eat Swiss cheese and take a bite out of that faint-hearted attitude. To be mentally sharp, use sharp cheddar! Springwater sprouts are ideal for seed-planting interviews; use ranch dressing if you're interviewing for an outdoor job and perhaps a peppercorn dressing to protect your ideal job from other seekers!

Prospect Pancakes

Makes 4 servings

Oats represent the providence and prosperity that we all hope to gain from our work. To them we've added energy herbs and fruit to open the doors for abundant opportunities and/or options in your career.

2 cups oatmeal
½ cup all-purpose flour
2 tablespoons granulated sugar
2 tablespoons brown sugar
1 teaspoon baking soda
1 teaspoon baking powder
½ teaspoon salt
¼ teaspoon cinnamon
¼ teaspoon clove
2 cups milk
½ cup strawberry juice
2 large eggs
¼ cup (½ stick) butter, melted
1 teaspoon vanilla extract
Cooking oil
Maple syrup

Magical preparations and candles: Since one of the chief goals of this breakfast is providing a physical and mental boost for the day, place three candles on your kitchen table—one red (for physical energy), one yellow (for the conscious mind), and one in your favorite color to represent the self. Light them saying:

> *The flame of power I claim* (red candle)
> *The flame of insight and perception I claim* (yellow candle)
> *The flame of self confidence I claim* (your candle)

Leave these burning all the while you prepare this dish.

☙ In a large bowl combine all the dry ingredients, making sure the spices, baking powder, and baking soda are well integrated. Slowly add the milk and juice to make a thick batter. Beat the two eggs separately, then fold them into this blend. Whisk in butter and vanilla repeating an adaptation of the previous verbal component while you stir. For example, chant:

> *Power I claim*
> *Perception I claim*
> *Confidence I claim*
> *Insecurity tamed!*

Chill slightly for a thicker batter.

Meanwhile, prepare a skillet with cooking oil. Pour out ¼ cup of the batter on the frying surface at a time. Wait for bubbles to appear evenly in the surface of the pancakes (this is a good time to etch a dollar sign in them for prosperity), then turn over and cook the other side. Serve with real maple syrup so those opportunities flow as liberally as the maple trees in spring!

Adaptations: Instead of syrup, serve the pancakes with preserves to likewise preserve your job, or with a variety of fresh fruit to open a wide variety of opportunities.

DESSERT

"Wow Them" Pineapple Cake

Makes 6 to 8 servings

The whole purpose of this cake is to literally turn the business world on its ear (upside down) with your aptitude! The pineapple in the recipe also makes people more congenial toward you (in early American decorating schemes, the pineapple represented hospitality and welcome).

- **3/4 cup plus 2 tablespoons (3/4 stick) butter**
- **3/4 cup dark brown sugar, packed**
- **Maraschino cherries (optional)**
- **6 slices of pineapple**
- **1 1/2 cups flour**
- **2 teaspoons baking powder**
- **1/4 teaspoon salt**
- **1/4 cup plus 2 tablespoons (3/4 stick) unsalted butter, softened**
- **1 cup granulated sugar**
- **2 large eggs**
- **1 teaspoon vanilla**
- **1 tablespoon rum flavoring**
- **1/2 cup pineapple juice**

Magical preparations: In what line of work are you employed? Think of a simple emblem that represents that work. For example, someone who works in computers might use a square (the computer screen). Pattern that image in the pan using maraschino cherries before the pineapple is placed therein to literally bake your intention into the cake.

Candle types: Choose a color suited to your career and dab the candle with pineapple scented oil.

Preheat the oven to 350 degrees F. In a large frying pan, melt the butter, slowly adding the brown sugar to it. Toss the pineapple slices liberally into this mixture saying:

Sweet hospitality, open opportunity's doors to me!

Place the pineapples evenly in the bottom of a 9-inch round cake pan that's well oiled (these go *over* the cherries if you've chosen to use them). Set this aside.

Next, blend flour, baking powder, salt, and butter together until creamy. Slowly beat in the sugar, followed by the eggs, vanilla, rum flavoring, and pineapple juice. Pour this evenly over top of the pineapples, then bake for 45 minutes. Let this cool for about 7 minutes. Loosen the sides of the cake and flip it out onto a serving platter. As you turn out the cake say

With a turn of a cake, a turn of luck, a turn of fate
Let my talents flow, constraints abate!

Remove any pineapple or cherries that don't come out of the cake pan, and place on top of the cake.

Adaptations: If you wish, drizzle with sweet cream or rum-flavored whipped cream, both of which sustain the magic you've created, adding a slightly protective dimension. For more personal clarity, intermingle the pineapple slices with oranges slices in the same manner as the pineapple. For wisdom in your interview, add thinly sliced apples or peaches.

Butter Up the Boss Blend

Makes about 4 cups

This spiced butter is lovely with sweet toast, dessert pancakes, or even as a garnish to vanilla ice cream. The walnut here provides sound reasoning skills with which to present your case, and the pumpkin represents having many feasible possibilities, thereby increasing the chance of success.

Zest of 1 orange or zest of ½ orange and ½ lemon removed in wide strips
3½ cups pumpkin puree
2 cups light brown sugar, firmly packed
3 tablespoons orange juice
3 tablespoons lemon juice
1½ teaspoons ground cinnamon
¼ teaspoon ground allspice
¼ teaspoon ground ginger
Pinch of ground cloves
⅓ cup toasted walnuts, finely chopped

Magical preparations: I'm assuming you're making this dish for a positive conversation with your employer regarding your present and future position. With that in mind, you need to prepare your ideas clearly. Make a list of what you'd like to cover and dab the paper with a bit of rosemary oil to support your conscious mind and take it with you to the meeting.

Candle types: Put your list for the employer on a table and surround it with candles while you're making and enjoying this dish. As you set the candles in place add an incantation like:

Like these candles, let my talents shine
Throughout this meeting, clear thoughts be mine.

In a saucepan, simmer the orange zest in 2 cups of water for 10 minutes. Drain and mince it fine. Measure out 1 tablespoon and reserve the rest. Combine the following ingredients in a nonaluminum pan: pumpkin, orange zest, sugar, orange juice, lemon juice, cinnamon, allspice, ginger, and cloves. Bring to a boil over medium-high heat, stirring constantly. Lower the heat and simmer the mixture, stirring regularly until it thickens, about 15 to 20 minutes. This is the point at which you can adjust the blend to suit your tastes. Stir into nuts and then cool. You can choose to can this, or just store it in the refrigerator.

Adaptations: I like to make this into a truly buttery blend by mixing some of the spiced pumpkin mash into softened butter. Etch an image of your goal into bread before toasting, then liberally apply your butter to smooth the way toward that goal.

MONEY MEALS

Always remember, money isn't everything—
but also remember to make a lot of it before
talking such fool nonsense.

—EARL WILSON

Nearly everyone I know has had at least one moment in their lives when money was lean. During that period stress levels increased, people got grumpier in the household, and there seemed to be an overall air of worry and frustration. That's all perfectly normal. We live in a society where we need money to survive. However, there's nothing keeping us from using magic to try and ease both those constraints and the tension they bring. This isn't a "get rich quick" scheme—it's just simply proactive spirituality focused on helping in times of need.

Speaking of which, be prepared for the ways in which the universe may choose to meet your candlelight recipe's request. If you have a job, you might be offered more hours. If you're unemployed you might find a job that isn't quite your ideal, but pays the bills. The second happened to me. I enacted a candlelight recipe to open the path for a job that could pay for medical insurance. What I was offered was a position decorating commercial Yule trees for the holiday season. While it wasn't permanent, nor exactly what I envisioned myself doing, it did pay the insurance costs for six months. I could have turned it down, but that would have been like spitting at a gift for which I asked. So as you're doing money magic, keep in mind that there will be some type of balance point that you will need to honor to make everything come together.

Potential Money Components

- *Aromatics:* Allspice, ginger, cinnamon, dill, clove, marjoram, mint, basil.

- *Candle types:* Square candles are a good choice since they represent earthly matters and foundations.
- *Color:* Silver, gold, and lush green.
- *Candlelight recipe ingredients:* Berries, cashew, grape, maple syrup, oat, banana, fig, pear, onion, pecan, pea, barley, egg, rice, pineapple, pomegranate, sesame, peanut, pine nuts, wheat, basil, parsley, lettuce, cabbage, spinach, tomato, milk, alfalfa, kiwi, oats, salt, sugar.
- *Crystals, metals, stones:* Jade, agate, brass, moss agate, moonstone.
- *Decorative touches:* A bowl full of coins, or perhaps a cornucopia filled to overflowing with change.
- *Timing:* Noon. Full moon. Sundays. Taurus, Virgo, Pisces, or Aquarius moon.

APPETIZER

Prosperity Pasta

Makes 2 servings

The wonderful green noodles in this recipe represent your money, whereas the garlic sauce neatly surrounds it with protective energy. This way when you really need money, you can "bank on it" being there.

½ pound spinach noodles
3 garlic cloves
3 tablespoons olive oil
½ cup fresh chopped spinach
½ cup grated Asiago or fresh Parmesan cheese

Magical preparations: Make yourself a karmic piggy bank. To do this you'll need a plain bank (that can be painted, and that has a plug in the bottom), some black and white paint, and a special "seed coin" (perhaps a silver quarter or a coin that bears your birth year on it).

On the side of the bank paint a yin and yang symbol, which represents equitable balance in all things (including your money). After the paint dries, take the seed coin in hand (over the opening for the bank) saying:

What I place herein
Multiply and bless threefold
To others in charity
And to myself, to hold

Put the seed coin in the bank and your loose change every day. When the bank is filled, give the proceeds to a good charity (all but the seed coin, which remains in the bank to bring the blessings back to you).

Candle types: I like to leave a candle adjacent to my karmic bank and light it with a wish when I put the change inside.

Bring a large pot of water to a full rolling boil and add the spinach noodles (the color and leafy nature of spinach both encourage a flow of money). While these cook to a tender stage, begin sautéing the garlic and chopped spinach in the olive oil. Drain the noodles, adding the garlic blend and tossing gently, focusing on your goal, until well coated. This is an ideal time to add an incantation like:

Oodles of noodles, with prosperity green
Bring me more money than I've ever seen!

Serve with Asiago cheese sprinkled liberally on top in the pattern of a dollar sign. Eat, and watch with joy as cash stays where it belongs—in your pocket and the bank!

Adaptations: For more protective energy, add 2 tablespoons diced onion with the garlic during the sautée process. For more prosperity, dice up precooked broccoli spears and blend them with the noodles and garlic.

BEVERAGE

Oppulent Eggnog

Makes 4 to 6 servings

Some cultures including the ancient Chinese believed it was from an egg that the entire universe came forth, so why not look to this symbol of beginnings and creation for prosperity when needed?

12 egg whites and yolks (separated—note that 12 is the number of completion and fulfillment)
1½ cups sugar
¾ cup whiskey
¾ cup brandy
½ cup rum
2 cups heavy cream, lightly whipped
ground nutmeg for garnish

Magical preparations: Choose the flavor of your brandy and/or rum so that it corresponds to the area of your life that's led to the need for improved financial flow. For example, if poor health has drained your resources, apple would be an excellent choice.

Candle types: Match the color and aroma of your candles to the brandy or rum flavors you've chosen.

Beat the egg whites until stiff, gradually adding in ¾ cup of the sugar. This is where you get a lot of energy for your spell because the eggs seem to multiply before your eyes, so add an incantation like:

Eggs multiply before my eyes
So money grows by and by
And as this beverage passes my lips
Renewed prosperity in each sip.

Set aside the egg whites. Beat the egg yolks until they are thick and pale, adding the remaining ¾ cup sugar. Gently stir in whiskey. Fold the egg white mixture into the yolk mixture, slowly adding the brandy, rum, and cream. Beat the mixture well. Sprinkle the top of the eggnog with the nutmeg to taste.

Rags to Riches Wine

Makes 4 to 6 servings

When you need to increase your bottom line so you have enough to cover a future goal, this wine is a great helpmate. By the time it finishes aging, the wealth should be well on its way!

2 chamomile tea bags
2 cups boiling water
1 (750-milliliter) bottle semi-dry white wine
½ cup sugar
⅓ cup orange juice, well strained (or pulp free)
¼ cup rum
1 tablespoon raisins
1 tablespoon chopped mixed dried fruit
1 cinnamon stick
⅛ teaspoon ground nutmeg

Magical preparations: Since the magic here is aimed toward increasing your "bottom line," it helps to have your checkbook or budget handy so it can absorb the energy you're creating. Before starting the spell recipe, place your hands (palm down) over these items saying something like:

Spirits of prosperity I behoove
Let my wealth continually improve!

Keep this item near where you're working.

Candle types: surround your checkbook with candles after energizing it with your incantation. This way it will absorb the energy you're creating, and that which the candles provide.

Steep the tea bags in the 2 cups of boiling water and let it stand until heady. This transfers the energy of the herbs to the water. Strain off the liquid and set aside.

Combine the tea with the remaining ingredients in a non-aluminum pan over a low flame. Simmer until the sugar dissolves and taste for sweetness. Adjust by adding more sugar (sweeter) or a bit of lemon juice (tarter). Bottle the entire blend in glass and let sit for 1 week, shaking daily saying:

Good credit with low interest rates
By my will, constraints abate!

Serve warm when you need to manifest the money more quickly, or cold so you can keep a cool head and spend it wisely when the line of credit arrives.

Adaptation: Substitute a berry-flavored brandy for the rum to manifest bounty.

MAIN DISH

Profit Pancakes

Makes approximately 20 small pancakes

Oats is considered a sustenance grain, and therefore a contributor to providence. It's also considered a "fertile" grain that keeps money multiplying once it comes.

½ cup old-fashioned oats
1 cup cream
1 cup (about 3 medium) mashed ripe bananas
2 large eggs, beaten to blend
1 teaspoon ground cinnamon
1½ cups pancake mix
6 tablespoons butter
Extra cream (if needed to smooth batter)
Maple syrup
Fresh fruit (your choice)

Magical preparations: Take some extra oats and place them in a green or gold-colored piece of cloth to make a sachet with a silver or gold-tone coin minted in the year of your birth. As you tie it into the bundle, using four knots with a green string or yarn, add an incantation like this at each knot:

With the knot of one, my spell's begun
With a knot of two, prosperity true
With a knot of three, money to me
With the knot of four, wealth pours!

Keep this with you in the sacred space while you cook, then store it with your checkbook.

Candle types: Use four candles to provide earth-oriented energy that supports your goal.

Combine oats and cream in large bowl. Let stand until oats are soft, about 15 minutes. Mix in mashed bananas, eggs, and cinnamon. Gradually stir in pancake mix (batter will be very thick, but you can adjust the texture to your personal taste by adding more cream).

In a large skillet, melt the butter and begin to cook coin-sized pancakes. Let these fry on each side until golden brown. Flip over, and if you want sketch a symbol of your goal in the side facing you. When the pancakes are done, put them in a low heat oven until you finish the batch.

Serve with real maple syrup (remember like attracts like, and real maple syrup is considered a "luxury" item) and fresh berries or other fruit on top.

Adaptation: For a symbolic color, add a few drops of green food coloring to the pancake batter.

Funding with Feta Rolls

Makes about 30 rolls

Pine nuts, like other nuts, symbolize abundance and fertility. To this we're adding rice for providence and dill and mint (money-oriented herbs). With the cheeses, this is especially good for helping ease financial stresses in relationships.

14 ounces diced tomatoes
1 cup long-grain white rice
1 cup thinly sliced green onions
½ cup finely chopped fresh mint
½ cup finely chopped fresh dill
¼ teaspoon cardamom
½ cup pine nuts, toasted
⅓ cup extra-virgin olive oil
2 large garlic cloves, minced
Pinch sugar
50 grape leaves
¼ cup fresh lemon juice

Dip

1 cup plain yogurt
4 ounces feta cheese, crumbled
1 large green onion, cut into 1-inch pieces
¼ teaspoon grated lemon peel
¼ teaspoon onion powder

☙ Puree all these ingredients together, then chill until the rolls are completed.

Magical preparations: Take a few of the extra pine nuts outdoors. Hold them in your hand thinking of your specific financial need (be very clear about this). Sprinkle the nuts toward the north with your wish. Add an incantation like:

As the birds and winds take these seeds
Return to me with what I need!

Birds will carry your needs on the winds.

Candle types: In keeping with your magical preparations, write the amount of money that you actually need on the candle's wax using a toothpick.

☙ Put the tomatoes with their juice in large bowl. Add the remaining ingredients except for grape leaves and lemon juice. Set aside.

Preheat the oven to 350 degrees F. Rinse grape leaves under cold water. Drain well. Lay 6 to 8 of these in the bottom of an ovenproof dish. Cover bottom of heavy large Dutch oven with grape leaves (about 6). Place 1 grape leaf on work surface, vein side up; put about 1 tablespoon rice mixture in center of leaf. Fold sides over filling then roll it up tightly like you might an egg roll. As you do, focus on capturing your prosperity and keeping it safe. The neat thing here is that these really look like little rolls of cash!

Place in the baking dish, seam side down. When you're done with the leaves and filling, pour lemon juice over top of the rolls. Cover these again (as you did the bottom of the pan) with 6 to 8 grape leaves. Pour a little water in the bottom of the pot so the rolls are about three-fourths covered. Top the pan with aluminum foil and bake until the water has been absorbed. This takes about 40 minutes. Serve with the dip.

SIDE DISH

Currency Cabbage

Makes 4 servings as a side dish

This dish originated in Germany where it is consumed during the Christmas season to inspire abundance, especially in the area of goodwill, kinship, and a sense of welcome. Better still, cabbage protects your abundance once it's obtained!

1 small head of cabbage
4 cups sangria or sweet red wine
1 teaspoon cinnamon
1 teaspoon salt
2 tablespoons butter
2 teaspoons sugar
1 apple, grated

Magical preparations: Pour out a small cup of sangria or apple juice before you begin making the recipe. Bless the cup by holding it in your strong hand (the one you write with) saying:

Minding dollars, minding cents
I cast this spell for abundance
Directed by will and by my inner witch
In all things I will become truly rich

Candle types: Repeat the incantation three more times while you light your chosen candles (four being the number of earthly things).

Slice the cabbage, thinking about eliminating any barriers between yourself and wealth as you slice. Place in a large bowl with the wine, cinnamon, and salt, and soak overnight (or at least 8 hours). Blend and mix it regularly (this is a good time to recite your incantation from the preparation process again). Drain, reserving the liquid.

Melt the butter in a frying pan, transferring the shredded cabbage into it. Brown gently, sprinkling sugar over top to help caramelize the mix. Return the wine blend to cabbage and simmer for 50 minutes. Add the apple and cook for 15 more minutes.

Think fond thoughts of family and friends as you eat this and watch them return that fondness threefold.

Adaptation: If you're not fond of apple, this is quite tasty with sliced carrots. You will want to steam the carrots to firm-tender stage and add them during the last 15 minutes of cooking as you would the apple.

In the Green Dressing

Makes 2 cups

The energy from this dish comes from its rich, green coloration. Additionally the three herbs herein (basil, dill, mint) were all used in prosperity magic. Use this on top of a nice lettuce side salad.

1 cup watercress leaves, packed
3/4 cup (or more) plain yogurt or sour cream
1/3 cup mayonnaise
2 tablespoons chopped fresh dill
2 tablespoons chopped fresh basil
2 tablespoons chopped green onion
1 tablespoon chopped fresh mint, packed
1 teaspoon garlic powder
1 teaspoon red wine or balsamic vinegar

Magical preparations: Stick with your green theme, perhaps adding highlights of gold. Don green clothing, decorate with greenery, and have green plates on which to serve your salad!

Candle types: Again, green and gold, perhaps carved with dollar signs.

In a saucepan, boil watercress for 30 seconds. Drain. Pat watercress dry. Transfer into a blender. Add all remaining ingredients and puree until smooth. Pour this over the top of any salad, or even potatoes. Don't forget to pour in a clockwise direction, or even create the image of a dollar sign with the dressing while saying:

Times are lean,
So let my spell be keen
Luck, turn around, bring in the green

DESSERT

Crisp Cash

Makes 6 to 8

There's nothing quite so nice as a crisp bill, which is why grandmothers everywhere give them as gifts. This lightly sweet appetizer builds on that tradition and symbolism.

1½ pounds frozen mixed berries
¼ cup sugar
1 cup flour
¾ cup oats
⅔ cup dark brown sugar, packed
½ teaspoon ground ginger
¼ teaspoon ground nutmeg
7 tablespoons chilled unsalted butter, diced
Cream or vanilla ice cream

Magical preparations: Building on the idea that one should give to receive, take a small bill (say $5) and wrap it in paper three times saying:

To one in need, this bill goes
There too, the money flows
And like a wave that moves to the sea
So prosperity returns to me!

Put it in an envelope, mailing it to someone anonymously, then go ahead and prepare this candlelight recipe.

Candle types: Improve the results from the spell by putting the envelope under the base of your chosen candles while you make this candlelight recipe.

Preheat the oven to 375 degrees F. Mix the berries with the sugar and flour and toss until coated. Place this in a well-greased 9-inch pie pan and set aside. In another bowl blend the remaining ingredients together, cutting in the butter until its well integrated. If this doesn't hold together when pinched, add a few drops of water until it does. Sprinkle this evenly over the berries (move clockwise, and pattern the last bit like a dollar sign to manifest that cash quickly). Bake for 1 hour.

Serve with warm cream or vanilla ice cream, both of which encourage insightful use of the cash that comes your way.

Adaptation: Add shaved almonds to either the berries or the topping for even greater prosperity power!

Fast Cash Custard

Makes about 3 cups or 4 servings

The eggs and cream in this recipe attract money, while the sugar makes its receipt ever so sweet and timely! Add a little green or yellow (gold) food coloring to improve the symbolic value.

2 eggs
2 egg yolks
½ cup sugar
2 cups of light cream
1 vanilla bean
Crushed nuts for garnish (optional)

Magical preparations: When I think of needing money quick, I think of my ATM card. So take a moment before preparing this candlelight recipe to bless that card. The goal is to be able to access money when you need it most! To accomplish this, wait until the moon is full (for similar financial fullness) and hold the card in both hands saying:

Cash, come quick
Magic here bind
When I need money, prosperity's mine!

Keep this in your wallet and repeat the incantation mentally each time you use the card to increase the overall effect.

Candle types: Four green or gold candles would support this candlelight recipe nicely.

❧ Combine the eggs, egg yolks, and sugar in a large bowl and beat them until they double in volume (about 5 to 7 minutes). This symbolically doubles the financial base with which you're working!

In a nonaluminum pan, warm the light cream and vanilla bean together. Make sure this does not boil. Remove the vanilla, and transfer the liquid to a double boiler. Add the egg mixture. Continue cooking in the top of the double boiler (over water) for 25 minutes or until the custard thickens. Remember to stir clockwise constantly and visualize money falling into the pan (think pennies from heaven with more oomph)! If you wish, you can repeat the previous incantation at this juncture too!

Spoon out into dishes and chill. Makes about 3 cups.

Adaptations: Any of the herbs or fruits mentioned under candlelight recipe ingredients in the beginning of this chapter could be added in the form of an extract for variety or slightly different focal points. For example, if I needed extra physical energy to go out and seek my fortune, I would use ginger to flavor the custard.

Frugality Apples

Makes 3 servings

There are going to be times when everyone has to pinch pennies. This sweet dessert makes that process a little less painful, and adds a hearty dose of wisdom so you use your resources carefully.

3/4 pound apples (your choice, but green emphasizes money)
1 tablespoon butter
1 1/2 tablespoons maple syrup
1/2 teaspoon maple extract
1/2 tablespoon water
Cinnamon and ginger to taste

Magical preparations: Use a variation on an old divination method to find out how long you will need to make resources last. Hold the first apple in the bunch in hand and count the number of turns it takes to twist out the stem. This number equals the number of days, weeks, or months.

Candle types: Whatever the results from the divination, use that number of candles to give you strength and endurance to last that amount of time.

Peel the apples clockwise, taking care not to break the peels if possible. This encourages more luck with the food magic being created. Core them, then cut into 1/4-inch thick slices. Save the peel and dry it for magical incense.

Carve a dollar sign into each slice, then sauté the apple slices in butter until golden brown to energize the magic (remember to keep your mind focused on your goal while you cook). To this, add the maple syrup and extract, water and personally preferred spices (about a pinch is plenty). As this cooks it creates a natural glaze.

Serve warm to allay indifferent feelings that often arise with constraint. Or eat just before you try to re-work your budget so resources get applied in the best possible way.

Adaptation: Toss in some nuts to bring a little humor into the picture (humor is a great coping mechanism), and let yourself get a little "nutty!"

9

Relationship Rounds

FOR FRIENDS AND FAMILY, LOVERS OR LIFE-MATES

You meet new people every day. Some you'll never see again. Some become acquaintances or co-workers. Some become friends and family. And some very special people turn into lovers or life-mates. Sorting all this activity out, however, isn't easy (let alone knowing what's really a healthy relationship and what's a dud). So we come to consumables that help tone down our hearts so that we can see clearly. Or, if we're already seeing clearly these foods and beverages can heat things up to a whole new level.

We'll start with Kinship and Friendship Food. These feelings are the foundations of any long-lasting relationship. Whether or not you want to take that relationship to the next level, these candlelight recipes help solidify the feelings of respect and trust you have for others.

Then there's Love's Delectable Delights. These have two goals. One is to help heal the wounded heart when love goes awry. The second is to take love to new heights when both people want something deeper.

And where there's love, there's Savory Sexuality and Sensuality to heat things up. Whether you're hoping to please or tease, these recipes give whole new meaning to "something's cooking in the kitchen!"

KINSHIP AND FRIENDSHIP FOOD

All love that has not friendship for its base,
Is like a mansion built upon the sand.

—Ella Wheeler Wilcox

Without food, friends, and family our lives would be far less rich and interesting. Nontheless, kinship isn't something that just happens and continues without some amount of honest effort on everyone's part. It takes a lot of listening, cooperation, and understanding for camaraderie to not simply remain consistent, but grow. Kinship and friendship fares foster the relationships that exist, or open the door to making new potential friends. It's also directed toward healing wounds that might develop in your relationships. Last, but certainly not least, friendship fare is directed at you—as to be a good witch, you also have to be your own best friend!

Potential Kinship Components

- *Aromatics:* Almond, apple, sweet spices.
- *Candle types:* Consider using two (or more) candles for your table, one for each person toward whom you're directing your energies.
- *Color:* Pink.
- *Candlelight recipe ingredients:* Berries, bread, butter, caraway, cardamom, celery, leek, lemon, bread, dill, lentils, lettuce, passion fruit, pineapple, rice, orange, cheese, warm foods, mulberry, pineapple. Picnic fare. Pizza. Macaroni.
- *Crystals, metals, stones:* Jade, pink quartz, pink tourmaline.
- *Decorative touches:* Prepare your serving space in such a way as to please your guest(s) and honor their favorite colors, aromatics, etc. Yellow roses are a good choice for fresh flowers.
- *Timing:* Gemini, Aries, and Aquarius moon. Waxing or full moon. Any day in June.

APPETIZERS

Alliance Meatballs

Makes 10 servings

The power of almond is that of vigilance. In fact, in Hebrew the almond tree is called "watchful one." Friendship requires that kind of ongoing awareness and dedication if it's going to last. So, make these meatballs (wrapped neatly around the almond surprise center) when your friendship needs a tune-up.

1½ pounds lean ground steak
2 large eggs, beaten
¼ cup Italian style bread crumbs
1 teaspoon cornstarch
2 tablespoons grated onion
¼ teaspoon ground black pepper
¼ teaspoon ground nutmeg
1 teaspoon sea salt
¼ teaspoon garlic powder
Whole almonds (1 per meatball)
2 tablespoons virgin olive oil
4 tablespoons cornstarch
1 tablespoon soy sauce
3 tablespoons wine vinegar
⅓ cup water
½ cup brown sugar, packed
1¼ cups pineapple juice
1 (20-ounce) can pineapple chunks
1 red onion, peeled and sliced
2 red bell peppers, seeded and sliced

Magical preparations: Consider the specific area of your friendship that seems to have been lacking. Focus on that in setting up your sacred pantry, choosing colors, aromatics, etc. Also pick up the phone and call your friend! Open the way for the energy you're creating to begin its work.

Candle types: One to represent you, one for your friend, and one for the friendship itself. Light the two for you and your friend, then light the friendship candle when you're done preparing this dish.

Blend together ground beef, eggs, bread crumbs, cornstarch, grated onion, pepper, nutmeg, salt, and garlic powder. Form into 1-inch balls around one almond each saying:

Peace to our hearts
This almond imparts
Pure intention wrapped around
The magic abounds.

Heat oil in a skillet and brown the meatballs evenly. Set aside on paper towels to drain.

In a large saucepan, combine the remaining 4 tablespoons of cornstarch, soy sauce, vinegar, water, brown sugar, ginger, and pineapple juice. Cook until thickened, stirring constantly. Add the meatballs, pineapple chunks, sliced onion and green peppers. Cook for 5 minutes or until thoroughly heated.

Hearty Lentil Helpmate Soup

Makes 8 servings

This dish was said to keep Vikings healthy and hearty. Share it with your friends when they're under the weather or in need of Viking-like fortitude.

1 ounce butter
8 ounces lentils
1 medium carrot, diced fine
2 stalks of celery, chopped
1 small turnip, diced
1 medium parsnip, diced
Fresh ground salt and pepper to taste
50 ounces soup stock (chicken is a good choice)

Magical preparations: Your friends should be involved in the making of this meal if possible. If not, minimally have a picture of them handy so you can direct the energy more effectively. Also consider working on this dish around two in the afternoon (the number stresses partnership).

Candle types: One for each person to whom the candlelight recipe is directed, with colors and aromas chosen by that individual's needs.

In a large frying pan, place the butter and sauté the lentils and vegetables therein. Season with salt and pepper then add to the stock. This needs to come to a full rolling boil while you chant:

Bubble up strength, set the magic free
Bubble up for ______, grant vitality!

Fill in the blank with your friend's name. Once your broth is boiling, turn it down and simmer for a full two hours. Adjust the seasoning before serving.

BEVERAGES

Hospitality Ade

Makes 2 servings

Pineapples were a favorite decoration at the turn of the century, being carved often in wood as a sign of welcome. Here you're making a lovely beverage with which to welcome your friends on their next visit!

4 slices pineapple, chopped
2 teaspoons superfine sugar
3 ounces brandy
1 cup crushed ice
Club soda
2 slices lemon
2 pineapple candy sticks

Magical preparations: If you can find a whole pineapple at the store and cut it into two "cups" for this beverage the symbolism would be very supportive and the flavor is outstanding. As you remove enough pineapple from the center of your cups you might wish to incant something like:

There's room in my home and my heart for ______
Through this beverage my hospitality, impart

May our time be sweet, may our time be fun
By my will this spell's begun.

Candle types: Individual candles are nice here. You could even adorn them to represent your friend(s) in some way, like making a paper tie for the candle of the friend who's an accountant. This makes a very sweet visual presentation. Just take care to remove any flammable items before lighting.

☙ Put the pineapple, sugar, brandy and ice together in a shaker to mix thoroughly. Strain off into 2 glasses. Finish filling with a little club soda, then adorn the drink with the lemon slice and pineapple.

Solidarity Cup

Makes 8 (1-cup) servings

When I was growing up I was taught that a true friend stands with you in difficult situations. The ancients sometimes gave the gift of an apple to symbolize just this kind of undaunted friendship and love.

8 cups apple cider
3-inch cinnamon stick
10 whole cloves
1 navel orange, sliced crosswise
2-inch piece of peeled fresh ginger, cut into 6 slices
Sugar or honey to taste

Magical preparations: Take an apple and cut it in half. On a piece of paper write down the situation that's brought you and your friend to this point of standing your ground in a united front. Put the two halves of the apple on each side of the paper and secure them with a white string (for resolution). Bury this in the ground to provide a firm foundation, and so that something positive grows from this situation.

Candle types: Pick out a candle to represent the problem and let it burn completely away. Ritually dispose of the wax.

☙ In a large saucepan, combine the cider, the cinnamon stick, the cloves, the orange, and the ginger and simmer the mixture for 20 minutes. Stir counterclockwise to decrease negativity saying:

Together we stand, we shall win the day
All maliciousness and negativity, keep neatly away
Our friendship is true
United are we
By our wills, this spell is freed!

Strain the mixture through a fine sieve into a heatproof pitcher, sweeten with sugar or honey and serve the mulled cider warm.

Advisory Wine

Makes 3/4 gallon

In the Bible the mulberry tree becomes an adviser and diviner for David. Its leaves shake to warn him it's time to move upon the Philistines. It is also the tree of wisdom. So, we'll be making this wine to have on hand for those times when your friends need good council.

6 pounds ripe mulberries
2 pounds sugar
1 pound chopped golden raisins
1 berry tea bag
1 orange, sliced
6 pints water
Wine yeast (your choice)

Magical preparations: I've always felt that sound advice comes from both the head and heart. With that in mind, bless your ingredients both by sunlight and moonlight to get the best head-heart balance possible.

Candle types: In keeping with the idea of balanced insights how about one white or silver candle (moon) and one yellow or gold (for the sun).

In a nonaluminum pan, boil the water adding the sugar and stirring until it's completely dissolved. Put the remaining ingredients except for the yeast into the pan to simmer for 10 minutes, then remove from the heat. When the mixture reaches room temperature add the yeast suspended in 1/4 cup of warm water. Let this sit covered with a heavy towel for 4 days (stir it once a day). This is a good juncture to add any verbal component you wish like:

In each sip, wisdom lies
Help me in my task to advise!

Strain into another container (I use old glass wine bottles with balloons affixed to the top). Store this in a cool, dark area for 2 months, then strain again. Repeat a third time in 2 months. Place in a corked container and let it age. One year is good for a lightly sweet blend.

MAIN DISH

Companion Chicken

Makes 2 servings

Chicken inspires healthy interactions while the citrus in this dish provides sweet clarity, and a little unexpected adventure to your friendships.

1 tablespoon cornstarch
1/4 teaspoon salt
1/8 teaspoon cayenne pepper
Pinch powdered ginger
2 tablespoons soy sauce
3 tablespoons cooking oil
2 boneless/skinless chicken breasts, cut in 1-inch pieces
1 cup green pepper strips
1/4 cup chopped green onions
1/2 cup chicken broth
1 cup fresh pink grapefruit sections

Magical preparations: Using the tip of a sharp knife etch each chicken breast with the initials of the people for whom they're being prepared.

Candle types: Choose the color or aroma of your candles so they better reflect you and your friend. If your companion enjoys working magic, have him or her carve their candle with meaningful emblems so they become an active participant in creating energy.

❧ Light your candles. Put them near the working area where it's safe (i.e., they won't get knocked over). Keep your intentions in mind as you do, and perhaps add an incantation like:

> *Friendship good, friendship true*
> *I extend true friendship from me to you!*

In medium bowl, mix together cornstarch, salt, cayenne pepper, ginger, soy sauce and 1 tablespoon of the cooking oil. Add chicken to cornstarch mixture, coating all sides; let stand 10 minutes. Meanwhile in large frying pan, heat remaining 2 tablespoons cooking oil. Add chicken mixture and stir-fry 3 minutes over medium heat or until light brown. Stir in the remaining ingredients but for the grapefruit and lower the heat for 5 minutes. Finally add grapefruit, continuing to cook until the citrus just warms.

Serving suggestion: You serve your friend, your friend serves you! Therein is the perfect exchange of energy.

Pal-Around Party Pizza

Makes 5 servings

Pizza is a kinship food. It's something around which friends gather to share fun moments and good conversation. Better still, it's a circle that surrounds and supports whatever energy you put in it. You can pattern the toppings in special ways to express your goal too!

3 tablespoons olive or vegetable oil
1 loaf defrosted bread dough
30 ounces pizza sauce
12 ounces shredded mozzarella cheese
16 ounces sliced pineapple
1½ cup diced ham
1 large red pepper, cut into rings
Maraschino cherries
Slivered almonds

Magical preparations: The bread dough needs to rise twice, first in its normal form, and the second time after you stretch it to fill your pizza trays (this will actually fill two normal sized pizza platters). While you're stretching it add a verbal component like:

Stretch good feelings
Stretch the fun
By my will this spell's begun
Within a circle spicy and sweet
Wonderful friendship grows replete

Candle types: Tropical scented (coconut, pineapple, etc.) is nice to match the pizza. I'd also have one candle for each of your guests to take home with them.

Preheat the oven to 375 degrees F. Grease your pans with the oil. Stretch the dough to fit your two pans, then put your sauce, cheese, and toppings on. Bake about 25 minutes until the crust is fluffy and browned. Cut in squares for easy feasting and well-grounded energy!

SIDE DISH

Make Your Acquaintance Fritters

Makes approximately 1 dozen

The cinnamon in these fritters has strong lunar associations in magic, and was even thought by the ancient Chinese to have been grown on the moon. This provides great psychic energy when meeting new potential friends. To this foundation we add mangos, which promote good feelings and even love between people, and leek for courage.

FRITTERS

2 leeks, split in half
2 eggs, beaten
1 package fine matzo meal
Salt and pepper to taste
½ teaspoon ground cinnamon
Oil for frying

SAUCE

18 ounces ripe mango pulp
5½ ounces dates
2 (1-inch) cinnamon sticks
1 tablespoon ginger paste
4 cups water
9 tablespoons sugar

Magical preparation: Since the goal here is to "meet and greet" and hopefully open some friendly doors, you could make yourself a friendship charm using a carnelian for effective communication. Wrap this in a pink cloth saying:

> *Words be wise, words be kind*
> *In this charm, my magic bind*
> *And if the fates are meant to be*
> *Bring friendship to _____ and me* (fill in blank with person's name you're meeting)

Candle types: I'd actually wait to choose a candle until after your meeting so you can find one that best represents this new person and your hopes for him or her. For example, a very upbeat person might be represented by a brightly colored candle.

Begin by boiling the leeks until tender. Drain and chop them finely. Let drain of any excess water. Turn these into a bowl, adding the eggs, matzo, and seasonings. While you're mixing, warm oil (into which you'll be dropping the fritters, so make it deep enough). Use 1 tablespoon full of fritter mix at a time, browning for about two minutes per side. Put these on paper towels to drain.

For the topping/dipping sauce (which can be made ahead of time for convenience), perhaps wait until the moon is waxing to full so that you add even more lunar energy to the topping. To the mango, simply dice the dates and place the ingredients in a pan and bring to a low rolling boil. Remove the cinnamon sticks before serving (serve warm for warm emotions, cold to keep a cool head).

DESSERT

Friendship Fudge

Makes 16 (2-inch) squares

In Babylonian stories a mulberry tree built understanding between families after their children, much like Romeo and Juliet, died underneath in a secret tryst. The tree represents wisdom (something very helpful in all relationships) and good luck.

1½ cups ripe mulberries **2 cups butter**
2 cups sugar

Magical preparations: You may want to have an item that represents each of your friends toward whom you'll be directing your energy. This improves the focus of the spell.

Candle types: Surround the mulberries for a few minutes with your chosen candles, even as you want to surround your friends with love and kindness.

Cook the mulberries. Mash and drain through a fine sieve to obtain the juice saying:

> *Pure juice, pure intention*
> *My friendship, love and support to all I now mention*
> _____ (list the names of your friends)

You need about ⅔ cup of juice total. Mix this with the sugar and butter and cook over low heat until sugar dissolves. Turn up the heat slightly, bringing everything to a boil without stirring until you reach the soft-ball candy stage (240 degrees F). Remove from heat; cool until lukewarm and beat with a wooden spoon until mixture looses its gloss. Press into a 9 by 9-inch buttered pan and cut into squares before the candy firms up. Keep in a tightly covered dish or this will lose moisture very quickly. The airtight container is also a good symbol for preserving your magic until most needed.

Tropical Amity Cake

Makes 4 to 6 servings

Passionfruit is used by homeopaths and herbalists to reduce physical "inflammation." We're using that symbolism on an emotional level in this recipe when the communications in a friendship have become inflammatory. While not all friends are friends for life, it's nice to have closure without hurt feelings. The coconut here provides you with an intuitive edge.

3/4 cup sifted self-raising flour
3/4 cup coconut
3 eggs
1 cup raw sugar, processed very fine
6 ounces passion fruit pulp
2 tablespoons lemon juice
1 teaspoon lemon rind, fresh
1 teaspoon vanilla powder
1/2 cup icing sugar

Magical preparations: Sounds to me like you need to get away from it all—so decorate your space with a tropical flair that mirrors the ingredients and hopefully lightens the mood.

Candle types: White for peace, or black to banish your negativity.

Preheat the oven to 350 degrees F. Grease a small square pan. Add the flour to the coconut. In another bowl lightly beat eggs and sugar, then add passion fruit pulp, juice, and rind a little at a time. Fold the dry ingredients into this blend. Pour into the pan and cook for 20 minutes until firm. While you're waiting mix the vanilla powder, sugar and rind together saying:

Where hurt feelings lie, let these sweet spices allay
Let this spell instill peace; let it begin this very day!
Emotions boiled over,
The truth has bubbled free
Now it's time for closure,
Between me and thee.

Sift this evenly over the top of the cake and share it with your friend while you're talking things out.

LOVE'S DELECTABLE DELIGHTS

Love from one being to another can only be that two solitudes come nearer, recognize and protect and comfort each other.

—HAN SUYIN

Some claim that money makes the world go around, but there is a small optimistic voice inside me that says it's really love that drives everything. The problem is often our perception of love. If you say that word, most folks automatically think of romantic or sexual love—not the love of an art, the adoration of a child or pet, or the fondness between friends. Now, since we've already talked about kinship, we need not rehash that subject. When you work with these recipes, however, please keep in mind that this creature called love is much larger than we normally give it credit. These recipes were designed with that multidimensional characteristic in mind. Let your love out of the "box" to grow into whatever it needs to be!

The only caution with love's delights is that this is not an emotion that should be constrained or manipulated in any way. You can offer love, but you cannot force it. Inevitably trying to do so magically or mundanely will blow up in your face and leave several broken individuals in the wake. So in preparing these dishes keep in mind the words "release" and "allow"—you create and release the energy and allow a person to accept it or not. This way you never hinder free will, which is the truly loving thing to do!

Potential Love Components

- *Aromatics:* Allspice, almond, bay, cinnamon, vanilla, fennel, anise, clove, violet.
- *Candle types:* While it's a tad corny, consider getting a heart-shaped candle since you're focused on matters of the heart.
- *Color:* Red (also most really rich colors like deep satiny purple).

- *Candlelight recipe ingredients:* Apricot, barley, beet, berries, brazil nut, brussels sprouts, cheese, guava, mango, honey, lamb, orange, peas, pumpkin, quince, strawberries, sweet potatoes, tomatoes, cardamom, cherry, currant, ginger, kiwi, plum.
- *Candlelight recipe ingredients (sensual):* Banana, carrot, coriander, hazelnut, mango, mik, mint, peach, pear, pomegranate, asparagus, cashew, chocolate, eggs, figs, licorice, mint, olive, sesame, shellfish, vanilla, all aphrodisiacs.
- *Crystals, metals, stones:* Amethyst, onyx, jade, lapis, moonstone, pearl.
- *Decorative touches:* As with friendship dishes, you should decorate to please your guest. If you're working alone and directing loving energy to someone, then have a picture of them present (or something personal to help connect you).
- *Timing:* Aquarius or Pisces moon; full moon, Fridays; Valentine's Day. Beltane and Summer Solstice.

APPETIZER

Passionate Sweet Potato Ravioli

Makes 2 dozen ravioli

I'm fond of lightly sweet foods for love, since love should be sweet but not "syrupy" (IMO). The potatoes in this recipe give love solid ground upon which to grow into fullness.

1½ pounds sweet potatoes
2 tablespoons golden brown sugar, packed
¼ teaspoon ground nutmeg
1 teaspoon minced garlic
1 teaspoon finely ground ginger, fresh if possible
2 green onions, finely chopped
2 large egg whites, beaten until foamy
48 wonton wrappers

Sauce

¾ cup butter
1½ tablespoons balsamic vinegar
1½ tablespoons chopped fresh thyme
Chopped toasted almonds for garnish

Magical preparations: Do something sweet or thoughtful for your mate today. That will set the tone nicely for this Candlelight recipe.

Candle types: I suggest pink because you don't want a "pushy" love, but rather something gentle and insightful.

Pierce potatoes on all sides with a fork. Cook in a microwave on high until soft (about 6 minutes). Cool slightly. Cut potatoes in half, scooping out the potato flesh into large bowl (you need two full cups of it, packed tight). Mix in brown sugar and seasonings.

Place 1 wonton wrapper on work surface. Brush this lightly with beaten egg whites. If you wish, pattern your strokes so they form a heart. Place a full tablespoon of the potato filling in center. Top with another wrapper. Press edges together to seal. In this form you can deep fry them, or boil them, topping with the butter sauce.

To make the topping that literally butters up your mate, melt the butter in a pan, cooking it until it browns lightly. Stir it clockwise, patterning your movements to again make a heart in the bottom of the pan. Keep an image of your loved one in mind as you do so. Remove from heat, adding vinegar and thyme. Toss the ravioli with the butter and nuts just prior to serving.

Remember Me Violets

Makes 3 to 4

Violets have a flavor akin to mild greens or peas. In the Victorian language of flowers it means "you are in my thoughts." A folk name for them is "heart's ease." The flower was also a common component in love divinations.

1 small head leaf lettuce
½ cup young, sweet violet leaves
12 (½-inch) tips spring tarragon
2 tablespoons chopped lemon balm
¼ cup sweet violets
3 tablespoons olive oil
1½ tablespoons rice wine vinegar
Salt and freshly ground pepper to taste

Magical preparations: Since the violet brings to mind the person you love, it's nice to spend a few minutes in quiet meditation about him or her. Think of all the things that attracted the two of you to each other, and direct warm, loving thoughts in his or her direction.

Candle types: Violet colored and scented are definitely the way to go!

Wash the greens, herbs, and flowers and pat them dry with clean kitchen towels. Tear into bite-size pieces. This might be a fun time to remember the child's game "loves me, loves me not" by reciting that while you break up the salad. (Just make sure to end on *loves me*!) Toss all, except for violets, with the olive oil, vinegar, salt and pepper. Arrange the violets on top before serving (pattern them into a heart!).

BEVERAGE

Tropical Temptation Rum Punch

Makes 6 servings

Everything in this recipe is ideally suited to taking a gentle love and heating up some real excitement. Mango represents love in India, Guava is favored in Latin America for inspiring passion, and pineapple creates a sense of welcome.

1 1/3 cups gold rum
1 1/3 cups frozen passion fruit-flavored juice cocktail
1 cup mango nectar
1 cup guava nectar
2 tablespoons (or more) fresh lime juice
4 cups ice cubes
6 fresh pineapple wedges

Magical preparations: Put on something sexy! You're hoping to please and tease, and clothing helps with that by signaling your partner as to what's on your mind. As you dress, visualize red, sparkling light filling your aura (especially erogenous zones).

If you wish, toss those clothes in a dryer with passionate herbs like cinnamon and ginger for an aromatic energizing beforehand.

Candle types: Vibrant red, for passion.

Mix gold rum, passion fruit, mango, guava, and lime juice in pitcher (add more if you wish after tasting). Pour punch into 6 glasses. Garnish with fresh pineapple wedges and serve.

MAIN DISH

Adoration Shrimp

Makes 4 servings

Shrimp is among the foods thought to inspire love and passion. When combined with honey, another love food, it makes a delectable, intimate treat for two!

1 cup flour
¼ teaspoon salt
Freshly ground pepper to taste
1 egg lightly beaten
⅔ cup water
Vegetable oil for deep frying
1 pound medium shrimp, shelled
2 tablespoons cornstarch
1 tablespoon sesame oil
2 tablespoons honey
¼ teaspoon ginger
½ teaspoon crushed garlic
1 tablespoon sesame seeds

Magical preparations: Use some ginger incense to bless your sacred pantry. Walk clockwise around the room with it burning and say something like:

Bless the power of love
As below so above
As shown without, so it grows within
Loving feelings to grow as this spell begins

Candle types: Red's a good choice if you're hoping for passion. Perhaps light it at the end of your blessing.

Combine flour and salt and pepper in a bowl. Add the egg (at room temperature) and water. Stir until smooth and set aside while you heat the cooking oil. Put about 1½ to 2 inches of oil in a wok until medium hot, about 375 degrees F. Roll cleaned shrimp in cornstarch, then dip in the batter. Coat evenly, letting excess drip off. Fry these, a few at a time, in the hot oil. Cook until golden brown. Remove and drain on paper towels.

Repeat the frying process until all shrimp are cooked. In a small saucepan, heat the sesame oil, adding the honey and spices. Toss the shrimp with this to coat well. Serve with rice or noodles, zucchini, or other vegetables. By the way, these make good finger food, so don't hesitate to feed each other!

Appreciation Pasta

Makes 4 servings

Cheese was often part of wedding rituals in ancient times, in part because it was considered a gift from Apollo's son, Aristaeus. Aristaeus means "very good" and this recipe is just that—very good tasting and very good for creating loving energy.

3 tablespoons garlic, minced
½ teaspoon dried rosemary, crumbled
1 tablespoon butter
1 tablespoon olive oil
¼ cup brandy
1 cup heavy cream
⅓ cup basket cheese, crumbled
¾ cup cheese (your choice) crumbled
½ cup freshly grated Parmesan and Romano mixed
¾ pound pasta (your choice)

Magical preparations: To honor Apollo, open your kitchen curtains wide to receive sunlight and let that wonderful warmth bless your food and your efforts. Lighting a yellow or gold-colored candle will also work if it happens to be a cloudy day.

Candle types: Yellow and gold are Apollo's colors.

Sauté the garlic and herbs with the butter and olive oil until golden brown and very aromatic (love tends to be effected strongly by aromas). Add the brandy and the cream to this slowly, stirring constantly. Cream has very nurturing energy.

Once this is well mixed, begin adding the cheese a little at a time. Allow the cheese to melt and mingle, continuing to simmer for 10 minutes after all have been added to integrate the flavors and the associated energy fully. Note that you will need to keep stirring this to avoid separation or sticking (remember to turn your spoon clockwise to invoke the best possible energy).

While the sauce simmers, bring the pasta to boil in a large pan. Cook until tender, drain, then put into a large bowl. Pour the sauce over the pasta, mixing until well coated. As you stir the blend add an incantation like:

love be quick, love be kind
help me Aristaeus, a lover find!

Adaptations: Play around with different types of cheese to attract specific kinds of lovers. For example, if you want a spicy lover, use a hot pepper cheese, or for a mature lover, use a well aged cheese.

Cut the Baloney

Makes 1 serving

Think someone isn't being wholly honest about a relationship? Well cut through the phoney baloney right away with this tasty, and simple sandwich!

2 slices garlic baloney
1 small onion, sliced
½ green pepper, sliced
Butter
¼ cup mozzarella or other favorite cheese
Roll or bread
Lettuce for garnish (optional)

Magical preparations: The night before making this spell recipe, sleep with a sunflower under your pillow. According to rural folklore this will help you sort out truth from lies or game playing in any relationship. To improve the results gained, whisper an invocation to the petals before you put it in place like:

Shadows fade, lies behold
By my will, the magic unfolds!
Sunflower, reveal the truth like the sun
When I wake the spell's begun

Take the flower out from under your pillow and into the sacred space of the kitchen while you're cooking. Afterward release its petals to the earth with thankfulness.

Candle types: Match them to the color of the sunflower you used in the spell.

Take the two slices of baloney and cut them into strips (this cuts through the bull that's keeping the truth from you). Put them in a frying pan with the onion, green pepper, and butter. Stir counterclockwise as you fry to banish lies. As the onions and baloney get browned, top with cheese (this symbolically heals things once the truth comes out). Serve on your favorite roll or bread, garnished as desired.

Adaptations: If you feel you need extra protection in this situation, add just a bit of chopped garlic when frying. If this relationship is particularly loving add a slice of tomato to the top of the sandwich (the love apple).

SIDE DISH

Serenity Barley Salad

Makes 4 servings

Everyone deserves at least one relationship in their lives where they feel completely safe and secure. This recipe helps bring such a relationship your way, or fosters one that already exists, and is particularly suited to a family to inspire greater unity and trust.

½ cup pearl barley, presoaked
1½ cups canned broth (your choice)
1 large green pepper
1 small red bell pepper
2 large plum tomatoes, seeded, chopped (about 1 cup)
1 cup fresh corn kernels
¼ cup chopped green onions
2½ tablespoons orange juice
2 tablespoons olive oil

Magical preparations: You will need a pouch, box or other small storage container that you can leave somewhere undisturbed for this spell. You will also need a picture of the individuals you wish to safeguard. Place the picture(s) in the container saying:

Protection within, this spell begins
With magic pure, keep our family secure

Close the box and wrap it with a white ribbon or piece of yarn so the top doesn't come off accidentally. Keep this near your stove somewhere safe (this is the heart of the home). This is also the location where it will absorb all the good energy from your kitchen magic.

Candle types: While you're working on this spell recipe you can surround the box with candles, which also symbolizes protection.

Place the barley in a pan with your chosen broth over a medium heat. Bring this to a low rolling boil, continuing to cook until the barley absorbs most of the broth. Dice the peppers, putting them with the barley, tomatoes, corn, onion, juice, and olive oil in a mixing bowl. This mixture coats the barley in protective energy. While you're mixing try adding an incantation like:

Here place my magic, my will affect
To preserve, love, and forever protect!

Add a little salt and pepper to personal taste. Serve when warmed through for a similarly warm, cozy relationship and home.

Adaptation: Substitute rice for the barley to produce a relationship that is both emotionally and financially secure.

Take a Chance on Me Crab

Makes 3 servings

Every once in a while there's a person that seems wholly inaccessible and unreachable, even as a friend. When this happens, and you'd like some magic to open the door and put that individual on "notice" that you're interested, this is a good recipe to help break down the barriers.

1½ pounds crabmeat
2 tablespoons butter
1 tablespoon olive oil
1 (16-ounce) can spinach
2 cups grape tomatoes
½ cup yellow tomato, diced
1 shallot minced
1 teaspoon basil
⅓ cup olive oil
¼ cup balsamic or white wine vinegar
1 teaspoon fresh lemon juice
Salt and pepper to taste

Magical preparations: This spell is designed only to make the desired person aware of your interest, NOT manipulate his or her interest in you. Consequently, it's important to preface this Candlelight recipe with a prayer that allows the universe (or your pantry protector) to use your energy in the best possible way. One example directed to Kama would be:

Kama, god of love, born from Brahma's heart,
See my desire, hear my wish
Let _____ know my feelings but
Be not constrained by them
For the greatest good, and it harm none
So be it.

Candle types: Put out one candle that represents you, and one that represents the person toward whom you hope to make some headway. Light yours at the outset of the candlelight recipe, and then light the second from your candle when you're done cooking up the magic.

Sauté the crabmeat in a combination of butter and olive oil. Drain on paper towels and set aside, keeping the meat warm. Next, lay out the spinach in a lightly oiled, ovenproof pan (feel free to pattern it symbolically if time allows). Place the crabmeat evenly over top.

In a separate container mix all the remaining ingredients to create a dressing, and spoon this evenly over top of the crabmeat. Warm in a 350 degree F oven for about 10 to 15 minutes (to generate energy and warm hearts) saying:

Let barriers melt away in the heat
Let eyes see true the intention of my heart
Interest be known; goodwill impart

Serve. Watch for opportunities to present themselves within the next few days.

By the way, if you have any of the sauce left over it's quite tasty on chicken or salads, both of which emphasize healthy relationships.

Adaptations: If you're not sure that your intentions are wholly honorable in this situation, add a little onion and garlic to the sauce to purify those motivations.

DESSERT

Breaking Up Is Hard to Do Iced Dessert

Makes 1 to 2 servings

This wonderful no-guilt dessert is perfect when you want to get out of a relationship, when you'd like an over-amorous lover to cool off for a while, or when you need to improve your spirits after a nasty split up.

⅓ cup diced strawberries
⅛ cup coconut-flavored rum
1 banana, peeled and halved
1 cup raspberry sherbet or frozen yogurt
1 cup coconut sherbet (or other favorite flavor)
1 tablespoon fresh sweet coconut for garnish

Magical preparations: If this recipe is directed at cooling off a lover, take his or her picture and freeze it in an ice tray before starting the spell. This literally puts their attentions "on ice."

If you need to prepare for a split up or heal your heart, cut out a piece of red paper in the shape of a heart and apply some salve to it. Fold this in on itself three times saying:

Peace of mind, peace of soul,
Peace of heart, make me whole.

Carry this charm with you when cooking and thereafter until things have settled out.

Candle types: In keeping with the "cool" theme, chill your candles before using them.

☙ Marinate the strawberries overnight in the rum. This purifies the energies in the berries so only pure feelings, without guilt or remorse, remain. Place the banana halves in a large bowl with the sherbet or yogurt neatly on top. Garnish with strawberries and a sprinkling of coconut. Eat slowly, letting the sorbet melt in your mouth even as you want your sadness or misgivings to melt away!

Adaptations: For greater healing power put some whipped cream on top. Cream symbolizes the mother aspect of the goddess who is always there when we need comforting.

Dating Game Brownies

Makes 20 brownies

Cook these delicious mate-attracting treats to sweeten your love life, whether you're looking for a man or a woman! As you prepare them visualize the perfect companion in as much detail as possible.

1½ cups (3 sticks) butter
12 ounces bittersweet chocolate chips
6 large eggs
1¼ cups flour
1 cup unsweetened cocoa powder
3 cups sugar
½ teaspoon salt

Magical preparations: Grab a handful of bread crumbs and take them to an eastern-facing window of your home or apartment. Hold these for a moment thinking of all the best attributes you'd like in a boyfriend or girlfriend. Finally, release them to the four winds, which will carry your wishes out to the world as you begin the Candlelight recipe.

Candle types: Use pink to inspire friendship (which is a good foundation on which to build something more intimate).

Preheat the oven to 375 degrees F. Pre-prepare a 13 by 9 by 2-inch pan with oil and light flour. Don't forget to draw hearts in the oil with your finger! Next, melt the butter and chocolate together in a saucepan. When the butter and chocolate are fully melted and blended, whisk in the eggs one at a time, followed by the dry ingredients, while saying:

Loving glances
Sweet romances
Thru this wonderful treat
My true love to meet!

Bake the batter for 45 minutes. Cool and enjoy! Consider sprinkling a little powdered sugar on top to make your new relationship all the more sweet, then keep your eyes open for that perfect partner to come along soon.

Adaptations: Use white chocolate for a blond partner, mint extract for a wealthy mate or one with green eyes, or use butterscotch flavoring for a red-headed mate.

SAVORY SEXUALITY AND SENSUALITY

Understand that sexuality is as wide as the sea.

—DEREK JARMAN

Sexuality is a hot topic (no pun intended). The saying goes: Sex sells. Well, that's not the reason it's included in this book. Rather, it's because humans are sensual beings. There is no reason anyone should have to live without passion or pleasure. These dishes are intended to spice up your love life as a helpmate to your lover. (Both of you to each other!) The foods of passion should be ones toward which, well, you're passionate! They should also be filled with aroma and have a strong visual impact so they awaken as many of your senses as possible. Finger foods can also be a lot of fun. (Feed them to each other!)

Potential Sexuality Components

- *Aromatics:* Vanilla, lavender, jasmine, cinnamon, anise, clove, ginger, mint. Non-edible: patchouly, vetivert, or musk.
- *Candle types:* You can't beat candlelight for romance and to help put people in the right mood. The less fluorescent lighting the better for these candlelight recipes!
- *Color:* Rich red or other lush, inspiring hues.
- *Candlelight recipe ingredients:* Oysters, asparagus, almond, arugula, avocado, licorice, mustard, pine nuts, truffles (the mushroom), beans, chartreuse, brandy, plum wine, blackberry, sesame, caraway, cardamom, parsley, olive, berries (especially strawberry), chocolate, rosewater, mangos, yams, fig, candy, peaches, honey, cherry, carrot, fish, shellfish, wine.
- *Crystals, metals, stones:* Carnelian, bloodstone.
- *Decorative touches:* Let yourself be the decoration for this meal—dress in a sultry pleasing way!
- *Timing:* Spring, May Day. Virgo, Aquarius, and Pisces moon. Wednesdays and Fridays.

APPETIZER

Lusty Oysters

Makes 2 servings

I know of no one who doesn't think of oysters when they think about aphrodisiacs. Better still, oysters naturally stimulate psychic awareness so we can anticipate our partners and please them even more!

¾ cup salad dressing
1 green onion, minced
2 tablespoons dried cranberries, chopped
2 tablespoons orange juice
5 tablespoons yellow cornmeal
2 tablespoons flour
16 ounces shucked large oysters, halved, drained well
1 garlic clove, quartered
¼ cup olive oil

Magical preparations: You can take one of the oyster shells and use is as an eros charm. Rinse it off in hot salt water first, then situate any small oblong stone or object inside (this symbolizes sexual union). Tie the two halves of the shell together around the object with a red or purple ribbon (the color of passion) while saying:

Two minds, two hearts, two bodies
Connected in mutual pleasure
Protected by trust
And warmed with love.

Keep this charm in the kitchen with you while you make this dish, and then perhaps leave it in the bedroom where it can effect the most good.

Candle types: Use another oyster shell and affix your candle into it, using it as a drip catcher!

Begin by mixing the salad dressing with onion, cranberries, and 1 tablespoon of the orange juice. Set this aside to use as a sauce. If you wish, you can repeat the incantation used for the charm at this point to empower the sauce with your magic and will.

In another bowl, mix the cornmeal, flour, and remaining orange juice. Coat the oysters with this mixture and keep handy for frying. Using a nonstick frying pan, heat the garlic and olive oil together, removing the garlic when it smells aromatic. Turn the oysters into the heated oil, frying on each side for 2 or 3 minutes until browned. Serve with a hearty portion of sauce drizzled over top (don't be afraid to get creative with the pattern in which you apply the sauce!).

Adaptation: Lemon juice is a suitable substitute for orange juice, inspiring love and happiness in your physical encounters.

BEVERAGE

Mombo Mango

Makes 2 servings

Throughout India, mangos are planted with ritualistic diligence and care. For example, they're always grown in pairs (as mates). Thus it's not uncommon for weddings to take place in mango groves, which also neatly provide fertility should the couple wish it.

3/4 cup frozen mango-peach juice concentrate, thawed
3/4 cup white rum
1/2 cup orange juice
1/4 cup sugar
1/2 pound frozen unsweetened sliced peaches
1/2 pound frozen strawberries
Fresh mint sprigs for garnish

Magical preparations: Do everything you can in pairs (pairs of glasses, plates, etc.) so that you're encouraging "mating" energy.

Candle types: Yep you guessed it—two. Light them saying:

One for me, one for thee
By this spell, our passion's freed!

Combine mango-peach juice concentrate, rum, orange juice, and sugar in blender. Add half of frozen peaches and strawberries and puree. Slowly add remaining fruits, blending until mixture is smooth and thick, stopping to stir as needed. Pour and garnish with a fresh mint leaf (which also makes you kissable!).

MAIN DISH

Castle in the Sky Mustard Sauce

Makes 3/4 cup of sauce

Who of us doesn't have at least one fantasy that really gets our juices flowing. Well, why not be a little "saucy" about it too! Enjoy this sauce (ideally on a fish main dish) then act out your fantasy with a consenting partner and see what magic you can make together!

1/4 cup sweet mustard
1 teaspoon dry mustard
1 teaspoon whole mustard seeds
1 teaspoon black pepper
3 tablespoons ginger brandy (or plain)
1 tablespoon tarragon
2 tablespoons olive oil
1 1/2 tablespoons white wine vinegar
2 teaspoons honey

Magical preparations: Since this is YOUR fantasy—you decide! If you're going to need a costume or other supplies to make that dream into a reality, by all means assemble them near the sacred hearth so they can absorb the energy you're creating.

Candle types: Keeping with the castles in the sky theme, if you have a hanging candle lantern that would be very fitting.

Stir the mustard and pepper with the brandy, making sure to move clockwise to attract positive energy from which to manifest your fantasy. Continue stirring until the dry mustard dissolves in the brandy. Now add the remaining ingredients, mixing well, and saying:

Dreams and fantasy here with magic tossed
Passionate energy, sealed within this sauce

Chill overnight before using. This can be applied as a grilling sauce (if you want to light a real fire under yourself and your partner), a marinade (to warm things up slowly), or as a serving sauce.

Adaptations: To protect your privacy during those intimate moments, add a teaspoon of garlic powder to the sauce. Or, change the flavor of the brandy to better suit your goal. For example, use a strawberry-flavored brandy for a very loving fantasy encounter.

Just Ducky Desire and Devotion

Makes 2 servings

In China and Japan ducks represent sexual happiness, devotion, and beauty, especially in marriage.

10 ounces boneless duck breast
1 teaspoon five-spice powder
1 tablespoon finely chopped fresh ginger
3 scallions
Salt and pepper, freshly ground
4 ounces sesame oil
1 cup golden plum wine
2 cups chicken stock
1 ounce butter

Magical preparations: Physical devotion and happiness are not simply a matter of magic, they're also a matter of maintenance. Think about this entire night as an opportunity to reconnect and do things with or for your partner that sometimes get lost in a hurry-up day. Take it slow!

Candle types: Lots of 'em! Go for romantic and sensual.

Put the duck breast in a bag or pan with the five-spice, ginger, scallions, salt, pepper, and sesame oil. This is where it gets saturated with extra energy so add an incantation like:

Passion and devotion
Put the magic in motion!

Preheat the oven to 400 degrees F. Heat skillet on moderately high heat, do not add any oil. Sear duck breast skin side down, brown both sides. Transfer duck to ovenproof plate and cook the duck in the oven for 10 minutes for medium rare. Pour off grease from the skillet, add plum wine. Add duck and stock and season with salt and pepper and reduce the sauce to 1 cup. Then incorporate the butter to the sauce and set aside and keep warm. Remove duck from oven and let it set for 5 minutes before slicing.

Temptation Savory Chicken

Makes 4 servings

What is it that you most crave in your physical expressions? Tenderness? Joy? Playfulness? Intensity? No matter that craving, or to whom it's directed, this dish creates the right auric energies to express that desire effectively to your partner.

2 tablespoons (¼ stick) butter
4 boneless chicken breasts, sliced in ½-inch pieces
½ teaspoon dried rosemary, salt, and pepper
⅓ cup frozen orange juice concentrate, thawed
⅓ cup canned chicken broth
2 tablespoons brandy
Mandarin orange slices (optional)

Magical preparations: Expressing your desires often functions hand in hand with self-confidence. To help with this, take a long hot bath that's scented with heather (for attractiveness in women) or a musky/spicy aroma like cinnamon (men). Chant to yourself as you de-stress and soak, simple affirmations like:

I am attractive
I am worthy to give and receive love
I am a passionate person
I am a strong, sensitive lover

As you chant, remember to visualize the upcoming encounter in the best possible light. When you're done, dry off and go make the magic meal that everyone will later crave!

Candle types: Surround your magical bath with aromatherapy candles to put yourself in just the right mood.

Heat a frying pan in order to melt the butter. Meanwhile, rub the chicken with the rosemary herb blend (magically this will make for a more memorable encounter). Add this to the butter and sauté for 3 or 4 minutes on each side until lightly browned. Add orange juice concentrate, broth, and brandy, simmering for another 5 to 10 minutes until the chicken is fully cooked. Remove the chicken from the sauce so this can thicken (about another 5 minutes). Add the mandarin oranges to the sauce just prior to serving, pouring the sauce over the chicken as you say:

Today I don't want to behave
Give to me that which I crave!

Just be careful what you wish for!

Adaptation: Choose a brandy flavor that further refines your goal, like cherry for delightful and loving physical expressions.

SIDE DISH

Sexy Shrimp

Makes 2 servings

Eating shrimp, for me, is a sensual experience in itself! Our ancestors must have agreed, as they often ate shrimp to inspire passion and desire. If you're not fond of shrimp, any shellfish can be used in this provocative recipe.

Oil for deep frying
2 eggs
1⅓ cup flour
1 teaspoon salt
2 teaspoons sesame seeds
1 cup flat beer or water
1½ pounds large shrimp

Magical preparations: Consider some of the physical or emotional characteristics of your lover and adapt the recipe accordingly. For example, is he or she dark haired? Use dark beer! A blonde? There are blond beers on the market too! Are they highly energetic? Sprinkle the batter with something a little spicy like cayenne or ginger. Note that if you're not already in a physical relationship you can choose these ingredients according to the type of lover you most desire.

Candle types: Match the color of the candles to the hair or eye color you desire in a lover.

Start heating the oil in a deep pan or fryer, enough so that the shrimp will not touch the bottom of the pan as they cook.

Put the eggs, flour, salt, sesame, and beer into a bowl and stir well (clockwise) until the batter is smooth saying:

Egg and magic in every bite
So too our passion shall ignite
Salt and beer and sesame
Give to us [me] our [my] fantasy!

Dip the shrimp into the batter so that they are evenly coated and deep fry until golden brown so the shrimp become as "hot" as you wish your date to be! Serve with cocktail sauce or a hearty portion of savory butter (consisting of 1 tablespoon toasted sesame seed, 1 teaspoon Worcestershire sauce, and a hint of garlic). Eat creatively!

Adaptation: If you've ever had fruited fish, it's an interesting taste sensation. In this case you could substitute plum wine for the beer for a slightly fruity flavor, and serve it with orange butter. The plum inspires healthy physical interest, while orange motivates devotion.

DESSERT

Desire Me Melon Ice

Makes 2 servings

It is said that Apollo gave humans melons as a precious food that fills us with wonderful flavors and desires. In fact, an early writer said that if you try one bite of melon, you must try more! Sex should be like that!

3 pounds honeydew melon balls
½ cup plum wine
2 teaspoons fresh lime juice
½ cup sugar
⅛ cup finely diced candied ginger

Magical preparations: Try a little aromatherapy around your home (and especially the area in which you wish to make love) to boost energy, confidence, and interest. If you're allergic to incense use simmering potpourri made from culinary herbs, or diluted essential oils dabbed in strategic locations. Some scents suited to this task include dragon's blood, daisy, lemongrass, patchouly (go light on that), vanilla and violet.

Candle types: Match the candle's aroma to your other aromatics, or blend it so it supports your goal.

The simplest way to prepare this is to put the honeydew melon through a food processor, pureeing until smooth (which also magically smoothes the path ahead, and makes the transition from an every day "date" into a passionate encounter far less bumpy). Use the plum wine and lime juice for liquid as needed. Whip this with the sugar and ginger, then place it on a large nonstick pan in the freezer. When the mixture reaches a semifrozen state, return to the blender for a frothy texture saying:

Energy grow higher and higher
Fill this dessert with sweet desire!

Serve immediately and watch as excitement fills the air, sending chills down your lover's back.

Adaptations: You can use all kinds of liqueur in this recipe for varying effects. For example, if you want to excite desire in a relationship that's been damaged somehow use a melon liqueur which promotes healing. Add a hint of peaches or vanilla extract for wisdom in choosing bed partners. Or, try adding a little rosewater to improve your sexual self-confidence!

Fantasy Stuffed Figs

Makes 2 servings

Romans often drank wine with pine nuts feeling it would give them the durability to last through long orgies. Stuffed into a womb of figs, this provides you with the wisdom to use your energy wisely.

½ cup pine nuts
8 ounces cream cheese, softened
2 tablespoons grated orange zest
10 fresh figs, washed, stems removed

Magical preparations: I strongly suggest getting plenty of rest before making this dish. You're going to need it!

Candle types: This is your fantasy so choose the colors and scents accordingly.

Preheat the oven to 350 degrees F. Spread the pine nuts on a baking sheet and lightly toast them. Remove them from the oven, blessing them by saying:

> *All night long, just like the song*
> *Let our passions last until dawn has passed*
> *Let our love inspire an inner fire*
> *All night long, just like the song*

Cool.

Meanwhile in a small bowl, combine the cream cheese, cooled pine nuts, and orange zest, mixing until smooth. Slice each fig in half lengthwise. Press about a tablespoon of the cream cheese mixture into the cut side of each fig half.

Adaptation: You can use a flavored cream cheese (like pineapple) if you wish.

10

Wholeness Harvest

REAPING HEALING, LONG LIFE, AND HAPPINESS

As the last part of our exploration in candlelight recipes, we're turning to those things that inspire physical, mental, and spiritual wholeness. The entire holistic movement is focused on the goal of treating people on all levels of their Be-ing. This is very sensible, and we're going to follow suit magically.

For the mental part of the equation, we have forgiveness fare. When there are open wounds between you and other people, especially family, it cannot help but weigh down your thoughts. Additionally, sometimes we need to forgive ourselves. Accomplishing this isn't always easy, however; there's a lot to work through and release. Forgiveness fare opens that path and smoothes the way a bit.

For spiritual matters, we look to Protection and Safety Selections for proactive energy. The goal of these dishes is keeping us out of negative energy flows, breaking bad habits, and keeping the sacred pantry safeguarded against any ill will. Make these on a regular basis to keep your whole home, and everyone therein, surrounded with shielding vibrations.

Last, but not least, there's Vital and Healthful Helpings. When we're sick, out of sorts, or just "off" somehow, these candlelight recipes inspire restored balance. When we're healthy, these meals keep us vital and strong to face everything that life tosses our way with renewed vigor.

FORGIVENESS FARE

Inner peace can be reached only when we practice forgiveness. Forgiveness is letting go of the past, and is therefore the means for correcting our misperceptions.

—GERALD JAMPOLSKY

People are not perfect. Everyone makes mistakes, and sometimes those mistakes leave behind hurt feelings. And while one should always hold tight to the lessons of life, the pain need not always remain. When you're ready to forgive and put the past behind you, use these recipes to help heal your heart, mind, and soul. If the other person or persons involved are willing, they should join you for this meal as a sign of compromise and a new start.

Potential Forgiveness Components

- *Aromatics:* Violet, lavender, mint, coconut, vanilla.
- *Candle types:* Each person involved can bring one candle to represent their part in this situation. As the meal progresses, and it applies positive energy to the situation, the candle slowly shrinks even as you want negativity to wane. Bury the candles or dispose of them ritually to leave the past in the past.
- *Color:* White for peace; also possibly pale blue for hope and renewed happiness.
- *Candlelight recipe ingredients:* Raspberry, all cool items (for a cool head), parsley, all white foods, bamboo shoots, citron, date, marigold, pineapple, raisin, wine, potatoes, ground vegetables, apple, apricot, barley, licorice, peach, berries, sugar, sweet potato.
- *Crystals, metals, stones:* Alexandrite, moonstone, a plain rock that can be buried.
- *Decorative touches:* Stick with calming colors and music. Anything that inspires a sense of safety and ease in your

environment. Healing can't begin where there's too much of tension.

- *Timing:* Aries or Libra moon. Waning moon to decrease bad feelings. Dark moon to let things rest and heal.

APPETIZER

Roasted Regret Vegetable Soup

Makes 6 servings

Everyone has regrets, but this is one dish in which you can roast that negativity away, and begin building something positive in its place. Barley is sacred to Demeter, who provides us with nourishment for body and soul. It was often laid upon the altar as an offering, and utilized in folk healing to rid the body of infection. Thus we have the symbolism of cleansing away and renewal.

Nonstick vegetable oil spray
4 large plum tomatoes, halved lengthwise
3 medium carrots, peeled and quartered
6 ounces fresh mushrooms, thickly sliced
1 large red or Spanish onion, cut into 1-inch wedges
1 red bell pepper, quartered
1 medium zucchini, halved lengthwise
3 garlic cloves, unpeeled
2 tablespoons olive oil
Salt and pepper
8 cups canned vegetable broth
3 large fresh thyme sprigs
1 bay leaf
1 cup pearl barley

Magical preparations: Forgiveness isn't something you only give to others, you also need to direct it to yourself. Meditate on the situation that left you with regrets. Know it is in the past and release it. Turn your attention to the present and what changes you can make to improve matters, including making this dish to help the healing begin!

Candle types: Let the candles chosen for this candlelight recipe completely melt away even as you wish your regrets to disappear (but not the lessons learned).

Preheat the oven to 400 degrees F. Prepare a baking sheet with nonstick spray. Toss the vegetables and garlic with olive oil then disperse them on the tray. Season with salt and pepper. Roast for about 1 hour until the vegetables are tender and slightly browned. Dice the roasted garlic, cut the vegetables into bite-size pieces, and transfer them to a large soup pot.

Pour in the broth, thyme, and bay leaf. Bring the entire soup to a low rolling boil. Take one half of this and puree it. This is a good juncture to utilize a verbal element like:

The past is gone, the actions set
Remove from me those last regrets
Cook them down to digestible pieces
This spell, right now, all regrets—releases!

Add the barley to the remainder and boil for about 40 minutes. Return the puree to the pot and allow the soup to thicken to personal taste. The flavor of this soup improves by letting it set overnight and rewarming.

Visionary Violet Garnishes

Makes 1 cup

Some situations take a fresh perspective in order to find a way to fix things. In mythology, Aphrodite grew jealous toward dancing girls she noticed Amor (the God of Amorous feelings) admiring. Aphrodite grew jealous and struck them so hard they turned violet. Amor, regretting his lack of tact in admiring them, turned them into the lovely flowers called violets. Here, we wish to likewise turn a bad situation around and make it into a "positive."

Violet flowers freshly picked (use approximately 1 cup of flowers with 1 egg white)
1 egg white
Superfine white sugar

Magical preparations: Since you're trying to change your perspectives and turn things around, begin by changing your routine this morning. Don't follow the same old personal patterns, but mindfully switch them. Afterward, and before making this candlelight recipe, stop and ponder how making that small change has altered the way you feel or think. Apply the same idea to your situation in the way you look at it. Try a new angle!

Candle types: Carve the image of an eye into the top of the candle saying:

Open my eyes to see the possibilities before me

Now carve a heart below the eye saying

Open my heart to compassion and proper intention

Now carve a hand below that saying:

I offer my hand in peace

Gather your violets or get organic ones at a flower shop. If possible prepare this dish at dawn for hopefulness. Rinse and pat dry. Leave on paper towels while you make up the egg. Beat the egg white until it's frothy (but do not allow to get stiff as you would for a meringue). Dip each whole flower into the egg so it's evenly coated, letting any extra drip off. Now dip in the sugar, likewise letting excess fall off. Put these on a try lined with waxed paper in the refrigerator for 2 days. In this form you can keep the violets for about a month in a cool, dry location so long as you use an airtight container. Use to decorate beverages, cakes, salads, your main dish, the table, etc. with the magical flower of peace.

BEVERAGE

Explanation Marigold Wine

Makes 6 to 7 pints

Marigold flowers turn to follow the course of the sun throughout the day. Symbolically they represent worry and memories. When you find yourself worried about a forgiveness issue, and can't seem to find the words to explain it, turn and follow the light of the sun with the marigold. Magically it renews love and begins the healing process.

7½ pints water
2½ pounds granulated sugar
1 medium orange
1 quart organic marigold petals, firmly packed
½ pound chopped golden raisins
1 teaspoon yeast nutrient
1 packet wine yeast (note these last two items are available at hobby stores that offer brewing supplies)

Magical preparations: Definitely work in sunlight. Stop and close your eyes for a minute and let the warm energy begin restoring your ability to think and communicate clearly. Take that warmth into the sacred pantry with you.

Candle types: Orange, yellow, or gold are good choices in keeping with marigold hues.

In a large, nonaluminum pot, bring the water to a boil. Add the sugar, stirring until dissolved. Prepare zest from the orange peel and then extract as much juice as possible from the pulp (pouring that into the water). Put marigold petals, chopped raisins, and orange zest in nylon straining bag and tie closed. Put this along with the yeast nutrient into the pot of boiling water over bag. Set aside to cool, steeping much like a tea.

When the liquid reaches room temperature add activated yeast. Cover pot with a thick towel. Once a day, every day squeeze the bag to extract more flavor. On the fifth day repeat, getting as much liquid out as possible saying:

Release your powers into this drink
Help me to communicate, help me to think!

Allow the liquid to settle overnight and strain into a glass bottle. Affix a balloon to the top (this will keep the fermentation process from exploding the bottle). You will need to strain off the clear fluid after a month, and again after two months (this gets rid of the dead yeast at the bottom). Finally put into finishing bottles to age in a cool, dark area for 1 year.

Now, realizing that you may not want to wait a year to USE this, you can actually use marigolds and orange zest to make yourself a cup of tea to enjoy while brewing the wine.

MAIN DISH

Excuse Me Meat Balls

Makes 24 meatballs

The circle is a symbol of fulfillment and completion. Your effort to find or give forgiveness is part of walking life's circle, so focus on that movement—on moving forward as you shape each meatball. Better still the ground meat here (known for its ability to keep people planted in reality) provides foundations for a new start.

1 pound ground pork (use lean chops for best results)
3 tablespoons cracker crumbs
¼ cup finely chopped green onion
1 large egg
½ teaspoon salt
½ teaspoon ginger
Dash black pepper
2 cups sliced celery
2 cups sliced fresh mushrooms
2 tablespoons Worcestershire sauce
1 (8-ounce) can sliced water chestnuts, drained and chopped
1 (8-ounce) can bamboo shoots, drained
1 (6-ounce) package frozen pea pods, parboiled and drained
Salt and pepper to taste

Magical preparations: Since you're thinking circles in making the meatballs, how about also casting one to reinforce your focus on completion. Perhaps use an invocation like:

Powers of the East, bring the winds of change
Powers of the South, bring the fires of clarity
Powers of the West, bring the waters of healing
Powers of the North, bring the soils of enrichment
Let there be peace again
Let it start today

Candle types: Consider elemental candles combined with one to represent yourself, and one to represent the other people or persons involved in the conflict.

Combine ground pork, cracker crumbs, onion, egg, the 1/2 teaspoon salt, ginger, and pepper. Mix well. Shape mixture into 24 balls. Brown these in a large skillet, then remove and keep warm. Drain most of the pork drippings (leave a little), then add celery and sauté 4 minutes, stirring twice. Add mushrooms, Worcestershire sauce, water chestnuts, bamboo shoots, and pea pods. Reduce heat to low; cover and cook 5 minutes. Move the pork balls into this mixture and add salt and pepper to taste.

Adaptation: Pineapple adds a tropical hint and welcoming energy to this dish. You could also put an almond in the middle of each meatball for a little extra love.

Peaceful Solution Lavender Chicken

Serves 3 to 4 people

Lavender is a lovely herb whose aroma instills a sense of centering and peaceful awareness. Combined with the sweetness of honey, this should make for an ideal dish over which to talk things out.

Lavender Honey and Chicken

3 tablespoons honey
2 tablespoons water
4 sprigs fresh lavender flowers
1 tablespoon ground coriander seeds
1 tablespoon chopped fresh thyme
1 tablespoon soy sauce
4 garlic cloves, peeled and crushed
½ teaspoon five-spice powder
½ teaspoon ground cinnamon
½ teaspoon orange or lemon extract
¼ teaspoon kosher salt
¼ teaspoon black pepper
1 (4-pound) whole chicken

Sauce

1 tablespoon shallot, diced
½ ounce butter
1 tablespon each dry white wine and red cooking wine
Leftover lavender honey
1 teaspoon wine vinegar
Salt, pepper, and five-spice powder to taste.

Magical preparations: Highlight your working area with items in white or pale blue (colors that suggest peaceful intent).

Candle types: Likewise match your candles to those colors, and perhaps even carve a peace symbol into them.

Begin by placing the honey and water into a nonaluminum pot with the lavender flowers. Warm this until the flowers turn translucent then strain (squeezing the flowers to release as much flavor into the honey as possible). Put half the honey aside and then mix the rest with the herbs and spices. Brush this onto the chicken (or place under the skin) saying:

> *Make sweet our words, and honest our thoughts*
> *Let peace be born and last between us*
> *Apply this balm of understanding to our hearts.*

Leave the chicken covered overnight in the refrigerator.

The next day, roast the chicken at 375 degrees F for about 1 hour. Use the drippings to regularly baste or inject the bird and keep it moist. Meanwhile prepare your sauce. Sauté the shallots in butter, adding the remaining ingredients and the chicken's roasting juices. Boil to reduce. If you wish, you can whisk in more butter at the very end before serving (to butter up your guest).

SIDE DISH

Absolution Apples and Yams

Makes 4 servings

In Arabic, Teutonic, and Celtic mythology apples represent healing. New Guinea lore says yams or sweet potatoes have similar energy, specifically to restore one's health. Additionally the sweet potatoes were sacred to the ancient Semitic sun God Baal, thereby adding blessings to this blend to help everything work out right.

1 (22-ounce) can sweet potatoes or yams, drained
2 large eggs
2 tablespoons butter
1 tablespoon granulated sugar
½ teaspoon vanilla extract or powder
¼ teaspoon ground nutmeg
Salt to taste
1 (16-ounce) can apple pie filling

Magical preparations: Healing is a natural part of the forgiveness process, so you might as well start with yourself. Take a little dab of any cream used for "wounds" and dab it over your heart chakra:

Let me open to give and receive forgiveness
I am thankful for this opportunity to set things straight
And remove the walls between me and ______ (fill in with name of person toward whom this candlelight recipe is directed)
By my will, and this spell, so mote it Be!

Candle types: If you're focusing on self love and healing, try pink.

Preheat the oven to 400 degrees F. Lightly grease a baking sheet. Whip sweet potatoes until smooth in a large mixing bowl. Add eggs, butter, sugar, vanilla extract, and nutmeg; beat until well combined. Season to taste with salt. Form this mixture into six circles about 2 inches apart. Put a depression in each, filling the centers with the apple pie filling. This might be a good time to energize the sweet circles by saying:

Fill each bite with healing
Fill each bite with peace
Let the troubles be ending
Let forgiveness never cease.

Bake for 30 minutes.

Pardoning Nut Paste

Makes 3 cups

This is a Jewish dish called Haroseth (the H is pronounced like the end of loch*), typically served during Passover as a condiment. And just as God's wrath passed over the Israelites, this dish is well suited to helping ease the wrath of another, in hopes of building forgiveness.*

2/3 cup dried figs
2/3 cup dried apricots
1/3 cup pitted dates
1 1/3 cups walnuts, chopped and toasted
1/4 cup sweet red wine
1/4 teaspoon cinnamon
1/8 teaspoon ground ginger

Magical preparations: Bring a picture of the person from whom you wish forgiveness into the working space with you so you can direct your energy to him or her.

Candle types: Set a white candle for peace near the image you've just set up. Light the candle saying something like:

Bring us out of the darkness of anger
And into the light of understanding
Open the path between ______ and me
That our healing begins
Let the magic be freed!

The beauty of this dish is that it's fast and easy. Put all your fruits in a food processor and chop them fine. Stir in the nuts, wine, and spices. Serve hot or cold (but I think cold is better symbolically for a cool head).

Adaptation: I like to add 1/3 cup dried pineapple to this mix to encourage a hospitable atmosphere.

DESSERT

Apology Coconut Pudding

Makes 3 to 4 servings

I find that something sweet makes it easier to swallow my pride and apologize for those things that I've done wrong. Coconut adds a little luck to this equation so that things go smoothly.

1/2 cup shredded or flaked coconut
1/4 cup dry bread crumbs
1 cup cream
2 eggs
2 tablespoons butter
2 tablespoons sugar
1/8 teaspoon salt
Vanilla bean (optional)

Magical preparations: The ego can be a proverbial "hard nut to crack" so if you can get your coconut from a fresh shell, all the better. Focus on loosening yourself from pride (just like you're using energy to get into the coconut's shell and loosen the meat). If you wish, repeat an incantation like this one three times (once each for body, mind, and spirit so your entire self is in accord):

Where once there lived arrogance and pride
Let gentle words and modesty abide.

Candle types: One for each person who will be enjoying this dessert (and the conversation thereafter).

☙ Preheat the oven to 350 degrees F. Put all the ingredients in a blender (removing just a little of the interior from the vanilla bean). Whip until smooth. Bake for 1 hour. Serve with an expectant, welcoming smile!

Forgive and Forget Drops

Makes approximately 2 dozen drops

The key ingredient in these candies is the anise, which promotes loving energies and fresh, honest words while it soothes your nerves.

1 cup granulated sugar
1/4 cup packed brown sugar
1/4 cup water
1/4 cup light corn syrup
1/4 teaspoon anise extract

Magical preparations: Spend several days before preparing this recipe tape recording yourself. Listen to how you talk about the person or situation that led to needing forgiveness. Be aware of how your words "taste"—are they sour? Bitter? If so, you will need these to help sweeten your disposition too!

Candle types: I suggest using black to banish whatever negativities are impeding resolution. Also black is the color of release, and you want to release the past.

☙ Put the sugar, water, and corn syrup into a saucepan over medium heat. Stir. When the batch has boiled for the first time, scrape the sugar crystals down from the sides of the saucepan. Put a candy thermometer in the mix and cook without further stirring to soft-crack stage (290 degrees F on candy thermometer).

Remove saucepan from heat before adding anise flavoring. Stir gently. With a teaspoon, drop one at a time onto a greased baking sheet. Cool the drops completely by placing the sheet in a cool room. When firmed up, remove and wrap each one individually using waxed paper. Focus on your goal while wrapping and add an incantation like:

Candy sweet, candy fine
In your flavors my magic bind.
And when unwrapped, the spell begins
Forgiveness and serenity ultimately WINS!

PROTECTION AND SAFETY SELECTIONS

The desire for safety stands against
every great and noble enterprise.

—Publius Cornelius Tacitus

The world is not cut-and-dry, nor does it lack for dangers both big and small. From the moment we get out of bed in the morning until we go to sleep again all sorts of hazards lie in our wake. The person talking on a cell phone when driving, the friend who isn't being aware of his or her spiritual energy leaking all over your home, the random nippy dog, heck—even pollen is a small annoyance. The wise kitchen witch knows that forewarned is, indeed, forearmed. Therefore we create protection and safety dishes somewhat regularly so that proactive magic begins to saturate our lives, and keep us as safe as possible.

Potential Protection Components

- *Aromatics:* Basil, bay, dill, marjoram, clove, rosemary, almond.
- *Candle types:* You might want to put candles in your windows, or all around your working space. The first is an old bit of folk magic that's said to be protective. The second creates a circle of safety.

- *Color:* White or brilliant white-blue; red (especially against mischievous fairies).
- *Candlelight recipe ingredients:* Cactus juice, bananas, birch beer, nettles, radishes, red peppers, red beans or rice, garlic, parsley, black pepper, cayenne, sesame, broccoli, cranberry, olive oil, horseradish, brussels sprouts, leeks, mustard (whole grain), rum (and most "spirits"), prickly pear, chive or onion (red), pineapple, starfruit, eggs, sunflower seed, rhubarb, hot peppers, salsa, corn, vinegar.
- *Crystals, metals, stones:* Geode, eye agate.
- *Decorative touches:* Keep items in plain sight that make you feel wholly safe and comfortable in your space.
- *Timing:* Leo or Virgo moon, Tuesdays and Thursday. When the sun shines brightly.

APPETIZER

Retaliation Radishes

Makes 6 servings

Folklore tells us that eating radishes keeps one safe from his or her enemies, so this recipe is ideal when you know you have an adversary and have to face him or her head-on. The red color and zesty flavor makes this an ideal all-around protection food too.

1½ pounds red radishes
1 teaspoon salt
2 teaspoons sesame oil
2 teaspoons red wine vinegar
4 teaspoons soy sauce
2 teaspoons finely chopped onion (optional)

Magical preparations: In keeping with the color theme, don something red (really **red**). This makes a very positive statement about your power in this situation. Red's vibration is also that of vibrant success, and according to folklore it scares away mischievous entities too!

Candle types: Black for binding or brown to ground negative energies being aimed toward you.

⁂ Trim the tops and bottoms of the radishes and rinse them thoroughly in cold water to cleanse any unwanted energy. Using the back of a spoon or knife, crush them slightly to likewise crush any negativity aimed at you. Toss these with salt and let stand at room temperature for 15 minutes. Blend in the remaining ingredients, mixing until the radishes are evenly coated saying:

within me power burns
all ill will, my magic turns!

Chill before serving to help cool down an overheated situation.

Adaptations: Diced tomato and red pepper taste quite nice in this blend, and add even more protective energy.

Safeguard Sunflower Seeds

Makes one cup

Sunflower is particularly appropriate for protecting you during times of want. They were often eaten during times of famine. This flower also turns its head during the day to follow the light. Let it lead you out of the dark places.

1 cup sunflower seeds
1 teaspoon olive oil
1 teaspoon Worcestershire sauce
¼ teaspoon garlic salt

Magical preparations: Think sunshine and light. Use bright, lively colors in and around your sacred space (also in your clothing).

Candle types: Yellow or gold to honor the sun, and carve them with the image of the sun with long, reaching arms of light. When you light the candles you could add a corresponding verbal element like:

Turn toward the light, celebrate the day
Protection come
Keep all harm at bay!

Preheat the oven to 325 degrees F. Mix sunflower seeds with oil, Worcestershire sauce, and herbs until evenly coated. Spread on baking sheet. Bake about 8 minutes or until lightly browned. Note that oven temperature can cause these to brown very quickly so watch them. Add an extra dash of salt when they emerge from the oven

Adaptation: For more fiery protection, put a bit of hot sauce in the blend.

Sanctuary Cranberry Sauce

Makes 2½ cups sauce

The word "sanctuary" implies a great sense of safety—of knowing that the place and people therein are wholly protected. This sauce provides that energy. Besides enjoying it as an appetizer, you can eat it as a side dish, or as a garnish for meat and ice cream.

1 (12-ounce) bag of cranberries
1 seedless orange, peeled
1 (10-ounce) package frozen raspberries, thawed
½ cup firmly packed light brown sugar (or to taste)
¾ cup orange juice

Magical preparations: Since your home and kitchen are now a sacred space from all the magic you're creating therein, take a moment to bless this space or thank your pantry protectors for their aid. A simple prayer like this might do the trick:

> *Spirit of hearth and home, create here an atmosphere of safety and comfort. Surround this space with your protective power and bless it and the work of my hands with the light of love and joy. So be it.*

Candle types: In keeping with the prayer you could use a white candle. Alternatively make a special house candle that represents the spirit of your entire home and light it for this occasion.

Grind the cranberries and orange using a food processor or hand grinder. Symbolically this destroys any negativity. Place these in a saucepan with the remaining ingredients. Simmer for 30 minutes over a low flame, stirring regularly, until the sugar is completely melted and the blend thickens. Make sure to stir clockwise to attract more positive energy or counterclockwise to banish dangers while repeating an empowering phrase like:

Surround, surround, protection abounds!

Serve warm for active energy, or cold to cool down an overheated situation and inspire peace.

Adaptations: Pour this sauce neatly around pieces of poultry, symbolizing your desire to likewise surround yourself with protection. Alternatively, change the raspberries to strawberries, adding a hint of vanilla, to protect a marriage from negativity and strengthen loving energies.

BEVERAGE

Prickly Pear Protective Cooler

Makes about 5 cups

Native American shamans tell us that nature protects her greatest treasures by giving them natural features that make it hard for animals and people to handle them. Prickly pears are among these treasures, their skins being covered as if ready for a fight! We'll use that symbolism in this recipe to whip up some protective energy when you know a battle is on the horizon.

2 cups cold water or orange juice
1 cup ice
2 cups peeled, diced prickly pears (also called cactus pear)
¼ cup of sugar
1 tablespoon fresh lime juice to taste

Magical preparations: As you're whipping up this drink, visualize yourself surrounded on all sides by a mirrored bubble of energy, or by shields (anything that you associate with protecting you from a battle situation).

Candle types: Carve words or images into the candle that represent your battleground. That way as the wax melts, visually the problem disappears!

Put all the ingredients in a blender and whip until smooth. Strain through a sieve. If you wish, serve with a little ginger ale or soda water on top.

Adaptations: You can mix the fruit in this beverage so it better represents your goal. Add pineapple to insure you're well received in safe havens, strawberry to protect relationships, grapes to safeguard yourself psychically, etc.

MAIN DISH

Draw the Line Salsa

Makes about 3 cups salsa

Sometimes the greatest protection comes in the form of self-confidence—an attitude that says "Don't even try it." This spicy salsa energizes that kind of demeanor, adding a little personal zest for good measure. Use it on a meat main dish, or with chips as a snack.

2 tablespoons vegetable oil
½ pound beefsteak tomatoes, peeled and chopped
2 large yellow tomatoes, diced
2 yellow peppers, chopped
1 large onion, chopped fine
1 jalapeño pepper, minced
1 celery stalk, minced
1 small carrot, minced
½ cup red pepper, minced
½ cup red onion, minced
2 tablespoons lemon juice
½ teaspoon salt

Magical preparations: The way others perceive your level of confidence has a lot to do with auric energies. Before making this spell recipe, visualize pale red sparklers (like you see on the 4th of July) pouring down into your aura from above. These act like little balls of power and firm attitude spelled with a capital A! You will likely begin to feel a little warmer and more energized as the visualization takes effect. This is a good sign that you're doing it correctly. Allow some of these sparklers to pour out of your hands as you prepare the food.

Candle types: Draw a line on each of your candles showing definitively where you will not go beyond (just make sure your candle does NOT burn beyond that point). Put the candles safely away with the line mark on them after this spell until the situation has resolved. At that juncture I suggest ritually remelting the candles for another purpose.

This is marvelously simple. Dice up all the ingredients and put them in a large food storage container. Let them sit overnight, shaking regularly to integrate the flavors. Each time you mix them add an incantation like:

Pepper, onions, spices fine
Within this mix protection shines
Magic here with jalapeño minced
Too fill me with self confidence

Serve with tortilla chips and take a real bite out of your problems!

Adaptations: For even more flavor and safety, add some garlic juice (about 2 tablespoons) or 1 to 2 tablespoons minced garlic.

Shielding Pumpkin 'n' Squash

Makes 3 to 4 servings

Pumpkins appear most commonly around the Halloween holiday as a decorative or dessert item. In carved form they confer protection from any mischievous spirits, being a natural symbol of the golden sun.

Squash was a staple among the first settlers in the New World, often safeguarding people from starvation.

1 (5-pound) pumpkin
½ cup toasted walnuts
1 teaspoon butter
2 stalks celery
1 large Spanish onion, chopped
2 teaspoons fresh chopped garlic
1 cup sliced mushrooms (your choice)
2 cups cubed butternut squash
1 tablespoon ginger
½ cup bread crumbs
1 egg
1 tablespoon brown sugar
2 teaspoons soy sauce

Magical and Candle preparations: This is an ideal dish to prepare in the fall, so why not decorate accordingly? Buy an extra small pumpkin or squash and carve it like a jack-o'-lantern. Put a candle inside and light up your kitchen with watchful magic!

Clean out the pumpkin as you might for carving (symbolically this also cleans out any unwanted energy that's lingering around your home or life). Around the top rim, etch decorative magical carvings like runes to accent your purpose. Lightly oil the outside of the pumpkin, put the top on it, and place it in a baking pan with a little water in the bottom, baking at 350 degrees F.

While this begins to cook, in butter sauté the celery, onion, and garlic until lightly browned. To this add the mushrooms, squash, and ginger, cooking all for 10 minutes. Remove from the heat and toss the blend with bread crumbs, egg, brown sugar, and soy sauce. Pour this into the pumpkin shell, placing the lid back on top, and cook for another 45 minutes until the pumpkin is soft, saying:

Safety cooks from within
And this spell begins
All evil abate, it's time to celebrate!

When you serve this, move your kitchen pumpkin to the dining area to support and ignite your magic.

Adaptations: To protect a relationship add chopped almonds to the stuffing (about ¼ cup). Alternatively, to protect your mental well being use walnuts.

SIDE DISH

Defense Beets

Makes 6 servings

Beets are an ideal vegetable to safeguard those things and people you love during hard times, having been associated with love goddesses in ancient Greek tradition and thereafter. Additionally, this is a good dish to eat on Lammas to protect yourself from wicked fairies, who hate the color red. It's said that Lammas is one of the times during the year when the veil between worlds grows thin, and spirits and Devas can enter our world more easily.

3 pounds fresh beets
⅔ cup sour cream
2 tablespoons horseradish
½ teaspoon grated lemon or orange zest
1 tablespoon minced green onions
2 tablespoons butter

Magical preparations: Bring a picture of your loved ones into the sacred cooking space, or a representation of anyone/anything to which you want this magical energy directed. Put those photos or items in your line of sight so you can have a strong visual-emotional connection to the working, and focus the protective energy wholly on those individuals or items.

Candle types: Surround the photos and items with red candles and light them so the warm candlelight adds to the protective energy.

Wash and peel the beets. As you peel, think of this as if you were peeling away any barriers between the energy you're creating and the people to whom it's intended.

Bake the beets at 350 degrees F for 1 hour in a foil-covered baking dish with 1/4 cup of water in the bottom. Pour any juice from the beets into a saucepan and set aside.

When the beets have cooled, cut them into 1/4-inch circular slices (the circle represents wholeness and completion) and return them to the baking dish. In another bowl, blend the sour cream with the horseradish, beet juice (which provides lovely red color) and zest. Gently sauté the green onions in the butter, mixing these with the sour cream blend too. Pour this over the beat slices, and rewarm together. As you place this dish in the oven try adding an incantation like:

Within these beets are magic wards
Into each, my will is poured
Keep my love safe, by this magic charm
My love protects and preserves from all that would harm!

Adaptations: Nestle the beets on a bed of cooked spinach for the strength to withstand any difficulties. Or, eliminate the beets in this recipe altogether and use peas instead. Magically this "preserves the peas (peace)" in situations where you feel that anger and tension is causing peril.

Prop It Up Roasted Peppers

Makes 8 (2-skewer) servings

Humans have been growing and eating numerous kinds of peppers for thousands of years. They've also used them medicinally (in Asia, India, and China among other regions), and in rites of passage into adulthood (Mayan). In the Caribs tribe, peppers were rubbed on the body before battle to protect from injury and infection, making this dish ideal for safeguarding your health.

2 medium yellow or red peppers, roasted, cut into 16 small squares
16 ounces mozzarella cheese, cut into 16 cubes
16 fresh basil leaves
16 small cherry tomatoes
16 wooden skewers
⅓ cup Italian vinaigrette dressing (red wine if possible)

Magical preparations: Since we're focusing on protecting you physically wear white clothing. Also consider blessing a multivitamin and taking it before you begin the spell recipe. The blessing might go like this:

> *Lord and Lady, use this vitamin to support vitality in my mind, body, and spirit. Let it strengthen my immune system and protect me from illness.*

Candle types: Either white for protection or green for health and vitality.

Begin by roasting the peppers. Do this by arranging whole peppers on a foil-lined baking sheet. Place under broiler 2 to 4 inches from heat source. Use kitchen tongs to turn peppers as skin becomes blackened. Continue rotating peppers until skin is entirely blackened. Cool completely. Peel the blackest part of the skin with a knife and discard, then cut these into 16 pieces.

Next put one cheese cube, basil leaf, pepper square, and tomato onto the skewers. Repeat until the skewer is full. Put these in a shallow baking dish, pouring the dressing over top to marinate. Leave in the refrigerator marinating until you're ready to serve them. (Note: These are good cold or at room temperature, just pour off the excess marinade.)

Look After Me Leeks

Makes 4 to 6 servings

Leeks bear very similar superstitions and folklore as do all members of the onion family. The stronger the aroma—the stronger their protective powers! Combined with this we have horseradish. The French word for horseradish is raifort, *meaning strong root. According to the Delphic oracle of ancient Greece the radish is worth its weight in lead, the beet its weight in silver, the horseradish its weight in gold. I'm not sure about it being worth gold, but it's certainly worth its protective power in this dish, which in particular helps stave off the blues.*

4 leeks, trimmed
2 tablespoons butter
⅓ cup chicken broth
⅓ cup heavy cream
1 tablespoon horseradish, or to taste
Salt and pepper
3 tablespoons grated Gruyère

Magical preparations: The Oracle at Delphi was sacred to Apollo. To honor him in the sacred pantry play lyre music, burn lotus or orchid incense, and/or have pieces of alexandrite or tourmaline around your work space. If you're feeling adventurous here's a sample of a hymn to Apollo found at Delphi:

Oh, come now, Muses,
And go to the craggy sacred place
Upon the far-seen, twin-peaked Parnassus,
Celebrated and dear to us, Pierian maidens
Repose on the snow-clad mountain top;
Celebrate the Pythian Lord
With the goldensword, Phoebus,
Whom Leto bore unassisted
On the Delian rock surrounded by silvery olives,
The luxuriant plant
Which the Goddess Pallas
Long ago brought forth.

Candle types: Yellow or gold for Apollo.

Slit each leek down the side to about 1 inch of the base. Put the leaves of the leaks in cold water and rinse thoroughly. Set aside. Meanwhile, in a large skillet, heat the butter. Let the butter brown slightly then add the leeks. Toss. Add the broth and cream, cooking for about 30 minutes until tender. Transfer these by slotted spoon to another oiled, ovenproof pan. Add the horseradish to the sauce, seasoning it with salt and pepper, then pour this over the leeks placing the cheese on top. Slide this under the broiler for about two minutes until cheese bubbles. By the way, the cheese in this recipe adds a healing element, specifically to renew a sense of self love.

DESSERT

Concealment Rhubarb 'n' Cream

Makes 3 (1-cup) servings

When you're feeling overexposed to a person or situation, make this dish and fade neatly into the background. By removing your auric imprint from direct view, you also remove one source of exposure to whatever negativity plagues you.

3 cups rhubarb, trimmed and cut into ½-inch pieces
1 tablespoon orange juice
1 tablespoon gingerroot, minced and peeled
⅓ cup sugar
1 tablespoon butter
Vanilla ice cream for garnish

Magical preparations: A good activity to precede this spell recipe is something called a glamoury where you bring a specific desired energy into your aura, in this case that of camouflage. Go to your kitchen and see yourself in your mind's eye just as you are. Slowly, let that image begin to get fuzzy at the edges and blend into the background. Continue this way until you have completely melted your image into the room in which you're working. This is the metaphysical version of what a chameleon does in the wild!

Candle types: To mirror the rest of the candlelight recipe, whatever candle you use should not be directly visible to you while you're working. Perhaps have it in a covered container (like a lantern) or put it in another room.

Preheat the oven to 350 degrees F. Put the rhubarb, orange juice, ginger, sugar, and butter into an ovenproof dish. Bake covered for 20 minutes or so until the rhubarb is tender. Lather each serving with ice cream so that the rhubarb is completely covered from view (this strengthens your magic visually), and add an incantation at this juncture like:

> *What I do not wish seen is hidden away from those who would do me ill by my magic and my will. So be it!*

Enjoy!

Adaptation: After removing the rhubarb from the oven, let it cool and put it through the food processor to make a serviceable rhubarb spread for breads and meats. Again, make sure you spread the sauce in such a way as to hide what's beneath it to maintain the magical meaning of this dish.

VITAL AND HEALTHFUL HELPINGS

A healthy body is the guest chamber of the soul

—Francis Bacon

Mothers and grandmothers everywhere seem intent on reminding us that "if you have your health, you have everything." Well, maybe not everything, but being healthy certainly goes a long way toward happiness and contentment. As spiritually oriented people, however, we cannot simply focus on physical health in the holistic equation. We also have to nurture our mind and soul. These recipes help us to do just that!

Potential Healthful Components

- *Aromatics:* Allspice, basil, ginger, cinnamon, almond, thyme, lemon.
- *Candle notes:* Change the color of your candles to reflect the area of your life where you wish to bring health and vitality (like red for healthy relationships, or green for a healthy garden).
- *Color:* Sprout green (renewal), pale blue (peace), white (cleansing), and red for protection.
- *Candlelight recipe ingredients:* Dill, banana, kumquat, fig, pineapple, alfalfa, barley, oatmeal, rice, bran, soup, almond, berries, parsley, pear, cloves, beans, peanuts, spinach, peas, tomatoes, oranges, sesame, pinenuts, cabbage, milk, chicken, brandy, cucumber, garlic, honey, lemon, walnut, apple, eggs, cornmeal, onion.
- *Crystals, metals, stones:* Bloodstone, holey stones, amber, and coral.
- *Decorative touches:* Put a bundle of carnations, gardenia, and roses on the table to promote health and healing.
- *Timing:* Waning moon to decrease an existing problem, waxing moon to bolster overall immunity. Moon in any water sign (to cleanse), January for protection.

APPETIZER

Atlas Soup

Makes 4 servings

Or maybe that should be Popeye? Either way, with the hectic pace of many people's lives, ongoing strength and vitality is a tremendous blessing that this soup motivates.

2 pounds chopped frozen spinach
3 tablespoons butter
2 tablespoons flour
1½ quarts beef stock
1 teaspoon salt
¼ teaspoon pepper
⅛ teaspoon nutmeg
2 hard-cooked eggs, sliced

Magical and candle preparations: Take a red candle (for strength) into your cooking area. Carve it with an upward pointing arrow around the middle of the candle (this is the rune of the warrior—so you can fight what ails you). Light the candle saying:

The light of strength be mine
The light of vitality be mine
I claim the warrior's rune
Spirit, grant this boon!

Let the candle burn all the while you're preparing the candlelight recipe, then keep the wax remnants for any other strength-related spells.

Precook the spinach, then drain and set aside. Using a medium-size saucepan, melt the butter. Stir the flour into this slowly to make a paste. Add the beef stock to this about ½ cup at a time, stirring constantly. Cook over a low flame for 5 minutes. Add the remaining ingredients including the spinach, keeping only the eggs out of the blend. This is a good time to repeat the same incantation as that used when lighting the candle.

Cover for another 5 minutes. Serve, using the sliced eggs as a symbol of the sun's blessings, floating atop each bowl of soup.

Adaptations: Substitute broccoli for spinach to create a soup that protects health and strength once you've recaptured those energies. Or for a heartier blend, add a cup of diced, sautéed celery and potato during the simmering process. Magically the celery inspires intuitive insights into matters of health, and potatoes provide strong physical foundations in which good health can continue to flourish.

Fit as a Fiddle Chicken Soup

Makes 4 servings

Some students of language believe the phrase "fit as a fiddle" came about because fiddles were so precious to their owners that they took care of them fastidiously. This recipe takes that idea and combines it with hearty chicken soup so that you're reminded to take care of the most important person in your life: you! *The mushrooms in this recipe support the well-being of the psychic self.*

1 pound chicken breast diced
3 tablespoons soy sauce
4 ounces button mushrooms
1 tablespoon sesame oil
1 garlic clove (elephant), minced
1/4 teaspoon red pepper
1 can chicken stock
2 cups chopped red cabbage
1/2 cup diced green onion, with tops
sesame seeds (optional)

Magical preparations: You might want to consider working out before making this soup, and reciting healthful affirmations as you do so. For example, I often take a long walk and say things like "I am healthy" or "I am strong and fit" in rhythm with my movements. This puts out energy and helps get you into the right frame of mind for the meal.

Candle types: Something as bright and vibrant as you wish to feel.

Into a large saucepan, place the chicken, soy, mushrooms, sesame, garlic, and pepper. Lightly fry these for 3 minutes. Add broth and simmer until the chicken is cooked through. Stir in cabbage and onions, cooking for another 2 minutes. Top with sesame seeds to "open" the way for healthful energies.

BEVERAGE

Able-Bodied Eggnog

Makes 7 Servings

The egg has very ancient mystical connections. Among its many uses, sometimes people carried eggs when ill, then buried them to banish the sickness. Adapting this a bit, hold the eggs in this recipe before using them, and visualize your problems being absorbed by their healthy interiors. When you break and eat the eggs, it symbolizes breaking the power of sickness.

4 eggs, separated
½ cup sugar
¼ pint peach brandy
2 teaspoons rum or rum flavoring
¼ pint apple brandy
⅔ pint whole milk
¼ pint heavy cream
1 teaspoon vanilla extract

Magical preparations: Following the cue given by our ancestors, take one egg that you don't intend to use for cooking and keep it with you for a full day before making this candlelight recipe (you can hard boil it if need be to avoid mishaps). Then, just before preparing the eggnog, take the egg outside and crush it under your foot to break sickness' back.

Candle types: Choose the color and number here according to your need.

Using a hand mixer, beat the egg yolks and sugar together. When this thickens, add the remaining ingredients except the egg whites and vanilla. Chill.

Meanwhile, beat the egg whites until stiff. Fold these into the chilled egg mixture saying:

By eggs and cream and magic spell
Keep me energized and keep me well!
Within this eggnog drink so fine,
Healing powers now combine!

Garnish cups with a fresh slice of apple or mint leaves. Sip, visualizing the liquid as white light that fills every cell and leaves no shadows where any problems can dwell.

Adaptations: Play around with the flavors in this mixture. Berry brandy, for example, can be used if you've been suffering from emotional illnesses like depression to inspire joy. Alternatively, use citrus flavored rum for overall health.

MAIN DISH

Enlivening Sandwiches

Makes 2 servings

Peanut butter provides a stick-to-itiveness that's often necessary when we battle sickness and disease. Research has shown that a strong will and positive outlook accomplish much, and it can begin with this recipe.

- **½ cup chunky peanut butter**
- **4 large slices bread, toasted (your choice)**
- **8 slices bacon, cooked crisp and drained**
- **1 small delicious apple, peeled, cored, and sliced thin**
- **½ cup alfalfa or springwater sprouts**

Magical preparations: Take a little peanut oil or olive oil and dab it on the regions described below for a mini-self-blessing ritual. The idea here is to charge yourself with all the best possible energies so that you can fend off sickness head on:

Top of your head: *Bless me with the healing light of Spirit*
Third eye: *Bless my vision and fill it with hope*
Mouth: *Bless my mouth that all things consumed will be healthful*
Heart: *Bless my heart that I might love myself into wholeness*
Hands: *Bless my hands that I might honor my gifts and limitations*
Feet: *Bless my feet to ever walk the Path of Beauty*

Note: You may also wish to add a blessing to the specific part of your body that's in need.

Candle types: Dress your candles with a little peanut oil.

Spread peanut butter on two of the bread slices (don't be afraid to pattern it creatively—an inward spiral being a good symbol for internalizing healing energy). On top of this place four strips of bacon each, several apple slices, and bean sprouts. As you put the final piece of bread on top of each sandwich add an incantation like:

With this peanut butter, strong will—I muster
With bacon and apple—I will be well!
Now sandwiched within, let this spell begin!

Adaptation: Prepare the bread for this dish in a special way. Dip your index finger in a bit of water and etch one side of the bread with an emblem that represents fortitude or well-being. Toast the bread (the dampness will leave a white pattern, revealing the emblem), then follow the directions given above. Alternatively, change the type of bread to better represent your goal. Rye bread, for example, would help heal a relationship, and wheat would help heal a financial problem.

Mending Meatballs

Makes 2 servings

Circles are an ancient symbol of wholeness. In this case you'll be shaping a lot of little healing mandalas, and putting a little bit of recuperative energy into each!

1 tablespoon olive oil
1 small onion, chopped
1 small tomato, chopped
1 small red bell pepper, chopped
½ cup chicken broth
1 bay leaf
½ pound ground chicken
½ cup seasoned bread crumbs

1 egg
1 tablespoon chopped toasted almonds
1/4 teaspoon dried thyme
1 garlic clove, chopped
1/4 teaspoon smokey seasoning (liquid)
2 cups cooked rice

Magical preparations: Take a piece of paper and a marker or crayon whose color to you represents health (pale green is one common choice). Draw a circle on the paper saying the following incantation three times:

On this surface drawn round,
Health and wholeness shall abound!

Now either color in the circle or draw a symbol that equates to the type of health you desire (like a heart for circulation problems).

Candle types: Place the aforementioned charm underneath the candles' base. Put that candle and charm nearest the person who needs it the most at the serving table.

In a saucepan, place the olive oil over a medium-low flame. Add the onion, tomato, and pepper, stirring regularly until the vegetables are tender. I suggest stirring counterclockwise while focusing your mind on the problem so sickness wanes.

Slowly pour the chicken broth into this mix, and finally add the bay leaf. Simmer 30 minutes until thickened then turn down and keep warm for the meatballs.

Preheat the oven to 400 degrees F. Put all of the remaining ingredients into a bowl and knead until well blended. Shape into meatballs of any size and shape desired. Get a little creative! For example, returning to our earlier example about circulation, inspire a healthy heart by shaping them into little hearts while saying:

There's power in the blood
Today healing will start
To my heart, through all of me, health now impart!

Bake for 12 to 15 minutes until cooked through then serve with plenty of sauce over the cooked rice, which acts like a salve on your figurative wounds.

Adaptations: For more health-protecting power, wrap each meatball around a half clove of garlic. Or, to improve the health of a relationship, stuff the center of each with a piece of favorite cheese.

SIDE DISH

Essential Stuffed Tomatoes

Makes 6 servings

When tomatoes were introduced to Europe, people called them golden apples—likening them to the apples of Hesperides of Greek myths. This fruit was said to bestow eternal life and health on those who ate of it. Here we combine tomatoes with healthful brown rice for a very "good for you" side dish.

2 teaspoons butter
½ cup chopped onion
1 cup uncooked brown rice
1 cup chicken broth
1 tablespoon lemon juice
½ tablespoon fresh lemon zest
3 tablespoons fresh chopped parsley
6 large tomatoes
1 cup shredded cheese (your choice)

Magical preparations: To what area of your life are you applying the energy of this food? Use a toothpick to draw an image of that (like a spark or flame if directing it to spiritual health) on the tomato skin. Focus on your goal!

Candle types: Rub a little lemon oil or juice into your candle. This aroma brings cleansing into your sacred space so that healing takes place in the best possible atmosphere.

Place butter and onions in a frying pan and cook the onions till tender over a medium heat. Add rice, chicken broth, lemon juice, and zest. Bring everything to a full boil. Reduce the heat and cook covered for 45 minutes (rice should be tender). Remove from the heat, stir in the parsley, and put the top back on the pan. Set aside for a moment.

Core the tomatoes, removing some pulp from the center. As you do this, think about anything that you feel is adversely affecting your health and imagine digging that out too! If you want, add an incantation like:

Troubles, sickness, disease, I command you away
Only that which is helpful and healthy may stay!

Try to leave about 1/4 inch all around the outside edge intact so the tomato will hold up in the broiler. Fill the tomatoes with the rice and top with your chosen cheese. Using a baking dish to hold the tomatoes, broil them until cheese melts.

DESSERT

Cure-What-Ails-You Crumble

Makes 2 servings

This lightly sweet dish is good for whatever's ailing you, especially emotional distress. The juice of the banana is said to inspire delight (and happiness is a very powerful healer).

2 large bananas
1/8 cup all-purpose flour
1/8 cup brown sugar, firmly packed
1/2 cup rolled oats
1/4 teaspoon cinnamon or ginger
2 tablespoons (1/4 stick) butter, cut up

Magical preparations: Make yourself a little amulet that will help protect your heart from more emotional upheaval. Begin by drawing a red heart on a piece of paper. Cut this out, and apply any type of healing lotions to the center of the heart saying:

Healing within (fold the heart in half with the
salve inside)
By my will, this spell begins
Protection and safety, within these creases
(fold the heart in on itself again)
This amulet's power never ceases!

Candle types: Bring the charm with you into the kitchen while you work so the protection will go into place immediately after healing begins. Place it near to a white candle.

Preheat the oven to 400 degrees F. Slice the bananas in half the long way. If you wish, you can etch into them simple words or symbols that represent your goal at this juncture, then place the bananas flat side down in a well-greased 9 by 13-inch pan.

Put the flour, sugar, oats, cinnamon, and butter in a bowl. Cut the dry ingredients into the butter, working the blend so that the butter is evenly distributed. This is an excellent time to focus on cutting apart the power of disease and sickness. Sprinkle this mixture evenly over the bananas and press it in a bit using the back of a wooden spoon (this helps it stick to the bananas). As you press down on each slice, visualize white, purifying light filling the bananas and say:

All negativity out, only happiness stays
Healthy body, healthy mind, healthy spirit,
now and every day!

Bake for about 15 minutes until golden brown. Repeat your incantation just prior to eating to internalize wellness.

Adaptations: Add 1 teaspoon of berry-flavored brandy to the topping. Magically this motivates pure, unbridled joy which has tremendous healing power.

FINAL WORDS

I hope you enjoy these recipes as much as I and my family have in putting this book together. Tinkering in your kitchen should be fun (there's lots of good, sacred energy in laughter). It also should be fulfilling. I've done my best to provide you with good ideas and constructs that will inspire many, many more magical meals everyday of the year. Eat and drink well, with Spirit as your co-chef!

SUGGESTED READING

If you're interested in learning more about kitchen magic and the history and lore of all kinds of foods and beverages, these books are a good place to begin:

Ainsworth-Davis, James Richard. *Cooking Through the Centuries*. London: Jim Dent and Sons, 1931.

Andrews, Tamra. *Nectar and Ambrosia*. Oxford: ABC-Clio, 2000.

Arnold, John P. *Origin and History of Beer and Brewing*. Chicago: Wahl-Henius Institute of Fermentology, 1913.

Beyerl, Paul. *Herbal Magic*. Custer, WA: Phoenix Publishing, 1998.

Cunningham, Scott. *The Magic in Food*. St Paul, MN: Llewellyn Publications, 1991.

Davidson, Alan. *The Oxford Companion to Food*. New York: Oxford University Press, 1999.

De Cleene, Marcel, & Lejeune, Marie. *Compendium of Symbolic and Ritual Plants in Europe*. Ghent: Man and Culture Publications, 2004.

Gordon, Leslie. *Green Magic*. New York: Viking Press, 1977.

Hale, William. *Horizon Cookbook & Illustrated History of Eating & Drinking Through the Ages*. New York: American Heritage Publications, 1968.

Hechtlinger, Adelaide. *The Seasonal Hearth*. New York: Overlook Press, 1986.

Hylton, William H., & Kowalchik, Claire, ed. *Rodale's Illustrated Encyclopedia of Herbs*. Emmaus, PA: Rodale Press, 1987.

McNicol, Mary. *Flower Cookery*. New York: Fleet Press, 1967.

Roberts, Annie Lise. *Cornucopia—The Lore of Fruits & Vegetables*. New York: Knickerbocker Press, 1998.

Tannahill, Reay. *Food in History*. New York: Three Rivers Press, 1973.

Telesco, Patricia. *The Herbal Arts*. Secaucus, NJ: Carol Publishing Group, 1998.

———. *The Kitchen Witch's Cookbook*. St. Paul, MN: Llewellyn Publications, 1992.

———. *A Witch's Beverages and Brews*. Franklin Lakes, NJ: New Page Books, 2001.

Visser, Margaret. *Much Depends upon Dinner*. New York: Grove Press, 1986.

———. *The Rituals of Dinner*. New York: Grove Weidenfeld, 1991.

Wolf, Burt. *Gatherings & Celebrations*. New York: Doubleday Books, 1996.

INDEX